P9-DFT-457

MARRYING JONAH

AMY LILLARD

ZEBRA BOOKS
KENSINGTON PUBLISHING CORP.
http://www.kensingtonbooks.com

ZEBRA BOOKS are published by

Kensington Publishing Corp.
119 West 40th Street
New York, NY 10018

Copyright © 2017 by Amy Lillard

All rights reserved. No part of this book may be reproduced in any form or by any means without the prior written consent of the Publisher, excepting brief quotes used in reviews.

To the extent that the image or images on the cover of this book depict a person or persons, such person or persons are merely models, and are not intended to portray any character or characters featured in the book.

If you purchased this book without a cover you should be aware that this book is stolen property. It was reported as "unsold and destroyed" to the Publisher and neither the Author nor the Publisher has received any payment for this "stripped book."

All Kensington titles, imprints and distributed lines are available at special quantity discounts for bulk purchases for sales promotion, premiums, fund-raising, educational or institutional use.

Special book excerpts or customized printings can also be created to fit specific needs. For details, write or phone the office of the Kensington Sales Manager. Attn.: Sales Department. Kensington Publishing Corp., 119 West 40th Street, New York, NY 10018. Phone: 1-800-221-2647.

Zebra and the Z logo Reg. U.S. Pat. & TM Off.

First Printing: April 2017
ISBN-13: 978-1-4201-3977-8
ISBN-10: 1-4201-3977-0

eISBN-13: 978-1-4201-3978-5
eISBN-10: 1-4201-3978-9

10 9 8 7 6 5 4 3 2 1

Printed in the United States of America

MORE THAN FRIENDSHIP

"I could use a friend, Sarah Yoder." He took her hand into his, lacing their fingers together.

Night birds called and katydids sang as they sat there on the banks. The world seemed suspended, as if they were the last two people on the Earth. He could almost close his eyes and imagine it so. Just the two of them all alone. No Lorie. No Zach Calhoun. No church. No censure.

Her hand was warm in his. He could feel every breath she took as he sat next to her, their backs braced against the old fallen log. In that moment it was easy to imagine that it was just the two of them, and nothing existed outside their warm cocoon there by the pond.

How easy it would be to kiss her, pretend that it was only the two of them. No one existed anywhere else in the world.

He was just so tired of fighting, struggling, wanting things he couldn't have. And there was Sarah sitting beside him. Sweet, warm, loving Sarah. Sarah who once upon a time had loved him beyond measure. He could use some of that right now, to be loved without question. Had anyone ever loved him like that? He didn't think so. And he needed it. Oh, how he needed it.

He didn't think, didn't allow himself anything other than to feel. He leaned in and pressed a kiss to her lips. . . .

Books by Amy Lillard

The Wells Landing Series

CAROLINE'S SECRET

COURTING EMILY

LORIE'S HEART

JUST PLAIN SADIE

TITUS RETURNS

MARRYING JONAH

E-Novellas

The Quilting Circle

MORE THAN FRIENDSHIP

MORE THAN A PROMISE

MORE THAN A MARRIAGE

Published by Kensington Publishing Corporation

Chapter One

Sarah turned in a semicircle, surveying the crowd around her. So far the back-to-school day was playing out better than she could have dreamed. Families sat on blankets and quilts underneath the warm Oklahoma sun, eating sandwiches, chips, and baked beans.

There were nine families in her school. Nine families and twenty-two scholars. Plenty to keep her busy all year long.

"Sarah! Sarah! Sarah!"

She turned as Prudy Miller came running across the playground toward her.

"Will you come have dessert with us? *Mamm* brought plenty enough. Shoo-fly pie," the young girl singsonged.

Sarah searched her brain for the nicest possible way to refuse. It wasn't that Gertie Miller's pie wasn't worthy. Her recipe might have even been the best in the district. But Prudy Miller was Jonah Miller's sister, and Sarah had vowed to stay as far away from Jonah as possible.

There had been a time when Sarah would have done just about anything to get such an invitation. Eating dessert with Jonah, sitting underneath the blue sky, their knees almost touching—it was the stuff dreams were made of.

But she had held that dream too long. Jonah didn't want her. And even though Lorie Kauffman had married her *Englisher* boyfriend almost two months ago, nothing had changed. Jonah still loved Lorie and had no interest in anyone else.

That was when Sarah had decided to give up. What use was there in loving a man who didn't love her back?

"Sarah!" Prudy tugged her hand, peering up at her with tawny eyes so much like her brother's. But whereas Jonah's hair was the golden color of newly harvested wheat, Prudy's was as dark as the finest chocolate.

"How about I go over and say hello again?"

"And eat pie?"

Sarah placed a hand over her stomach. "Not this time. I couldn't hold another bite." *Lord forgive me the lie.* But self-preservation had to take precedence. She couldn't go sit so close to Jonah. Not yet. Not when her resolve to move on was still so new.

Prudy looked mildly disappointed, but tugged her to the blanket where her family was seated. "Look! I have Teacher."

Eli Miller frowned a bit as Prudy dragged her into view. Sarah wasn't sure what Jonah's father thought about her. Since Prudy was just starting school this year, Eli had been off the school board for several years. But she was certain the other members had filled him in on all the troubles she'd had.

This year was going to be different. *She* was different. She had made up her mind. She might not ever get married and have a family, but she was going to be the best teacher the district had ever seen.

"Hi, Sarah." Buddy Miller was on his feet in a second.

"Sit down, Buddy," Jonah coached.

He obeyed in an instant.

Buddy was a little different than most folks. Down syndrome, she thought they called it, though he was the only person she knew who had it. Not that she truly knew what it was, just that Buddy was a little slower than most folks. His face was a little broader and his speech not as clear. But the Lord had given him a good heart and a loving family. He couldn't ask for more than that.

"Hi, Buddy. Jonah." Sarah was proud of herself. Her voice didn't sound the least bit breathless as she uttered his name. She turned to Jonah's mother. "How are you today, Gertie, Eli?"

"*Gut, danki*," they said together, each nodding.

"Do you want some pie?" Buddy asked.

"She's too full," Prudy said.

"Prudy." The warning came from her mother.

Sarah was careful not to let her gaze stray to Jonah. "*Danki*, Buddy, but Prudy's right. I have already eaten way too much."

The young girl gave a self-satisfied smile, then plopped down between her oldest brothers. There were two more Miller boys: Aaron, who was about to marry Mary Ebersol, and Jonathan, who was still running around. The Millers also had a daughter, Hannah, who was Sarah's age. The two were close friends, though Sarah hadn't expected Hannah to come today. She was too busy building her home.

A home like Sarah would never have.

"Well, I hope you enjoy the rest of the picnic."

She turned to walk away and her gaze wandered toward Jonah. She couldn't help it. Despite her vow to forget him, she was just so aware of his every move, his every breath.

He looked . . . heartbroken, sad, and her heart went out to him. He had taken his breakup with Lorie badly.

He smiled at Prudy. It was the only time his face relaxed

and his eyes lit up. It shouldn't be that way. She couldn't believe it was God's will for him to be so unhappy, and she said a small prayer that one day he would heal and find that happiness he deserved.

"She's pretty."

Jonah tore his gaze from Sarah's departing back and settled it on his brother. Until Buddy had spoken, Jonah hadn't realized he'd been staring, watching Sarah walk away. "You think so?" He'd never given the matter much thought. He supposed that Sarah Yoder was attractive enough, with her dark brown hair and crystal-blue eyes.

"*Jah.*" Buddy smiled in a dreamy sort of way.

Jonah lightly pinched him on the arm. "I think somebody has a crush on somebody."

Deep rose flushed Buddy's cheeks. "No." But Jonah could tell. Not that anything could ever come of it. He had heard his parents talk too many times when they thought no one was listening. *Mamm* and *Dat* weren't even sure if Buddy would ever leave the farm, much less find a love of his own. It was sad really, given the size of his heart and his kind nature. If they stayed with tradition, Jonathan would inherit the farm and most likely the care of Buddy to go along with it.

"I think she's pretty," Prudy chimed in. "Does that mean that I have a crush too?"

Jonah smiled at his baby sister. At six, Prudy was definitely a late blessing in their lives. *Mamm* and *Dat* had thought they wouldn't have any more children after Jonathan was born. Now he was nearing seventeen while Prudy was just starting to school.

"Maybe," Jonah said.

Buddy shook his head. “She’s a girl, and a girl can’t have a crush on her teacher.”

“I can too.” Prudy stood, her anger shining in her red cheeks.

“Shhh . . .” Jonah pulled her into his lap. “Of course you can.”

Meanwhile *Mamm* soothed Buddy. She caught Jonah’s gaze over his brother’s shoulder. A helpless light flickered in her eyes and then it was gone.

He knew his parents weren’t sure what to do about his brother, but they had to believe that God would show them the way. The good-natured Buddy had grown increasingly irritable over the last couple of months. Jonah had believed at first that the sensitive boy had just been picking up on Jonah’s own agitation, but now he was beginning to think otherwise. Maybe Buddy was starting to realize the differences between them all. If that was the case, Jonah wasn’t sure what to do either, except to be there for him and pray daily.

Calmer now, Prudy pushed up from his lap and flounced over to get another piece of pie. Jonah’s gaze wandered around the area, taking in who had come to the back-to-school picnic.

But his stare settled on Sarah once more. He couldn’t pin it down, but there was something different about her. Something he couldn’t name.

“She is pretty.” His mother’s words were low and close by, as if she had moved near when he wasn’t looking. “Fancy, but pretty.”

“I suppose.” What could he say really? Was Sarah fancy Amish? He supposed that according to his mother’s standards, she was.

“She’ll make someone a good *fraa*.”

“*Jah*,” he murmured. He’d been hearing comments

like this from his mother ever since the wedding. Lorie Kauffman and Zach the *Englisher*'s wedding. He had started off gently explaining to *Mamm* that he had no interest in getting married. Not now, maybe not ever. But it seemed his mother had wedding fever. His brother Aaron was promised to marry Mary Ebersol, the bishop's daughter, in a couple of months. The whole house was in an uproar as she sewed shirts and prepared for the big day. It was only natural that she wanted Jonah to get married too. After all, he was the oldest aside from his sister Hannah and she had married Will Lapp last year. If Buddy never married . . . well, that left Jonathan until Prudy came of age.

"Of course, if she likes teaching . . ."

It was a lead-in and he knew it. What Amish woman would rather teach the scholars than raise a family of her own? Amish women were raised to want a husband and a family. Big families filled with laughing kids and more cousins than they could count. Once upon a time Jonah had thought he'd have that with Lorie, but that dream was long gone.

He ignored his mother's less-than-subtle attempts at dragging him into a conversation he didn't want to have, one in which she would extol the merits of marriage and the love of a good woman. "There's a volleyball game at Obie Brenneman's next weekend."

"Are you going?" His mother's eyes lit up like the amber lights the town put up around October. He knew she wanted him to stay closer to home, and since Lorie . . . well, he'd been spending a lot of time in Tulsa with Luke Lambright and some of his English friends.

"Maybe." He shrugged as if it were no big deal, but at least he'd gotten the conversation away from Sarah Yoder. He didn't want to talk about her.

His gaze followed her around the playground. She walked

from one family's blanket to the next, talking and laughing and seemingly oblivious to his stare. He just couldn't figure out what was so different about her, and heaven help him, he was intrigued.

"I wanna go," Buddy said. "Can I go? Can I?"

"Buddy, no," his mother said. "That's for the older kids."

"But I'm older than Aaron and Jonathan, and they get to go."

"Buddy . . ."

Buddy ducked his head. "I know what you're going to say. That's different."

Jonah turned back to his family, his mouth open to offer to see after Buddy at the game, but he knew his mother wouldn't want him to interfere. He didn't understand why his parents were so against Buddy socializing, but he knew they had their reasons. Still, he couldn't help feeling for his brother, so different than anyone else in Wells Landing. "I've got an idea," he finally said. "Why don't you and I go over to the Hein ranch."

Ezra Hein had married Lorie's sister Sadie. Even though Ezra was a Mennonite, the families had remained close. And Jonah knew that Ezra would welcome Buddy's visit. Buddy loved watching the bison roam around the pasture. Up until earlier in the year, Ezra had also kept a few camels, but Jonah had heard that he'd sold those off to Titus Lambert. It was a good ways out to Ezra's, but it would be worth it to keep the smile on Buddy's face.

"You mean that?" his brother asked.

"Of course I do." Never mind that it would give him the opportunity to talk to Sadie and see if Lorie was truly happy. That was all he had ever wanted, her happiness. He just always thought he'd be the one to give it to her. Not some smooth-talking *Englisher*. And once he knew she was happy . . . well, maybe then he could learn to move on.

At the thought, his gaze drifted back to Sarah. That was what was different. Not so long ago she would have done anything to sit next to him, talk to him, make sure that he knew she was around. And today? She had barely looked at him. Hadn't spoken to him at all, and refused his sister's invitation. An invite that could have landed them side by side eating pie.

Everyone knew that Sarah had a crush on him, but it seemed as if that time was over. Maybe, like Lorie, she had found someone else. Or maybe she had just given up on him ever noticing her. Whatever it was, he had noticed the change immediately. And it set well upon her shoulders.

"Look! Look!" Buddy hopped out of the car and raced toward the fence, pointing at the bison as he ran.

Jonah chuckled and got out of the car, their driver following suit. Bruce Brown was one of the favorite drivers in these parts. A retired Air Force medic, he had fabulous stories to tell, and Jonah knew that Buddy loved to hear all about flying in an airplane.

Neither man spoke as Ezra Hein came out of the barn. He was dressed in blue jeans and a plaid shirt, black suspenders across his shoulders.

"Jonah," he greeted, striding toward them. "How are you?"

How to answer that . . . "I'm *gut*, thanks." So it wasn't the exact truth. At least it wasn't a lie either. He was making it. Just one day at a time, never looking beyond the next horizon. "And *danki* for letting me bring Buddy out today."

Ezra cast a quick look over one shoulder. Buddy was up on the fence calling to the bison, who munched grass and otherwise ignored him. "You're welcome anytime. I love having Buddy visit."

"How's Sadie?" Bruce asked. He had driven for so many in the community, it was as if he was one of them.

Ezra's face lit up at the mention of his wife. "She's good. At the doctor's right now."

"Did she take your mother in?"

Ezra's grin deepened. "We're having a baby."

Jonah's heart turned over in his chest. He recognized it for what it was. He was jealous. He wanted the same happiness that he saw on Ezra's face. But the chances of that happening now were slim to none. "Congratulations," he managed to choke out as Bruce shook Ezra's hand and clapped him on the back.

"Best news I've heard all week." Bruce puffed out his chest, almost as proud as the father-to-be himself.

"Absolutely." Jonah forced a smile. He was happy for his friend, but he felt as if a little piece of him had died.

He had waited for Lorie for so long. She had been unsure about joining the church, then when her father died, she had pulled even further away. She hadn't told Jonah the big secret, that she had discovered Henry Kauffman had had another life outside Wells Landing. One no one knew about. She had found a car, a grandmother, and an English beau for herself. She had found herself, and in turn Jonah had lost her.

He pushed those thoughts aside and centered his attention on Ezra. "That's really great news."

Ezra shot him a sympathetic smile. "How are you?" He had already asked that, but this time his meaning was clear. *How are you really?*

"I'm *gut*." It was almost the truth. Lorie was gone, and he was doing everything he could to heal his broken heart. One day soon, he truly would be good. Until then, he was confessing that every chance he got.

"Have you been over to Abbie King's?"

Jonah knew what he meant. Had he taken Buddy over there. "Not yet."

"I hear they have a really smooth operation going."

"With the camels?" Bruce asked.

Ezra nodded.

"That's pretty amazing. Camels in Wells Landing," Jonah said. So many changes in the last couple of years. Nothing should surprise him now. "Maybe I'll take Buddy over there next." He would do whatever he could to keep his brother happy, especially since their parents weren't going to let Buddy attend any normal youth functions. Maybe one day. But until then . . .

"Come on in the house," Ezra said. "Sadie left a pitcher of limeade in the fridge."

"I don't know, Sarah. Do you think he's sick?"

Sarah gave a cursory glance in the general direction of Jonah Miller. She didn't want her gaze to linger too long. There was already enough talk in Wells Landing about the two of them. Or rather about her and how she loved him to distraction. She had given up, and everyone was talking about the changes in her attitude toward Jonah. It wouldn't do to go back on that now.

She shifted on the bench where she sat next to her cousin. The evening had started off simple enough, a volleyball game just after church at the Brenneman farm. The younger kids were singing in the barn, but the recently married couples came to enjoy a little more fellowship and exercise. Almost everyone in their group had gotten married recently. Except for her. And Jonah Miller.

But she was happy. Her classroom was under control. She had worked extra hard this summer getting better learning materials and decorating the large one-room schoolhouse. Unlike many of the other districts in Pennsylvania and Ohio, Wells Landing only boasted two schools, with the rest of the scholars attending public school with the English kids until grade eight. Sarah worried about their minds and what they were learning in such a modern place. But the elders knew best. She had to trust them and God to take care of the youth.

Her thoughts tumbling one over the other, her quick look had turned into so much more.

"He looks . . . he looks . . ." She couldn't say the words. He looked terrible, gaunt. Sick, just like her cousin Libby had said. Heartbroken. He hadn't looked that bad at the back-to-school picnic a couple of weeks ago. Or had he? She had monitored her perusal of him then as well. He could have looked just as sad then, but she hadn't noticed because she was too busy trying not to notice anything at all.

"You don't think he really expected Lorie to come back, do you?" Libby asked.

Sarah didn't know for certain, but if his current state of decline was any indication, she would have to say yes. "I don't know," she murmured.

It was early September. Nearly three months since Lorie Kauffman had married the *Englisher* Zach Calhoun. Three months of Jonah dealing with the fact that she was never coming back.

"Poor Jonah."

"You know she's been gone almost a year now," Libby said.

"I know." Somehow Sarah managed to keep herself in place as she watched him. She wanted nothing more than to go to him, offer him comfort. Tell him all the things that had been bubbling up inside her for so long. But he had rejected her so many times, she wasn't sure she could handle any more. And she had given up. Nothing could be between them. She had settled herself to her life's calling: teaching. She had prayed and prayed about it, and she knew in her heart that this was what God wanted from her.

"Maybe you should go talk to him." Libby nudged her in the side.

Sarah shook her head. She had come here to watch volleyball and nothing more. She hadn't come here to make a fool of herself over Jonah Miller. Not anymore. Never again.

"If you're not going to talk to Jonah, then you should go see what Ben is doing."

"Ben Schrock?"

Libby nodded. "I heard that he really likes you."

"Libby," Sarah protested.

Her cousin shrugged. "If you won't go after a boy who likes you, then go get the one you want."

"I don't want Jonah Miller." And she surely didn't want Ben Schrock. He was . . . well, not Jonah. "Besides, you know I would never 'go after a boy.'"

"You know what I mean. You can make yourself known to them. There's nothing wrong with that."

No, she didn't suppose there was if she was Ivy Weaver. But she wasn't. She was plain ol' Sarah Yoder.

"Hey, Sarah." Sam Troyer suddenly appeared as if out of nowhere.

Sarah jumped, then quickly recovered. “Hi, Sam.”

He grinned at her, then swung around until he was sitting on the ground at her feet.

“I think I hear Joseph calling,” Libby said, referring to her longtime boyfriend, Joseph Byler. She waved and disappeared.

“Good.” Sam continued smiling as if he knew the best secret in the world. “I wanted to talk to you alone anyway.”

Sarah frowned. “You did?” Sam had a terrible reputation when it came to girls. He was an incurable flirt and flitted from one girlfriend to the next. Every unattached female in the district knew better than to take him seriously.

“*Jah*. I wanted to ask if I can take you home.”

“Today?” She studied his face, looking for signs that he was joking with her. He seemed serious enough. But why had he set his sights on her tonight?

“Of course today. When else?”

“I just . . . I mean . . .” What had happened? Sam had never paid her two seconds of attention. Now, all of a sudden, he wanted to take her home? “I came with Libby and Joseph.”

He waved away her words. “It’s okay. I’ve already talked to Joseph.”

He had? “I wish you hadn’t done that.”

“That’s me. A take-charge kind of guy. Are you ready?”

Sarah looked around. The crowd was beginning to thin. How had it gotten so late? She tried to spot Libby and Joseph in the few milling people left, but she didn’t see them anywhere. Knowing Joseph, he had taken Sam at his word. Joseph was nice enough, but not as smart as some.

He'd probably never given a second thought to the fact that Sarah might not want to ride home with Sam.

Only a few of the unpromised guys were left, Jonah Miller being among them. But she could never be as forward as to go right up to him and ask to ride home with him.

Besides, she had quit Jonah Miller.

No, she was better off taking her chances with Sam Troyer.

Chapter Two

Unbelievable!

Sarah stomped down the side of the road, thankful that at least it was summertime. Walking home in the middle of the night was bad enough; at least she didn't have to add cold weather to it. She supposed that was a blessing in itself. And one of the few she could count these days.

She hadn't done anything to deserve this. Nothing but try to move on. For all the good it did her. She might as well accept it right now. She was doomed. Doomed to live a loveless life. Doomed to be an old maid. Maybe she should just go ahead and move in the *dawdihaus* now and get it over with.

Whatever she did, it was time to forget about love.

She heard the *clip-clop* of horse hooves on the roadway and the *whir* of the carriage wheels as the buggy grew closer. Most likely another Amish youth on the way home. A young couple, perhaps newly baptized, just starting to date. They would be snuggled up in the buggy side by side talking about this and that and who won the last volleyball game. Really important stuff. Too important to do anything but pass her by.

She moved over, a little closer to the edge, but still on

the road. Oklahoma roads were notorious for having deep ditches on either side, and in the darkness, she couldn't tell how much was land hidden under the shadow of night and how much was empty air.

As the buggy grew closer, its lights lit the roadway ahead. Sarah didn't look up. She kept her head down and her eyes on her feet. Just her luck, the buggy slowed. But she walked on.

The driver pulled up next to her. She looked out of the corner of her eye and could only see one figure inside. A male. That meant it was an even younger Amish youth. Maybe a sixteen-year-old in his first year of *rumspringa*. If that was the case, he had slowed down to make fun. Perfect. Just perfect.

"Sarah Yoder."

He knew her name? She looked up and gave the driver her full attention. Her feet stopped beneath her as if stuck in a deep, thick mud. The buggy continued on.

"Jonah?"

The buggy stopped, and somehow she managed to get her feet in motion once again. She drew even with the buggy, circling around so she could see the driver better. It was Jonah Miller.

"*Oi*, Sarah Yoder. What are you doing out here all by yourself?"

She really wasn't in the mood for this. She propped her hands on her hips. "You're out here by yourself."

He seemed to think about it a minute. "O-kay. But I have a buggy."

Couldn't argue with that.

She opened her mouth to explain. But what was she really going to say? That Sam Troyer's offer to take her home had not been as sweet and innocent as she had first thought? Or that she had vowed to forget about Jonah so she had said yes to Sam? Or maybe she had simply chosen to ignore the rumors about Sam and take her chances. But that might lead to more questions. And she certainly didn't want to talk about how Sam had turned into a jerk and started saying hateful things, so she'd told him to let her out of the buggy immediately. No. That wasn't something she necessarily wanted to share.

"I'm walking," she said, looking off into the distance as if walking had been her plan the entire time.

"Are you walking home?"

She looked at the midnight-blue sky. It was after ten o'clock. The stars were out, the frogs and the night bugs were singing. Other than the occasional jackrabbit, not much stirred on the outskirts of Wells Landing, Oklahoma.

"Yes." Maybe direct was the best way to handle this. "I'm walking home."

He seemed to think about it a second. Or maybe he just hesitated. Whatever it was, he took a minute, then turned back. "Can I give you a ride?"

No! she wanted to scream. How many times in the past four years had she wanted to hear something like that fall from Jonah Miller's lips?

She wasn't sure she could count that high. But she'd spent four years, more than four years, hoping he would notice her. Hoping he would forget about Lorie Kauffman and give Sarah Yoder a try. But he'd never been able to. Now he wanted to take her home.

She thought about it a second. Other than her vow to give up on Jonah, there were enough stories about him to rival the ones about Sam Troyer. Stories about how he'd been dressing English and going to wild parties. There had been weeks this summer when no one had seen him. She was perfectly fine with that. It made forgetting him that much easier. But everyone knew how dangerous English parties could be. Why, just a couple of years ago, Emily Ebersol had gotten into an accident coming home from one such party. She had broken her arm and everything. Of course, now Emily was happily married to Elam Riehl. But that wasn't really the point, now was it?

She shook her head. What Jonah Miller did and who he hung out with was no concern of hers. She'd given up on him, and she didn't care what he did. Not anymore.

"No, thank you." She turned and started marching down the road once again.

He clicked his horses into motion and caught her easily. "Why not?"

She glared at him. "Because you are a boy, and I am done with boys."

"You're just going to walk home in the dark all by yourself? Can't be far. Like what? Maybe six or seven more miles. That shouldn't take more than a couple of hours or so. Maybe a little longer since it's dark. Of course, you could cut a half hour off if you cut across the field there by the bishop's house."

She wasn't going to stop walking. He could say what he wanted. But she had learned a valuable lesson tonight. Boys and men? They couldn't be trusted. The last time she checked, Jonah Miller fit that category.

"Of course you wouldn't want to walk across that field this late. I heard there were some coyotes out there."

She stumbled, then righted herself. She would find a big stick. That was all she needed.

"Go away, Jonah." Wow. Those were never words she

thought she'd ever say. But she had been a fool for too many years. No more.

"Fine," he said. He swung down from his buggy, grabbed the horse's reins, and walked beside her. "I'll leave. I'll leave you completely alone. But you have to tell me how you ended up walking out here in the middle of nowhere by yourself."

She shook her head. "It doesn't bear repeating."

"Why don't you let me be the judge of that?"

"Because it's my story."

He seemed to mull that over a minute. Not that she was watching him or anything. She was headed home, and that was all.

"If you won't tell me, then I'll guess. I saw you tonight at the volleyball game."

Wait . . . What? He saw her at the volleyball game? She didn't even know that he knew she was alive.

"And I saw you talking with Sam Troyer."

She stopped. "Maybe I was."

"No maybe about it. And I know Sam. So I figure he made a pass at you in the buggy and you told him to let you out. Am I right?"

Sarah lifted her chin. Why should she give him that satisfaction? "Go back to your English parties, Jonah. And leave being Amish to the rest of us."

"How do you know about the parties?"

"Everyone knows about them. It's all anyone can talk about these days."

"I see."

They walked in silence for a few moments. Surely he would give up and go home, leave her to her misery.

"Let me give you a ride home, Sarah." His tone changed,

became solemn, thoughtful, and concerned. "You can't walk all the way home from here."

Well, she *could*. But he was right. It would take her until the wee hours of the morning before she even made it to her driveway. And she was already tired.

"For Prudy," he said. "I can't have her teacher endangering her life on a dark road in the middle of the night."

She wanted to give in. Oh, how she wanted to give in. There wasn't anyone around to witness her weakness. She could have Jonah take her home, and no one need ever be the wiser.

"Okay," she finally said. She wasn't going to think about her vow to stay away from Jonah Miller. It was just a ride home. Nothing more.

"It's a beautiful night, *jah*?" Jonah peered out the window in front of them to the clear September sky. A million stars twinkled above them. Why he felt he needed to talk about them, well, that was another matter altogether.

Maybe because Sarah was sitting beside him, staring straight ahead. Not at all like the Sarah Yoder he had known before. Anger seemed to roll off her in waves. This was definitely a different side of her, and one he had never seen before. He wanted to smooth the wrinkle out of her forehead and put that smile back on her face, the smile he had seen her wear at the back-to-school picnic.

But everyone knew what Sam Troyer was like. He was what the English called a player. He liked girls and he liked to kiss and he had no qualms about kissing every girl who would stand still long enough he could get his lips on them.

So why was sweet Sarah Yoder out with a tomcat like Sam?

"Did you go to the game with Sam Troyer?"

Sarah turned to face him. Even in the near-pitch-black interior of the buggy, he could see the fire in her eyes. "No. Of course not." Her tone implied that he must think she was as dumb as a rock.

"But you were willing to ride home with him?" Everyone knew what that meant. A couple riding home together was as near a declaration to exclusively date as a person could get. At least it was where Sam wasn't included.

"Libby sort of abandoned me there."

"Your cousin?"

"Evidently blood is not thicker than water."

Jonah murmured something inconsequential, hoping his soothing tone was enough.

"I don't know who I'm the angriest with. Her for leaving me, Sam for . . . being Sam, or me for trusting either one of them."

"I guess it's a good thing I came along, then."

She half turned in her seat, her arm brushing against him as she shifted. The small touch shouldn't have sent little tingles racing along his skin, but it did.

"That's another thing," she railed. "You are the last person I would want to bring me home." She slapped her hand over her mouth as if she could stop the flow of her words. But it was too late, they had already escaped.

He drew back. "Me? What's wrong with me?"

She shook her head, and he liked the way her *kapp* strings danced around her shoulders with the motion. Her forehead furrowed as if she was trying to decide if she should say more or let it drop. Finally, she spoke. "If anyone finds out that you are taking me home, everyone will think I set it up so you would come along right when I needed you. It's always that way. I made a fool of myself over you, and I won't do it again."

It was no secret that she thought she had feelings for him, though he had never encouraged them. That wouldn't have been right. He and Lorie . . . well, there was no he and Lorie. Not anymore. Not ever again.

He turned his attention back to the girl sitting next to him. It was easier to think about her than all the mistakes he had made with another.

"You've given up on me? What exactly does that mean?"

"Exactly what it says."

He shook his head. "So you no longer want there to be a me and you as a couple?"

"Nope." She said the word with confidence, but he knew she was lying. Even through the night he could see the flush rise into her cheeks. It shouldn't have tickled him so, but it did. She was kinda cute when she blushed. His thoughts went back to the picnic and Buddy saying how he thought she was pretty. His brother was right. She was pretty. Even though she was mad enough to spit nails.

"There's something different about you tonight," he mused.

She shook her head. "There's nothing different about me, Jonah."

He didn't believe that. Maybe he had been away too long. Or maybe he hadn't paid enough attention to Sarah. They were almost halfway to her house, and for all her talk about expectations and rumors, he knew there was more she wasn't saying. He could almost feel the pressure in her as she sat beside him.

It was just a matter of time before she turned to him and said something. Said—

"I would have never treated you that way."

"I beg your pardon?"

She sucked in a deep breath. "Lorie. I would have never treated you like she did."

"*Jah?*" Well, he had never expected Lorie to either.

"You deserved better."

He wasn't sure how to respond. Everyone had been saying it was God's will and he needed to move on, find some sweet Amish girl and get married. They had been telling him that Lorie wasn't the one for him. He needed to forgive her, forget her, and move on.

But no one had ever told him that he deserved better. No one had ever said that they would have treated him better.

"*Jah?*"

"I cared about you, Jonah. I hated to see you hurt."

"That's sweet, Sarah." He wasn't sure what else to say.

"No," she protested. "It's not sweet. I cared about you and what happened to you. I would have been a *gut* friend to you, Jonah Miller."

She was sitting a little closer to him than she should, but he liked it. Yet it didn't feel like friendship. She wore such a frown on her face, he didn't think she even realized how close they were.

She smelled sweet. And next to her, he felt strong. Stronger than he had in a long time. Lorie was tall, almost as tall as he was. But Sarah was average height, maybe even petite. And next to her he felt like a protector, provider, more than friend.

"Why do you keep talking like it's in the past?"

"I told you. I gave up hope for the two of us a long

time ago." The words fell from her lips easier this time. And that surprised him that she could talk about it all so casually when he had been living it, doing everything he could to understand what had happened to his life.

"I'm sorry about that."

"About what?" she asked.

"About hurting you."

"No," she said softly. "You did nothing wrong. I did all of that to myself."

But he could have handled it differently. He could have been easier with her, helped her over her crush and not ignored it. "I guess we both made mistakes."

He had made more than his share, dressing English and going to parties where he had no business being. But he had wanted to know what in the English world was so appealing to Lorie. He'd drunk a little too much lately, but tonight he was stone-cold sober and yet his thoughts were no clearer.

But Sarah gave him hope. Like maybe he would come out of this eventually and be able to have a life again. Life after Lorie.

He enjoyed talking to Sarah. Funny, but he had never noticed before. She was easy to talk to. Candid and sweet. She was honest to a fault and smart. Why had he never noticed?

He inched toward her and pulled back on the reins to slow the horse's gait. No sense getting home too soon.

Sarah loved the warmth of Jonah next to her, the clean fragrance on his clothes and the scent that belonged to him alone. She closed her eyes and let it all wash over her.

How many times had she imagined this very scenario only to give up hope of ever having it come true?

And that she had confessed as much to Jonah? Well, she was glad it was dark in the carriage. She had embarrassed herself enough for one night.

"Sarah," he whispered somewhere near her ear. His breath stirred the strands of hair that had managed to wiggle free of her bob. That was the thing about her hair. It was forever doing what it wanted. There was no hope of taming it despite the amount of baby lotion she used to smooth down the flyaways.

"*Jah?*"

"Would you like to go down to the pond and talk?"

What she wouldn't have given to have him say that two months ago, two years ago. But now? She needed to go home. Where she belonged. Get some sleep. Forget tonight ever happened.

"Sure." Who said that? Certainly not her. But it hadn't been Jonah either. The words must have tripped from her mouth.

The last thing she needed to do was to be alone with Jonah. Or to talk with him.

She shook it off. Who cared? She wasn't in love with him. What was the harm? It wasn't like she would do something totally stupid. They could go down to the pond and talk for a while, then she could go home.

Besides, she enjoyed his company. All those years she had thought she was in love with him, she never really knew him. Tonight she got to see a glimpse of the real Jonah Miller. And she liked what she saw. He was caring and funny. Well, she already knew that. But he was also sweet and gentlemanly.

They could be friends. And she had a feeling that was what Jonah Miller needed right now. A real good friend.

Even though it seemed every time she had seen him since Lorie had gotten married, he was surrounded by a group of men, as if they were there to protect him from the world. But those times hadn't been often. She supposed he could use a friend right now. Maybe someone who wouldn't pass judgment and would just sit and listen. She could be that for him.

Neither one of them said a word as he drove them back to his family's land and to the pond that was a popular hangout when the sun was shining. No one would be there after dark, and he and Sarah could sit and talk as long as they wanted without being disturbed. He wanted to talk to her more. Wanted to find out why she could get through the numbness when no one else had been able to. He needed to discover the hows and the whys so he could correct that missing part and move on.

He tethered the horse at the edge of the field, making sure that beast and carriage were far enough off the road to protect them from any oncoming traffic.

Sarah climbed out of the buggy first. Jonah reached behind the seat and found the blanket he kept there for the winter months. They would need someplace to sit besides that dusty old log that had been there for ages.

He grabbed the blanket and a flashlight, then hopped down from the buggy.

"Are you coming?" he asked Sarah.

She looked to be a little starstruck. At least that's what the English called it. He wasn't sure exactly what that meant, but he figured it had something to do with freezing up from excitement. Or maybe it was nerves.

"*Jah, jah*."

She set her feet in motion and together they walked through the small thicket of trees and bramble that surrounded the pond. There were enough visitors to the pond each year that the path never grew up. Still, a person had to be careful in the dark.

Jonah shined the flashlight onto the ground ahead of them. "I know there's a hole up here somewhere. Be careful, we wouldn't want you to sprain your ankle."

She smiled at him and picked her way carefully along.

The pond looked so different at night, the water black. Something rippled the surface and he couldn't tell if it was a snake or a turtle. He hoped a turtle, or their conversation would be cut short before it had even begun.

The banks seemed different, empty, washed in moonlight.

He held part of the blanket out to her. "Help me spread this out."

She grabbed one end of it and draped it over the fallen log. He had left it doubled so the extra thickness cushioned his back as he settled down on the ground in front of the log.

Sarah seemed hesitant. Then she knelt down beside him. "It's a beautiful night, *jah*?" she asked.

"I believe we determined that." His words were without malice.

"Maybe it's so beautiful it deserves to be said twice."

He studied her for a moment in the shadows. "Why are you here, Sarah?"

"I thought you wanted to talk."

"No, really."

She shifted uncomfortably, then finally turned to face him. "I hate to see you hurting like this, Jonah."

"It wasn't like I couldn't see it coming."

"That doesn't make it right."

"No, I don't suppose it does." But getting angry and hating the world was only going to hurt him in the long run. Still, he wasn't quite ready to forgive and forget.

"Do you want to talk about it?"

He shook his head. He didn't want to rehash it all. Every time he told the story, it never changed. And that was what he needed, more than anything: a new ending.

"You can, you know. Talk to me. All I've ever wanted to be was a friend to you, Jonah."

But that wasn't true. Everyone in Wells Landing knew that Sarah had a crush on him. "I could use a friend, Sarah Yoder." He took her hand into his, lacing their fingers together.

Night birds called and katydids sang as they sat there on the banks. The world seemed suspended, as if they were the last two people on the Earth. He could almost close his eyes and imagine it so. Just the two of them all alone. No Lorie. No Zach Calhoun. No church. No censure.

Her hand was warm in his. He could feel every breath she took as he sat next to her, their backs braced against the old fallen log. In that moment it was easy to imagine that it was just the two of them, and nothing existed outside their warm cocoon there by the pond.

How easy it would be to kiss her, pretend that it was only the two of them. No one existed anywhere else in the world.

He was just so tired of fighting, struggling, wanting things he couldn't have. And there was Sarah sitting beside him. Sweet, warm, loving Sarah. Sarah who once upon a time had loved him beyond measure. He could use some of that right now, to be loved without question. Had anyone ever loved him like that? He didn't think so. And he needed it. Oh, how he needed it.

He didn't think, didn't allow himself anything other than to feel. He leaned in and pressed a kiss to her lips.

Chapter Three

She was such a fool.

Sarah stood off to one side pretending to listen to Libby, Julie, and Mandy talk about canning and such. She was watching Jonah. It was Sunday afternoon. A bright fall day in Oklahoma. It had been a month. A month and a half, since she and Jonah had gone to the pond. What a mistake.

"What do you think, Sarah?"

She jerked her head up as her name registered through her thoughts. "What?"

"I asked you about those new jars. Have you seen them? They're in colors. I mean, who wants to look at their food all changed like that?" Libby shook her head. "I don't know. I just think it's weird. Purple, blue, and green."

Sarah's attention drifted back to Jonah. "Weren't original Mason jars blue?" she asked absently.

Libby started to reply, but once again, Sarah stopped listening. She had tried to talk to Jonah so many times since that night. She thought they had shared something special. How wrong she had been. There had been no sharing that night. She had given, and he had taken and walked away. He looked up and caught her staring at him. She lifted her chin, unwilling to look away in embarrassment. She was not going to be embarrassed by what happened between them; she thought it meant something. It wasn't her fault if it meant nothing to him.

But what a fool she had been to think that she could go and sit next to Jonah Miller and just talk for hours on end.

"I'm just saying I think they're weird," Libby said.

It took everything Sarah had to stay in place. How badly she wanted to confront him in front of his friends, ask him why he was avoiding her. But she knew. He had taken what he wanted, knowing that she, in her adoration of him, would give it. They had sinned in the eyes of the Lord, the church, their families, and the community. And yet he stood over there like he didn't even know her name. She was such a fool.

"I think that would be fine," Julie said. "Sarah? Are you listening?"

Sarah turned her gaze away from Jonah and turned back to her cousin. "Yes. Of course. What?"

"I told you she wasn't listening," Mandy added.

"Let's all go down to Millers' Pond. This is probably the last day we will even be able to think about getting in the water."

It was early October, and before long the water would cool off and it would be too cold to get in the pond. They would still hang out there from time to time, but Julie was right. It was probably their last chance to go swimming.

Yet the last thing Sarah wanted to do was put herself in Jonah Miller's vision. In fact, she would rather avoid him like the plague than sit and watch him go through the motions of living while pining away for a woman he couldn't have. It was heartbreaking. "I don't think I'll go," she said.

"You have to come," Mandy said.

She didn't have to do anything.

"Please go with us." Julie squeezed her arm in encouragement.

"It wouldn't be the same without you," Libby added.

What could Sarah do but agree?

Jonah watched as Sarah looked away. He hated that shadow in her eyes, that ghost of betrayal and sadness. He didn't need her gaze on him to know that he had messed up. Really messed up. He didn't need her anger or her consternation. He knew.

"Are you going with us?" Obie asked.

Jonah dragged his attention back to the matter at hand. What to do after church. It was a question they had been asking themselves for years, ever since they were old enough to go to a singing. But things had changed. He looked at the faces of his friends standing around him. They were all married or engaged. All but him.

And Sarah.

"*Jah*," he said. Of course he would go. That was expected of him. That was what he was supposed to do. But he was just going through the motions until . . . until something happened.

It had been almost four months since Lorie had gotten married. He felt as if he were treading water, climbing uphill, walking through peanut butter. They were all inadequate descriptions. But he was growing weary, and there was no end in sight.

The conversation around him turned to who was driving, who was going, and what their wives were going to think.

His gaze drifted back over to Sarah. He wasn't really

avoiding her, not for the reason she thought. The truth was, he was ashamed. He hadn't been thinking clearly that night. That was his only excuse, the only one he had, anyway.

They dispersed, each man going to get his wife, and to Jonah's dismay, the second he was alone, Sarah broke away from the women and started in his direction. "Hi, Sarah."

"Can I talk to you for a second?"

He blinked. The last thing he wanted to do was talk to her, but how could he tell her no? "*Jah.* Of course." After all, what could she say to him in the middle of the Burkholders' yard with the entire church district milling around in one spot or another? The afternoon meal was over, and the sun was shining. It wasn't like she could pin him to the wall with questions he couldn't answer. Not with everyone watching.

"I thought you were my friend."

Maybe she could.

"Friends?"

"You heard me." She crossed her arms and shifted her weight. She was acting as uncomfortable as he felt. So why have this conversation at all?

"*Jah.* We're friends."

"And friends consistently ignore other friends?"

"I'm not ignoring you."

She laughed, though there was no humor in the sound. "Lying is a sin, Jonah Miller."

"I just don't want you to get the wrong impression."

"And what impression is that?" He squirmed under her steady stare. He could see the shame in her gaze, the pain and embarrassment, but she didn't look away. And he didn't know what to say.

She shook her head as she waited for him to answer. "I thought you were different," she finally said. "I thought you were a better person than that." Her shoulders were stiff and her chin trembled, but she held her head high as she turned on her heel and walked away.

He watched her retreating back, but had no words to say in his defense. She thought he was different? He had too. It seemed they were both wrong.

Sarah sat down on the edge of her bed and unpinned her hair. She had to admit it was her favorite part of the day. Sometimes her bob gave her a headache. She had to pull her wayward hair so tight to keep it under control, and she always looked forward to bedtime when she could let it down, brush it out, and release some of the tension on her scalp. She tossed the pins into the little dish she had sitting beside her bed, pulled the ponytail holder free, and began to brush out the tresses.

It had been three days since she had talked to Jonah after church. Tried to talk to Jonah. Her days were filled with teaching her classes and righting all the mistakes she had made last year. But at night, like now, her mind wasn't as occupied and thoughts of Jonah crept in.

Her sister Annie bounded in from the other room, in a flash of white nightgown and flowing blond hair. Annie hopped onto the bed, eyes sparkling. "Can you go to town with me tomorrow?"

"It's a school day." She didn't bother to remind her sister that as a teacher on probation, she couldn't afford to go flitting around town while someone else took care of her class. "If you wanted to go to town, you should have asked me Saturday. We could have shopped to our hearts' content."

Annie gave a pretty pout. Like that was unusual. Everything Annie did she did better than anyone else. It was simply her nature, one of the favored. "I didn't need to go then." She made a sad face. "I had forgotten my time was coming."

Sarah's brush stilled in her hair. How long had it been since she—

She jumped up from the bed and rushed over to the wall calendar hanging on the back of the closet door.

"What are you doing?" Annie asked, watching with wide eyes. But Sarah couldn't answer. Shock sliced through her like lightning, leaving her arms and legs weak, her fingers trembling.

She grabbed the calendar and flipped through the pages. So much time had passed since that night by the pond. How much time? One month? Two? How was she supposed to remember? How was she supposed to know? But if she couldn't remember all the details . . . How long had it been since she had her time? A while. That was all she knew. Longer than a month? She was pretty sure. But that could mean anything. She had known couples who had tried for a baby for years and years with still no success. Just because—

"Sarah? What's wrong?"

"Nothing," she lied. This couldn't be happening to her. Could not.

"You're as pale as a sheet. That's not nothing."

"I just forgot something is all. I'm supposed to take cookies for the scholars tomorrow." Nowhere near the truth, but perfect sister Annie didn't need to know that.

She shook her head. No. She was overreacting. She was worried for nothing. She had made a mistake and loved the wrong man. But that didn't mean God would punish her for it.

"Are you sure?"

"Positive." With slow, deliberate motions she rehung the calendar and turned back to her sister. Somehow she managed to paste an adequate smile on her face. At least she assumed it was genuine enough, for Annie stopped asking so many questions. "I'm just mad at myself for not remembering to make the cookies yesterday."

Annie tilted her head to one side as if studying her words from a different angle. Then she raised her shoulders in a quick shrug and hopped beneath the covers. "If you say so."

"I do." Sarah took a deep breath and exhaled quietly as Annie turned over and pounded her pillow into shape.

"Will you turn out the light?"

"Of course." As if led by a higher power, Sarah extinguished the light, then made her way to her bed. She was just settling down under the covers when her eyes adjusted to the darkness.

She couldn't allow the word to enter her mind. But it hung around the fringes, taunting her with the unknown. It had been more than a month. Probably closer to six weeks. And it wasn't like she was regular like Annie, just one more thing her sister did better than she did. Regular or not, she knew what she had to do. But in a town the size of Wells Landing, she wasn't sure how she was going to pull it off without everyone knowing before sundown.

Sarah stood in the grocery store aisle looking at box after box. They were all in pretty colors, pink, purple, and blue. School had let out a half an hour before and she only had a few more minutes before her parents started to wonder where she was. She needed to choose and get out. Before someone saw her.

She would get the pink one. She wasn't sure if it was any better than any of the other ones, but it claimed to give the most accurate results in half the time of the other leading brand. Not that she was in a super-big hurry to learn what a fool she had been. She took a step forward, hand out, ready to pick up the cotton candy–colored box.

The *squeak* of shopping cart wheels sounded behind her. She didn't turn to see who was coming, merely switched her attention to the other products stocked on the aisle. Something for bladder infections and an ovulation kit. Like either one of those was better.

She cast a quick look over one shoulder only to see an English woman pushing a toddler in the basket. Sarah heaved a sigh of relief when she didn't recognize them. The woman grabbed a package of diapers from the opposite shelves and tossed it onto the pile of groceries. She shot Sarah a quick smile, then continued down the aisle and turned the corner out of sight.

Sarah turned back to the rectangular boxes. Pink. Yes, she was definitely going with the pink one.

As quickly as possible, she snatched it off the shelf and hurried to the front counter. The checkout girl she had seen a hundred times. Her name was Kelsey and she was a senior at the high school. She was a nice girl, but Sarah knew she was bored in her job and talked to the customers way too much. If she went through Kelsey's line, her purchase would be all over the district before sundown.

She had never used the self-checkout before, but it was never too early to learn something new. Wasn't that what she was always telling her students?

She walked up to the counter studying the screen. She might just be an Amish girl, but she could do this.

Touch screen to start.

Sarah reached out trembling fingers and brushed them across the smooth television-looking device. Then she jumped as a voice spoke.

"Please scan first item."

Scan? Scan how? Then she remembered how the checkout girl would wave the products over the glass piece on the counter. She tried it, and thankfully it beeped on the first try. From there, it was a simple matter of stuffing the offending box into the sack and following the directions on how to deposit her money. As quickly as possible, she retrieved her change and receipt.

"Thank you." The security guard smiled at her as she started for the door. Had he seen what she had purchased? Did he know she was unmarried? Was he passing judgment on her as she nodded and walked by?

She pulled those thoughts in. There was no way for him to tell if she was married or single. Most *Englishers* knew that men grew beards when they married, but most had no idea of all the rules associated with aprons, apron colors, and what distinguished an unmarried woman from a married one. He couldn't know. He just couldn't.

Sarah tucked her package behind her seat and hopped on her tractor. She would put it in her dress, under her apron, and sneak it into the house and . . .

No. She would be better off to stop at the gas station on the edge of town and use their restroom.

The small cinder-block room reeked of urine and toilet bowl cleaner. The dual scent was nauseating and strange. Sarah let herself in with the key given to her by the attendant and locked the door behind herself. Thankfully she wouldn't have to buy anything in order to use the restroom.

She didn't need gas and she couldn't stomach any food or drinks. Her throat was tight, her belly flip-flopping. She knew it was merely nerves, but she wasn't sure how much more of it she could take. Her heart had been pounding in her ears ever since she had stepped out of the grocery store.

She took a deep breath and surveyed her reflection in the water-speckled mirror. She didn't look any different than she did any other day. Yet today could very well be life-altering. She was going to take the little box she'd bought at the grocery store, take the test, and see if she was pregnant.

She could barely stand the word in her private thoughts. She couldn't be pregnant. She just couldn't. But there was only one way to find out.

Her fingers flitted over her prayer *kapp*, then she reached for the plastic sack. She stuffed it in the trash and turned the box over in her hands. Her fingers trembled as she opened one end. There were instructions, written in English on one side and what looked to be Spanish on the other. Sarah scanned them. She had to pee on the little stick, wait two minutes, then she would have her answer.

She was a little nervous, peeing on something so small. But it seemed to be the way these things worked.

Somehow despite the tremor in her hands, she managed to get the second packaging open. There were two tests inside, but surely she could get it right the first time. She sucked in another breath and made her way to the toilet.

It was definitely tricky, but she managed to hit the mark. She finished her business and took the little plastic wand to the sink and laid it there. Now she had to wait for two minutes. Two full minutes. She didn't have a watch on, so she counted. One Mississippi, two Mississippi, three Mississippi, on and on. One hundred and twenty seconds shouldn't have taken so long.

Thankfully no one came knocking on the door wanting to know what she was doing inside.

It was time. She squeezed her eyes tight and reached for the little wand. *Please God*, she prayed as she opened her eyes and stared into the little window. *Please.*

Chapter Four

Sarah pulled her tractor to a stop. She could do this. She could.

She took a deep breath, then climbed down. Her gaze swung to the house, but all was still. She hoped he was home. Maybe she should have called to see before she drove all the way over. But if she called, then he would want to know why, and she wasn't prepared to tell him. And yet here she stood, palms sweaty, mouth dry. She started for the door of the house.

Someone must have seen her pull up. There was movement in the window, then the front door opened. Jonah stepped out onto the porch.

"What are you doing here?" he asked.

He looked the same as he always did, handsome despite the frown that marred his features. It was the expression he most used when he was around her. Except for that one night . . .

The wind stirred his straw-colored hair as his tawny maple syrup eyes narrowed.

"I need to talk to you." That was the one line she had practiced. The rest, she wasn't so sure about. Especially not with him glaring at her like she was the last person he wanted to see. She supposed that she was.

"Now?"

She had to remain strong. As much as it pained her, she had to keep her chin up and her backbone straight. She couldn't let him see how much his annoyance hurt her. "It's important."

He looked back at the door as if someone was waiting for him. Another girl? Had he finally decided to move on from his heartbreak? "Okay, fine." He shut the door behind himself and loped down the steps to her side.

She tried not to wilt with relief. There was still too much ground to cover to let her guard down now.

"Do you want to walk?" she asked. She kept her eyes forward and didn't let them stray toward the field of corn to her right, or more specifically, the copse of trees that hid Millers' Pond from view.

"Not really." He shoved his hands into the pockets of his pants and eyed her uncomfortably.

She looked back at the house. The Miller home was full. Jonah had three brothers and two sisters, and only one had moved out. Hannah had married Will Lapp last year. They had lived with the Millers for a while as tradition dictated, but had moved into their own home earlier in the year. That left four siblings plus his mother and father to overhear her shame.

"Let's walk over here." She started across the yard toward the small barn where they kept their horses. One must have heard them coming. The sound of his snort and his hooves pawing at the ground carried to her on the light breeze.

"What's wrong with you, Sarah?" He followed behind her. She could hear the reluctance in his steps.

Oh, the mistakes she had made.

What was wrong with her? "I think you know."

He shook his head, lips pressed together. He was going to make her say it, lay all of her shame out in the open for him to see. *But it's not just your fault.* He was a part of this. He'd had just as much responsibility for the outcome as she had. And yet the church wouldn't view it the same.

"I'm . . . I'm pregnant." She turned toward him to see if he heard.

But Jonah just stood there, his expression confused, dumbfounded even. "Jonah?"

It was as if she hadn't spoken his name at all.

How could two people be so dumb? How could they be so careless? But that wasn't even the worst of it. No, by far the worst was she knew in her heart that Jonah wanted nothing to do with her. He had avoided her from the time he had dropped her off at her house that fateful night until this very moment. And now? Now everything had changed.

"What?" He jerked his gaze from the ground back to her.

"Did you hear what I said?" It had been the hardest words for her to say. Ever. *Please don't make me say them again. Please, please, please don't make me say them again.*

He opened his mouth, closed it again, then somehow managed to speak. "You are? You're sure? Is it . . . ? I mean—"

"Of course I'm sure. Do you think I would be standing here if I wasn't?" What kind of person did he think she was? What kind of person was she that she had allowed herself to get in this predicament?

"I don't know."

"I'm going to pretend that you didn't say that." It might've been different if things between them had been . . . different. But they weren't. Somehow in a moment of weakness the two of them . . . And now . . .

"What are we going to do?"

It was perhaps the most intelligent thing he had said since she delivered her news.

But he wanted her to say it? How could she?

His eyes were blank, his mouth slack as if he were in shock. But how did he think she felt? She'd been walking around with this information for three days before she managed to get over here to talk to him. Three days of not being able to look anyone in her family in the eye. Three days of praying that it wasn't true. Three days of bargaining with God for a different solution.

But one didn't exactly make deals with God, and here she stood with only one option available that would help her save face, recover the faith and the standing in the community that she was about to lose.

"Jonah?"

"I need some time, Sarah." He turned as if he was about to walk away.

Her heart gave a painful thump in her chest. "We don't have much time."

He stopped. He knew what she said was true. It had been over a month already. Many more weeks and their secret wouldn't be a secret any longer.

"Tomorrow," he said, his voice strangled. "Give me until tomorrow. Come back then."

"I can't get another day off from school." She hated the tone of her voice, the hint of a whine that had crept in. She couldn't wait any longer. She just couldn't, but what she said was true. She had barely gotten this day off to come here. Her teaching job was already teetering in the balance. And of course this would push it completely over the edge. She could hear them now. Unfit to teach the scholars of the district.

He hesitated. She could see it in his eyes. This wasn't what either of them wanted.

Tears stung the back of her throat despite her vow not to cry. But there were too many things gone wrong, too much to recover from. She would lose her job, force Jonah to marry her, and deal with the shame that everyone in Wells Landing knew what they had done.

Yes, they would be forgiven. That was always the way. And she had wanted to marry Jonah for so long. But not like this. Never like this.

His breath was stuck somewhere in the middle of his chest, unable to actually get to his lungs. He couldn't inhale. He couldn't exhale. He could only stand and look at her. A strange buzzing started in his ears.

Sarah was pregnant.

Everyone in the district knew that she had had a crush on him since before they left school. And now they would know that he took advantage of her feelings for him on one warm September night.

Marrying Sarah was the last thing he wanted to do. He had never wanted to marry anyone but Lorie. Once she was off the list of options, he didn't think he would ever get married. He hadn't really thought about it, instead existing day to day, night to night, just trying to go forward. One foot in front of the other. One day at a time, and all those other encouraging things people said to get through a crisis. Say a prayer. He had prayed. Maybe not enough. That was the one thing he should've done more of.

"Jonah?"

He jerked his gaze back to her.

Her eyes were soft, misty with tears. This wasn't any easier on her. In fact, it might even be harder. He was a man, and people tended to forget the indiscretions of men, the sleights of faith and their mistakes, a lot easier than they did for the womenfolk.

"Just give me tonight, Sarah. Give me a day to get used to the idea. We need to make a plan to tell our parents." What was he going to tell them? The truth was the only thing. But how could he explain how he had stumbled across Sarah walking down the road? An angry Sarah who hadn't told him all the nice words about how wonderful he was and how terrible Lorie was. Sarah who laid it all out. A Sarah who, in that moment, had intrigued him. And in that moment of weakness, he had taken advantage of her innocence, her affections, her devotion to him.

"Just come back tomorrow," he said. "We'll figure everything out then."

He ignored the bruised look in her eyes and turned away, stalking back to the house.

Thousands of thoughts tumbled over inside his head. Beginning with what would he tell his parents? What would they say?

Would he and Sarah have to get married? Did they really have to?

That last one he knew the answer to, even if he didn't like it. Of course they did. Getting married would begin the forgiveness and healing for the community.

He stomped up the porch steps and into the house, careful not to let the door slam behind him. As usual his household was a loud mixture of shouting voices and sounds of living.

"Jonah?" His mother came out of the kitchen, wiping her hands on her apron. Gertie Miller was as round as she was tall, but to Jonah that just meant she gave the best hugs. Right now he could use one of those, but he was afraid if she touched him at all he would completely fall apart.

"Who was at the door?"

He gave a small shrug. "Sarah Yoder." Best not say any more than that.

His mother raised her brows in question. But he didn't want to explain. Not yet. Let them make their own assumptions. Maybe everyone would begin to think that he had wanted to be with Sarah and that because of that they had slipped up and made a mistake. And maybe if the district thought he wanted to marry Sarah, no one would express their pity behind his back.

Outside he heard her tractor start up and the gears grind as she backed out and chugged away.

"What did Sarah want?"

Jonah shrugged again. "We've just been talking lately."

"That's *gut, jah*. I thought she seemed . . . intrigued at the back-to-school picnic." His mother smiled, but the action didn't reach her eyes. "She's not quite your type, is she?"

"I don't know that I have a type."

His mother raised one shoulder in a semblance of a shrug. "She's just sort of . . . fancy, don't you think?"

"I haven't given it much thought."

"You should. Fancy Amish—" She shook her head. "They can be a different sort. Not the kind I would think you would want to get involved with."

If she only knew.

"I'll keep that in mind, *Mamm*."

"What's wrong, Jonah?"

He'd lost count of how many times people had asked him that tonight, and his answer had always been the same. *Nothing.*

But Ivan was more astute than the rest. Somehow his brother knew that Jonah's pat answer was just that.

"And don't tell me 'nothing' like you told *Mamm*. I don't believe it."

Ivan—though no one called him that, everyone simply called him Buddy—had what the doctors called Down syndrome. Jonah had heard it explained once, and it had something to do with chromosomes, which were something people couldn't see and a lot of Amish didn't know even existed. All Jonah knew was that his brother had a kind heart. He looked a little different than most folks. His eyes were a little too far apart and his cheekbones little flatter than most. Jonah knew his parents worried about Buddy. But Jonah knew. He might not be as smart as other boys his age, but he didn't have to have some fancy *Englisch* education in order to farm. He just had to love God, love the land, and do what he was taught to do.

"Go to sleep, Buddy."

"Not until you tell me what's wrong." His voice grew louder in the darkness that separated them.

Jonah shushed him to keep him from disturbing the rest of the house. He and Buddy had shared a room for as long as Jonah could remember. He had just turned three when his parents brought Buddy home from the hospital. He couldn't remember life without his special brother, who seemed more childlike than most and yet smarter by far than some.

"Girl troubles, Buddy." One particular girl, but he didn't need to tell his brother that.

"A girl?" Buddy asked. "Lorie? Did Lorie come back?"

Jonah's heart gave a heavy thump in his chest. Just the mention of her name could do that to him. "No, Buddy.

Remember? I told you that Lorie was going to be English now."

"She could come back as the English."

Jonah shook his head. "She got married."

"Oh. I forgot."

Jonah heard the springs of Buddy's bed squeak as he turned over to get more comfortable. "It's all right, Buddy. Just go to sleep, okay?"

"Okay."

Jonah heard his brother sigh and hoped he was gearing down. He loved Buddy with all his heart, but he needed time to think. That was all he'd asked Sarah for. Yet he didn't know what he needed to think about. He had no choice but to marry her. He might not love her, but he was responsible for the child she carried. He had to step up and do what was right. But still he needed to roll it around in his mind, get used to the idea, kick the tires, as the English said.

He was going to be a father. The thought sent a shiver through him.

"If it wasn't Lorie, who was it?"

Jonah bit back a sigh. "Sarah Yoder." He might as well tell Buddy the truth. Soon enough, Sarah was going to be a part of their family, like it or not. Best let Buddy get used to the idea now.

"I like Sarah Yoder."

The sweet innocence of his statement made Jonah smile. "Oh, *jah*?"

"She's pretty."

"You think so?" Jonah said as if Buddy didn't say those very words every time someone mentioned Sarah's name.

"*Jah*, and she's nice too."

Jonah usually considered Sarah to be a little on the

annoying side. Or maybe that was because lately it seemed that she was always around. Until this summer. Something had happened this summer, and suddenly Sarah wasn't underfoot. At first he'd thought it felt that way because he was spending more and more time in Tulsa with some of Luke Lambright's friends. But that night a few weeks ago, he'd realized that she simply wasn't hanging around as much.

At first he was relieved. Then a little perplexed. What had brought about her change of heart?

Jonah pushed those thoughts aside. Nice or not, crush or no, he didn't want to marry Sarah Yoder. And yet that was exactly where he found himself.

"Let's get some sleep, okay, Buddy?"

"Okay, Jonah."

Jonah turned over and stared at the wall. Their room was dark with only a few nighttime shadows moving around.

If only his thoughts could be as peaceful.

"Jonah! Jonah!" Buddy came loping in, bursting through the back door, his face flushed with pleasure.

"What? What?" he asked with a quick smile.

Buddy twirled his hat between his hands and grinned. "Sarah's here."

Jonah's heart gave a painful pound and his breath hitched in his chest. "Thanks, Buddy."

"Are you going to talk to her now?"

Jonah nodded and grabbed his hat from the peg by the door.

"Can I go too?"

"Not this time, okay, Buddy?"

Buddy nodded thoughtfully. "Right. Girl problems. I forgot."

"It's okay." Jonah settled his hat onto his head and started outside.

Sarah was just getting off her tractor when he jumped down from the porch. He didn't want her to go into the house, even though he should have invited her in, poured her something to drink, and led her to the sofa so they could talk this out.

There were too many ears inside.

"Let's walk," he said instead of a greeting. He grabbed her elbow and pulled her toward the road. "We can go down to the pond."

She dug in her heels. "I do not want to go back there."

"Right." He stopped. The pond was where they had—"We can walk down the road." He started down the driveway with her reluctantly plodding along beside him. "I know a place," he said, walking her across the road and into the cornfield there.

The stalks rustled like old bones. He pushed them aside to create an opening for her to duck inside. "No one will come looking for us here."

She looked up at the tall stalks. They were almost to his hat, but they were well over her head. "I could get lost in here."

"Just stay close to me." He took her hand and led her deeper into the rattling stalks. A few more feet in, he pressed down a couple of the stalks and sat on the ground, tugging her down in front of him.

She craned her head back, gazing up at the towering stalks that surrounded them. "It's really quiet here."

"It's a good place to think."

She leveled her gaze on him. "And talk?"

He plucked up a dirt clod and tossed it to one side. "And talk."

"Have you thought any more about it?"

Had he thought—? It was all he could think about. More times than not over the last twenty-four hours, he wished he could *not* think about it. "*Jah*. You?"

She nodded. "I guess we have a lot to do, huh?"

More than a lot. They had to tell their families, talk to the bishop, plan a wedding.

"I've got an idea. You might not like it," she said. "But I was thinking that maybe we could both invite our parents to Kauffman's and then we could tell them both there at the restaurant."

"It would definitely be easier telling them at the same time, but I don't think I can get my *dat* to go into town on a whim."

She frowned. "I didn't think about that."

He gave a quick nod. "I think we're destined to tell our story multiple times."

"Your parents, my parents . . ."

"The bishop."

"And then what?" Her voice cracked on the last word.

He sucked in a stabilizing breath. It didn't work, so he let it go. "Then we get married."

Her shoulders slumped. With relief? Did she think he wasn't going to marry her?

It wasn't like he'd said those words, and he surely hadn't given her any reason to believe in him. He should apologize, but he couldn't bring the words to his lips. Instead he stood and reached out a hand. "I guess there's no time like now."

She looked at his hand for what seemed like five full

minutes, then she laid her palm on top of his and allowed him to help her to her feet. "Now?" she squeaked.

He nodded and pointed to all the straw and pieces of dried grass that were stuck to her dress. "You have, uh . . ."

"*Now* now?"

"Yes, Sarah. You're already here. Let's get this over with."

They walked back to his house side by side. Jonah had dropped her hand as soon as she was on her feet, and she wished they were still connected. How could she go in and face his parents?

Everyone in Wells Landing knew that she had put herself in Jonah's path every chance she got. They would never believe that their meeting on the road that night was nothing more than a coincidence. And even worse, everyone would think that she had trapped Jonah on purpose. As if the shame of their sin wasn't enough, she had the added burden of unrequited love.

She shrank back. The closer she got to the house, the more she wanted to hop on her tractor and ride off.

Jonah stopped and looked back, waiting for her to catch up. "Are you okay?"

Was she?

She nodded slowly. It was a lie, but what choice did she have? Fine or not, she had to face Jonah's parents. It might have been better if they could have gone in as a couple. But they weren't a couple. They never had been.

He allowed her to go up the steps first, then opened the door for her. She stepped inside feeling like she was headed to meet her doom.

"Hey, Jonah. Hey, Sarah."

She turned to find Jonah's brother just inside the door. "Hey, Buddy."

He sidled closer to Jonah. "Did you get your girl problems worked out?"

Jonah turned a little red around the ears. "Uh, yeah . . . sort of." He coughed. "Are *Mamm* and *Dat* around?"

"*Dat*'s out in the barn bundling turnips to take to the auction and *Mamm* is in her sewing room. You want me to go get them?"

"Could you ask *Dat* to come in here? Tell him it's important."

"*Jah.* Sure."

Buddy disappeared out the front door, and Jonah continued through the living room and ducked into a door off to the left.

Sarah shifted her weight from side to side. She could hear their voices, but couldn't understand what they were saying. A few moments later, he came out of the room, Gertie Miller waddling behind.

"This better be important, Jonah, or I'm going to make you help me sew the rest of these shirts for the wedding." She stopped when she saw Sarah standing there. "Hello, Sarah."

She nodded in return. "Gertie."

"He's coming." Buddy burst through the back door, skidding to a halt next to his brother.

"Buddy, don't run in the house." Gertie's words seemed almost absentminded. As if they had to be said even though they were never quite heeded.

Sarah jumped as the back door slammed, and Jonah's father came into the house. "What's this all about?"

Jonah might have gotten his wheat-blond hair and maple syrup eyes from his mother, but he got his lanky height from his father.

Six-year-old Prudy Miller picked that time to come in from the outside. She held up the skirt of her dress with both hands, the fabric weighed down by random vegetables. "I got everything out of the garden, *Mamm*." She beamed, obviously proud of herself and her efforts. "Hi, Sarah." She looked from Sarah to Jonah, then back again as if trying to determine why her schoolteacher was at her house.

Gertie nodded toward the kitchen. "Go set them on the table. Didn't I tell you to get a basket?"

Prudy nodded, then skipped to the kitchen humming a little song under her breath.

"Where's Jonathan?" Jonah asked. His lips were pressed in a thin line and his forehead marred with a frown.

"He's getting the tractor ready to harvest the north field. You need him?" Eli Miller asked.

Sarah twisted her fingers together. How long were they to stand there and figure out where everybody was before sitting down to talk? She needed this over with five minutes ago.

"I need to talk to you," Jonah said. "Alone." He shot a pointed look at his brother.

Buddy might not be the most perceptive person at times, but Jonah's tone was clear. He glanced at all their faces, then sighed with disappointment. "I'll go see what Jonathan's doing." He shuffled out of the house, leaving Sarah, Jonah, and his mother and father standing in the kitchen waiting for what was next.

"Can we sit down?" Sarah asked. Her stomach was beginning to hurt, and her knees were shaking. She knew both were the result of nerves, but that didn't make it any better.

All three Millers swung their attention to her.

"*Jah*," Jonah said. "Let's sit down."

The four of them moved to the living room. Jonah's *dat* sat in a recliner while Gertie settled down in a wooden rocking chair. That left Sarah and Jonah to sit side by side on the couch.

She perched on the edge, unable to sit back and relax. She was entirely too nervous.

Jonah clasped his hands between his knees, then braced them on his thighs. Then he clasped them once more. It was no consolation to her that he was as uncomfortable as she was.

This too shall pass. Wasn't that what they always said?

"It seems that Sarah and I need to get married."

Eli's eyebrows shot toward his hairline. Gertie sat up a little straighter, rocking forward in her chair.

"What exactly do you mean, son?" This from his father.

Jonah sucked in a deep breath. He ducked his head over his hands as if praying for strength, then he leveled his gaze on his father once more. Sarah had to give him kudos for bravery. He looked his father right in the eye and said, "We're having a baby."

Eli blinked a couple of times as if trying to get a handle on what Jonah had just said. "I see." His gaze was centered on Jonah as if he couldn't bear to look at her.

Sarah wasn't sure what was worse, Eli's inattention or Gertie's condemning stare.

"How did this happen?" She looked from one of them to the other, her voice sharp.

Jonah opened his mouth, closed it again, then shook his head.

"That's not what I mean." Gertie pressed her lips together.

They were disappointed. In her? In him? In the fact that he would be tied to her forever?

Dear Lord, if this is truly Your will, help me through this.

Sarah gathered her gumption and stood. "We made a

mistake. I'm sorry. We're sorry. We are human and weak. But I have to believe that this is God's will and we must see it through." She was trembling when she finished, her knees shaking so badly she almost collapsed back onto the couch next to Jonah.

He stood, his body warm next to her, lending her his strength. Strength she so desperately needed.

Gertie and Eli watched them, not speaking, barely breathing.

Then Eli nodded. "*Jah*. That is how we must view this."

"Have you talked to the bishop?" Gertie asked.

Jonah shook his head. "You're the first we've told."

"Then you have a lot of work to do," Eli said.

"And a wedding to plan." Gertie shook her head. Sarah could almost hear her thoughts. So much shame. So much work still to do. And she was already sewing for one wedding now.

But Sarah knew. She and Jonah would only have a small service with just the immediate family. Not the celebration that her friends had enjoyed. Every Amish girl thought about her wedding every day of her life. Which siblings or cousins would stand up with them? Who would be invited? Who would be old enough to attend?

She pushed those selfish thoughts aside. She had created more work for both families. But she didn't have time to apologize.

Gertie shook her head. "I guess that's that, then, *jah*?"

Eli nodded.

Sarah stared at her fingers. They had told his parents, but there was still so much left to do.

"I could use your help in the north field," Eli said to Jonah, his implication clear.

Jonah coughed. "I think it's only right that we head over to tell Sarah's parents now."

Not that she wanted to. She wanted to crawl into a hole and never come out.

After her parents, they would need to have a word with the bishop.

So much to do. So many plans. So much heartache for them all.

Chapter Five

Hilde Yoder dabbed her eyes with the tail end of her apron and sniffed.

Sarah's parents had taken the news much like the Millers had, with a strong mark of shock and a little bit of disbelief. But instead of resigned and a little angry, Sarah's parents seemed sad.

She had disappointed them. She had let them down in one careless moment of weakness.

"I just never thought . . ." Her mother pressed her lips together, and Sarah's heart fell into her lap. She wanted to crawl under the table and pretend none of this was even happening, but she would have to come out and face it all eventually.

"I know." Her father cleared his throat and gave a small nod. Her actions had left a strong man practically speechless. "What do we do now?" he asked.

Mamm tried to smile, but the gesture fell short. "I guess we have a wedding to plan."

Sarah shrugged as if it were no matter. She was starting to become numb from the shame and disgrace. Maybe it was better that way.

"When are you going to the bishop?" Her father's shoulders sagged as he asked the question. She knew she had disappointed him. It had been the furthest thing from her mind that night. She hadn't been thinking about anything but Jonah and how easy he was to talk to when he wasn't mooning over Lorie. He seemed to enjoy her company, and the next thing she knew . . .

"I think we should go see if he's home now," Jonah said. "I want to talk to him before word spreads."

That way they could fight the gossip with their plans. And maybe then Sarah could pretend that this was what Jonah wanted as much as she did.

But she didn't want to marry him. Not like this. She had wanted him to love her in return.

Mamm looked at each one of them in turn. "This is the beginning of your story. It might be a little rocky, but you must own up to it. But from here . . . well, the rest of your story depends on you. You can make it happy or not."

They were wise words, but Sarah couldn't fathom them all in her current state. Once today was over, after they talked to the bishop, maybe then she could take out those words and glean more from them.

They rose from the table where they had been sitting and discussing their plans. Her father pulled Jonah to one side, talking in hushed tones only for him to hear.

"*Mamm*," Sarah whispered. "Is there another way?"

Her mother frowned. "What are you talking about, Sarah Sue?"

She swallowed hard. "Can you send me away somewhere? Do we have any family in Ohio or Pennsylvania? Someplace where I can go and . . . have the baby?"

Her mother blinked in apparent shock. "You don't want to marry Jonah? I thought you were crazy about him."

"I was. I mean . . ." She studied her fingernails, trying

to come up with the best explanation for how she felt. "I love him with all my heart. But he doesn't love me. Yes, I want to marry him, but only if he loves me in return."

Mamm shook her head. "Love comes. Love changes. You have to be patient. You have been given a special gift. Not everyone is blessed to have children. Look at Eileen Brenneman. Be thankful for the gift that God has given you."

"But—"

"Shhh," her mother said. "If it is God's will that you have this baby, then you must carry that out married to Jonah Miller."

Jonah pulled his tractor into the bishop's driveway and said a little prayer that the man would be home. He felt like he was carrying the weight of the world on his shoulders.

One bad choice and his life was forever altered. He might have understood what led him to Sarah if he had just come from an English party where people were drinking and making out all over the place. But no. He had just left a Sunday-night volleyball game.

He had no excuse for his behavior, no reasoning. They couldn't claim that they loved each other and couldn't wait. They could only say that they had made a mistake. And now they were paying the consequences.

Jonah and Sarah entered the house. "Bishop?" Jonah said in greeting.

"Just a minute" floated to them from somewhere in the vicinity of the Ebersol kitchen. But it was a female voice, most likely Helen, the bishop's wife. Then again, the bishop's household was full of daughters.

Sarah shifted in place next to him as they waited for

the owner of the voice to come out. Fortunately, they didn't have to wait long, and Helen appeared in the kitchen doorway.

She seemed surprised to see them standing there side by side. "Jonah Miller and Sarah Yoder. What brings you two out today?"

Jonah took his hat from his head and stepped forward. He cleared his throat. "We came to talk to Cephas. Is he around?"

"Last time I checked, he was fixing the back porch. We have a rotted board back there." She waved them toward the door. "Go on back."

"Thank you." Jonah nodded and started for the back door. Sarah was right behind him. He would have to get used to that. They would be expected to behave like a normal married couple.

He stopped, the realization of what was about to happen knifing through him. He was going to marry Sarah Yoder. How had his life gotten here?

They walked out onto the back porch to find Cephas Ebersol hammering down a new board. To call the space a porch was unflattering. Actually it was a raised deck complete with a barbecue grill, patio table, and beautiful potted plants. The bishop kept his house well-maintained, better than average. Jonah would like to have something like this one day. And then the question hit him. Where were they going to live?

Tradition dictated that they move in with her family for a few months after the wedding or longer, if their house was not ready. But there was no way he was doing that. He pushed the thought aside. First he had to get through whatever punishment the bishop doled out to them, the wedding ceremony, and a hundred other hurdles before he could think about where they were going to live.

"I didn't expect to see you today, Jonah Miller." The bishop thumbed his hat back to get a better look at the two of them. "Sarah Yoder. What brings the two of you here today? And don't say nothing, because I can see it on your faces."

He set his hammer down and turned to face them, giving them his full attention. It was one of the things Jonah liked most about the bishop. He was a good and caring man. He was fair, but he was tough. And in the past Jonah had admired many of his decisions. He just hoped that the bishop wasn't so hard on them.

"We wanted to talk to you before the rumor gets all around town," Jonah said.

"And what rumor would that be?"

"The rumor that Sarah and I—" He swallowed hard and fought to continue. "Are having a baby."

The bishop straightened, but his expression remained passive. "I see. That is a strong rumor. Is it true as well?"

"*Jah*," Jonah said. "That is why we would like to get married."

Cephas climbed up the steps so he was on the deck with them. "Let's go inside and talk." He took off his tool belt, deposited it on the patio table, then motioned them toward the house. The next thing Jonah knew, he was sitting at the table with the bishop, his wife, and Sarah. Everyone had a small plate with a slice of pie and a cup of coffee in front of them. He took a sip of his coffee, but no one was eating the pie. It was almost more of a nicety than a necessary snack.

"Marriage is a big step." The bishop looked at each of them in turn.

"We understand that," Jonah said.

"And you also understand that if you don't get married, then you will have to leave the church?"

"*Jah*."

"And how did you to find yourself in this situation?" Again he pinned them each with a stare, then qualified his question. "Most times if a couple comes to me with a similar situation, where they have strayed from their upbringing in this manner, they're usually already engaged."

Oh, how he wished she would stand up and spout all she had at his parents' house about being human and being weak, but she just sat there.

"We seem to have made a mistake," he said. "And now we need to atone for it."

"And you want to get married?"

"We do."

The bishop nodded. "Marriage is forever. Then again, so is having a baby. Are you ready for these commitments?"

"Does it matter?" Jonah cleared his throat. "That's not what I meant to say. It's just that—"

"You have to get ready," the bishop said. "You have to figure out how to let go of the past and look to the future."

The words washed over Jonah. He knew. That was exactly what he needed to do, but he hadn't figured out how yet.

"How do we do this?" Sarah asked.

He should have been the one to say those words.

"First, you'll need to go in front of the church and confess."

His heart sank at the thought. But it was necessary. Confessing would do away with any secrets. They could start fresh. But confessing would be uncomfortable. More than uncomfortable. Embarrassing. Shameful. Disgraceful.

"And after that?" Sarah asked.

The bishop spread his hands as if to say the rest would be up to them. "The church will vote. You can ask for leniency, especially since the two of you plan on getting married. That truly is your intention, right?"

"*Jah*. Of course." He finally found his tongue. "That was one of the reasons we came here."

"How quickly are you wanting to have the ceremony?"

"*Mamm* thought it would be a good idea if we could get married soon. Maybe right after Aaron and Mary."

"That's Gertie," the bishop said. "She moves quickly, *jah*?" He thumbed through a small leather-bound book until he got to the page he wanted. "Ah yes. How about the following Tuesday?"

So soon? Jonah nodded.

"That's fine with me. Sarah?"

She looked as if she had been glued into place.

"Sarah?"

"What?" She stirred and looked from him to the bishop as if trying to get her bearings.

"The Tuesday after Aaron and Mary's wedding. Does that sound all right to you?"

"For what?"

Had she not been listening at all? "Our wedding."

"So soon?" Sarah asked. She could hardly believe her ears. It was what she wanted, what had to happen, but it seemed so rushed.

"I think the sooner we get this matter cleared up, the better," Cephas said.

She nodded. "*Jah*. Okay then." Less than three weeks away.

The bishop cleared his throat. "Then there's the matter of the school board."

Sarah's heart sank to her toes. She knew this was coming. It had only been a matter of time.

"I'm sure they will request that you resign from your job as a teacher," the bishop continued.

Sarah somehow managed to nod. "I figured as much. *Jah*."

Unfit to teach the scholars of the district.

Helen moved toward Sarah, capturing her attention. "It's about more than the mistakes we make, Sarah. You will be a married woman and should be dedicated to building your home. Not teaching."

Sarah nodded. "I understand." And she did. But it didn't make it hurt any less. She'd struggled as a teacher, even though it had been the one thing she had wanted to do above all else. She was unable to get the older boys to do what she asked, and some of the younger ones too. The girls had seemed to take to her okay, but considering they were outnumbered two to one, chaos had ruled in her classroom as a first-year teacher. She had been planning to use this year to prove herself and show that she could be a good teacher. Now she had blown that. She would never get the chance.

"Your job will be to be a good wife to your husband and a good mother to your family." Helen's smile was gentle and encouraging.

Sarah just wished she could take it all in. So quick. So many changes. Too fast. Too many.

"I'll be in touch with everyone shortly," the bishop said. "I'm sure they'll want to meet with you tomorrow. I'll see if Emily can take over for you for the day."

"She can bring Sallie Mae here," Helen said. "I'll watch the baby for her."

"Thank you," Sarah said. What else could she say? Helen would watch the baby, Emily would take care of the school, and Sarah would give up her job.

And as easy as that, Sarah's life had been rearranged.

How she dreaded the meeting the next day, but it was one of those necessary things. And then a couple more days and they would stand in front of the church. It was almost too much.

They thanked the bishop for his time and headed back out to the tractor once again.

"What's wrong?" she asked him.

Jonah had said hardly anything during the last half of their visit. He'd simply stared at his hands braced in his lap and listened to everyone talk around him. Sarah couldn't tell if he had so much on his mind that he wasn't paying any attention to the things around him, or if he simply wasn't interested in responding.

"Why do I get the feeling you're mad at me?" Sarah asked, as she hurried behind him. His stride was much longer than hers.

"I don't know, Sarah. Why would I be mad at you?"

She studied his face for some hint of his feelings. But all she could discern was confusion, exhaustion, and a blaze of something she couldn't name.

"I can't read your mind, Jonah. If you have something you need to say, just say it."

"How did it come to this?" he asked.

She knew what he really wanted to know. How had they gone from casual acquaintances to planning a wedding in the span of just a few weeks? Because of one moonlit night. One bad choice.

She thought she would never regret the decision she had made then. She had made it thinking it would change things between them. Oh my, had it. She had hoped in those moments between kisses and more that Jonah would begin to view her differently. He would see her as someone he could care for. Someone he could spend the rest of his life with. All her talk of giving up on him and moving forward had been just that: talk. Words to convince herself that she wasn't really in love with him. But there in the dark, just the two of them, she couldn't lie to herself any longer. And when he turned to her for comfort . . .

But if she had known then that he would toss her aside, that he would forget what happened by the pond and ignore her for the weeks to come, she might have made a different decision.

Yet she couldn't look back at that. The decision had been made, a mistake to forge.

"If anyone should be angry, it should be me," she said. "Your parents look at me like I'm beneath them. Like I'm just some—" She couldn't even say the word. "Now I have to give up my job and stand with you in front of the church and tell everybody what we did. Stop acting like you're in this alone, Jonah Miller. This doesn't play with me at all." There. She'd said her piece. A lot of good it would do her. Jonah Miller was as stubborn as they came. And he seemed to prefer living in the past. Why couldn't he let go of Lorie? It was why he couldn't move forward. Well, that was fine with her.

"I'm sorry about your job," he said quietly.

She jerked her attention back to him. "You are?"

"I am. And you're right. We have to get up there and say things I never thought I would confess to another person. But I guess we have to do them together, *jah*?"

She nodded.

"Then maybe we should think about what we should say."

Sarah's throat constricted. Her heart pounded uncontrollably in her chest. Her hands were sweaty and her mouth was dry. She was supposed to talk to the school board like this? She could barely stand on her feet. She was embarrassed, shamed, nervous, and remorseful. It was an overwhelming combination.

"Sarah Yoder," the chairman greeted her as she stood before them. They came to her house, all four of them, and sat down at the kitchen table. They refused coffee and pie and told her to stand so they could see her.

How she wished she had resigned yesterday. She could have just told the bishop that she wouldn't be back to school as a teacher. They would have found someone. There was always a young girl wanting to teach school. And since a lot of the kids went to elementary school with the English kids, there were always more girls wanting to teach than schools available.

"*Jah?*"

"I believe you know why we are here today."

"*Jah.*"

"Last year, you had a hard time with your class, and the board decided to give you another chance. This year we find out that you have sinned in the eyes of the church and the Lord. We understand that you will be making amends for this to the church and to God. But that leaves us a couple of important concerns for this school year."

She dipped her chin, not really knowing what to say. She must not have been supposed to answer, for he continued quickly. "We hear that you are to be married soon, and as you know, married women do not teach in our schools. Being married means you need to focus on your family, your husband, and building a home for your own children one day."

Once again Sarah nodded, unsure of what to say and unable to speak past the lump in her throat even if she could.

"In light of this, we feel it's best that we replace you as

the teacher for this district with someone who will be able to better fulfill the duties of teaching our scholars."

"I understand," she said. Her throat tightened, her words choked.

"We also know that you might possibly have personal items in the school, and we feel you should be able to go get them as soon as class lets out today. Anything left after today will be turned over to the next teacher and will be either kept or disposed of by her. Do you understand?"

She nodded. "I don't have anything I need to get."

She had left a couple of things, a few personal items. A bottle of lotion and perhaps a pack of chewing gum. But whoever took her place could have them. Any decorations that she had hung for the scholars, she'd made for them, and she would leave them for the children. She couldn't face going back into that one-room schoolhouse just for items she could pick up again.

"Very well," the chairman said. "We wish you the best in your new endeavors."

Sarah nodded as everyone stood. She trailed behind them to the door and watched as they filed down the porch steps and onto their individual tractors. Five minutes later, everyone was gone.

She shut the door and managed to double back to the living room. She collapsed onto the couch, the weight of the world pushing her down. It could've been worse. She'd expected them to tell her how unworthy she was and how shameful her actions had been. But they hadn't. They seemed to know that she would be dealing with so much more in the upcoming days. They wouldn't shame her further. And for that she was grateful. One more hurdle she'd managed to clear. But in two more days she and Jonah would stand before the church and confess their sins.

The bishop had told her that he would recommend that they serve a two-week shunning. They would use those two weeks to reflect on their sins and get everything right with God before they got married. The wedding's October date was coming up so quickly it made Sarah's head spin. But everything seemed to do that these days.

She pressed a hand to her belly. She didn't know if it was stress or just the changes she was going through, but everything made her nauseous. Everything made her head hurt, everything made her dizzy. It was hard to eat and it was hard to sleep. And yet she trudged on, hoping that one day she would wake up and find this all behind her.

Chapter Six

Sarah sat across from Jonah at the kitchen table at the Ebersols'. It seemed she had been here so many times over the last few days. How ironic the church was held at their house this Sunday.

They were waiting on their time to go in, kneel, and confess before the congregation. Once they completed this task, they would hopefully have a two-week *Bann* that would end at the next church service. They would get married the Tuesday after that.

Married. That was the one thing she had dreamed of her whole life. All Amish girls did. She'd been raised to be a wife, whether it was to a farmer or Amish man who worked an English job, whoever she had the good fortune to fall in love with and marry. It was the one thing she wanted most.

And now . . . not as much. She still couldn't wrap her mind around the irony of it all. Two months ago she would have given anything to sit with Jonah at a youth group meeting or even just to have him talk to her. She knew that was just giving her more excuses to hang on and wait for him, so she had given up, vowed to move on. Now in just a couple of weeks she would be marrying him. And it was the last thing she wanted. At least, she didn't want it like this.

"Are you ready?"

She jerked her gaze up to Jonah's. He was staring at her, really looking at her like he had never looked at her before.

She shifted uncomfortably in her seat. "Does it matter?"

He shook his head. "I guess not."

"Do you think we'll get two weeks?" she asked.

He shrugged. "Hard to say. That's what the bishop said he would ask for, since we were doing everything in our power to right our wrongs."

Meaning they would confess, get married, and then raise their child in the church. It was all that could be asked of them.

"And then after that?"

Again he shrugged.

"We have a lot of decisions to make," she reminded him. There hadn't been a great bit of time over the last few days to start making those decisions, but they were coming up quicker than she would've liked.

"If you're talking about the wedding," he started.

She shook her head. "My mother's making my dress, your mother's making your shirt. All we have to do after that is show up." The guests were all in place and they weren't handing out favors.

"So what do you want to talk about, Sarah?"

She shook her head. It wasn't the time or the place. Not yet. But they had a lot to decide. A lot to discuss. It would have been easier to talk about had they been in love. He would share with her his plans for a home for them, where they would live and what they would do. She knew he would stay on the farm and help his father, at least for a time, and after that, who knew? He might get his own farm and plant corn and soybeans.

She pressed her hand to her belly.

"They're ready for you now," the deacon said.

Jonah shot to his feet, rubbed his hands down the front of his pants, then pushed his chair back to the table.

Sarah stood slowly, unwilling to hurry to what was essentially her doom. It was the last thing she wanted to do. The very last thing. But a necessary step in starting over. And that was something she desperately needed.

Two weeks passed in the blink of an eye and slow as molasses. There were times when she felt like she was on some type of whirlwind ride at the fair and other times when she thought this day would never come.

"Just four more days," Libby told her.

Sarah frowned at her cousin. "This isn't strange for you?"

Libby gave her a sad look. "Listen, not everyone manages to find love the same way."

Sarah shook her head. "And you think Jonah loves me?" Somehow she bit back her bark of incredulous laughter. As far as she could tell, Jonah pretty much despised her. He might have had one brief moment of weakness and thought about her a little differently. Or maybe it was because in that moment she wasn't so readily available to him. Whatever it was, she had followed him in that bad decision, resulting in a baby and a wedding, in that order. But now the moment was gone and they were doing their best to survive the consequences.

"He could. If he would let himself," Libby said. "Marriage is forever, Sarah. Just know that. If the two of you are ever going to survive this and hope to have a happy life, pray. It's going to take a little work. It's going to take some effort on both your parts. But it can be done. We just have to have faith."

"Faith in what?" She was running on a short supply of faith these days.

"That God's will can see you through."

Sarah couldn't think of one thing she would rather be doing less than sitting at her kitchen table facing off against Jonah and his parents. This was the meeting they'd been putting off from the very beginning.

"But tradition dictates that they should move in with us until they have their own house," her father said.

"I need Jonah at the farm," Eli Miller countered. He was the one saying the words, but Sarah knew they came from Jonah. She knew because he refused to raise his gaze to anyone sitting at the table. Instead he used his fork to cut tiny little pieces of piecrust into dust.

She wanted to reach across the table, grab his arm, yell at him to stop and pay attention, to care just a little bit. But she couldn't make him care. She couldn't force him to love her. She couldn't force him to want this, and that made her hate this all the more.

"I understand that," her father said. "It seems to me that we might have more room than is available in your house."

"Room is not the issue here," his mother said. "We need him to help take care of Buddy. They share a room, and if Jonah leaves, Buddy's schedule will be thrown off. We're fixing to bring in the corn. If you take him now, that's time away from being on the farm." His mother continued to list all the reasons why Sarah needed to move in with Jonah instead of the other way around. And moving in with his parents? It was the last thing Sarah wanted to do. They might be getting married in just a couple of days, but she couldn't lose herself like that. If she had to move in with the Millers, she would be gobbled up and would never be Sarah again.

Jonah stood abruptly, his chair scraping against the linoleum floor and teetering a bit before landing back on all four legs. "Sarah, may I talk to you?"

She looked to her parents, then to his, unsure what to say to that. Especially with him standing over her, his hand outstretched.

The implications were too great to ignore. This would be their marriage. Their life. They would have to make decisions. She hesitated a heartbeat more and slipped her hand into his. He helped her to her feet, then marched her out the door.

She stopped on the porch but he kept going, loping down the steps without a single glance back. He made it halfway to the barn before he realized she wasn't behind him.

"Are you coming?"

Once again she was left with a decision. She started down the steps. "Where are we going?"

"Somewhere we can talk. Alone." He ducked into the barn, leaving her to follow.

The dim interior of the barn was even cooler than the October breeze outside. The smell was familiar and comforting, hay and horse accented with a tiny bit of manure. It shouldn't have smelled good to her, but somehow it did. The smell was earthy and real and seemed to wrap its arms around her, comfort her. And that was the one thing she needed right then.

He settled down onto a five-gallon bucket while she leaned up against the stack of hay off to one side.

"I can't live here."

"You've already said that, but there are a lot of decisions, Sarah. I'm needed at the farm now."

"I don't understand. We're supposed to move in with my family, and we have so much more room."

Jonah shook his head. "I'm not worried about room. We have plenty. I'm worried about Buddy and Prudy and everybody else. Not sure how they would handle it if I just up and left."

She stared at him incredulously. "What about my family? Don't they count for anything? My sisters will have questions if I just leave one day."

"Be practical, Sarah."

"You know, I'm tired of everybody telling me to be practical. This is not a practical situation. I have to be practical about the wedding. I have to be practical about the living arrangements. What else do I have to be practical about?"

He crossed his arms and glared at her. "I will not live with your family."

"That's not fair to me at all."

"Fine. We'll live with my family for the first six months, and if in that time I don't buy you a house and get you a place of your own, then we'll move in with yours. Sound good?"

She couldn't say it was the arrangement she wanted. But it was better than nothing. Wasn't that what they said marriage was all about, compromise? "*Jah*. Fine. Okay."

"This is never going to work if we're constantly mad at each other," he finally said.

"You're the one walking around angry, Jonah. I didn't have anything to do with this."

"I never said that."

She laughed. "You didn't have to. Let's get one thing straight. I don't want to marry you. I even asked my family if there was something else I could do. Some place I could go and have this baby and no one need ever be the wiser."

He jerked back as if he'd been slapped. "You did what?"

She crossed her arms as his went slack. "You heard me. I asked if there was a way that I could get out of marrying you. You don't want to marry me. Why should we enter into a loveless relationship?"

This seemed to take a little of the zip out of his horse. "What did they say?"

"That there would still be love in my future. That many marriages started off loveless, but that didn't mean we couldn't find love one day. But I don't believe that will happen either."

He continued to stare at her as if he couldn't believe the words she was saying to him. But for so long she'd felt like she'd been doing everyone else's will. She had done what was expected of her, she had been patient. She had waited her turn, helped her fellow man, and it had given her absolutely nothing. Zip, zero. And just once she wanted a little more than that.

"Surprised?" she asked. "I'm marrying you because I have no choice. Don't expect me to love every minute of it. And don't expect me to allow you to take advantage of me. I won't be a dutiful wife while you do anything and everything that you want to do. That's not happening."

She pushed off from the hay bale and marched to the barn door, only then realizing that she might have said those words, but she had compromised on the one thing she didn't want to compromise on—where they were going to live.

Jonah watched her go, his jaw slack. He shut his mouth, lest any flies decide to come in, then pushed himself to his feet.

She didn't want to marry him? Wasn't that all she had wanted last year? She had managed to put herself in his path every available opportunity for months. At every event, he couldn't turn around without her being there. And now she wanted to deny that she cared about him?

He remembered their talk that fateful night down by the pond. She had told him that she had loved him and talked about it like it was over, like everything was in the past. Maybe she had loved him, but not anymore. She cared about him, but not like she used to.

He had walked around that volleyball game, the first Amish event he had gone to in a couple of months, but it hadn't felt the same. He hadn't wanted to be with the Amish, but the English world was starting to lose its charm. He couldn't find out what he wanted to know about Lorie and what drew her there. It was just a lot of drinking and girls in scandalous clothing, people who wanted to make out whether they knew your name or not. At first it had been a great deal of fun, then it just got boring. But when he'd come back to the Brenneman volleyball game, he couldn't find solace there either.

Now he was getting married to a girl who seemed to hate him. Where did he belong and what did God want from him? He wished he knew.

Jonah's words stayed with Sarah all through the remaining days before the wedding. Just last week she had witnessed the joining of Jonah's brother Aaron and Mary Ebersol. It had been such a happy time. Now she was getting married. Sarah felt sadder than ever.

But she had made her bed and now she had to lie in it.

"Are you ready?"

Sarah shook that thought away as her mother turned toward her. "*Jah*." But that was a lie. She wasn't ready for this. Not at all.

She had dreamed of her wedding day for as long as she could remember. Now she had no attendants and a small cake, and they would be home by five. Not the day she had envisioned by far.

But the saddest part of all was it didn't really matter. She was marrying Jonah Miller, like it or not.

Chapter Seven

Sarah wiped one arm across the back of her forehead and reached for the next bag in the back of the trailer. The last one. And then tomorrow they would go get the rest of her things from her parents' house. But for today, this was it.

"Here." Jonah nudged her out of the way. "Let me get it."

She wanted to tell him no, but she was so tired she didn't complain. It had to be the stress of the day mixed with the pregnancy exhaustion that she had heard everyone talk about that had her in such a state. As it was, she was about to fall asleep standing up.

Jonah lifted the bag with ease and carried it into the house. Sarah trudged behind him.

It was the last place she wanted to be. Jonah's mother and father had stayed behind to help clean up. Sarah was sure that Jonathan would be bringing Prudy and Buddy home shortly, but until then she was alone in the house with Jonah.

She pushed into the house behind him just as he headed up the stairs. Then it hit her all at once. They were married. *Married*. And as a married couple, would be expected to *act* like a married couple. Good or bad, right or wrong, love or not, they would be expected to carry on. And that meant sharing a room. Sharing a *bed*.

Her head began to pound. "Where are you going with my stuff?"

Jonah stopped on the fourth step up, but didn't turn around. "Upstairs."

"I can see *that*. But where are you *going* with it?"

"Sarah . . ." He continued up the stairs without even a quick glance in her direction.

"Jonah!" Her exhaustion vanished in an instant. She started up the staircase after him. "Where are you taking my things?" She had to hear him say it. This was something they had never talked about. They had only discussed that they would live here for the first six months and either move into their own home or stay with her family after that. Where they would sleep had never been brought up. But she couldn't imagine that the efficient Gertie Miller hadn't made arrangements of her own.

All during the ceremony Jonah's mother had dabbed at her eyes as if she was witnessing a funeral instead of a wedding. At first Sarah had tried to pretend that Gertie was overcome with joy at seeing her two sons get married. Then she started to wonder if maybe the joy was just for Aaron. But no, they were tears of sadness for Jonah. She was sure of it.

Jonah made his way down the short hallway at the top of the stairs. She followed him, but he acted as if she wasn't there. He stepped through the last door on the left and she trailed after him, not sure of what she was going to find.

Twin beds stood on opposite sides, their headboards pushed up against the outside walls with a curtainless window in between. Jonah tossed her bag onto the bed closest to the door, then turned to face her, his hands on his hips. His eyes blazed. "What?"

Sarah looked from the bed to her husband. Husband.

"This is your room." She wasn't positive, but it wasn't a question. She knew. She just needed him to confirm.

"*Jah*."

"I can't stay here with you." She wouldn't stay in here. Theirs wasn't a traditional marriage, and despite what his family wanted or thought, she couldn't stay here in this room with him. She wouldn't. Staying in his house was bad enough. She had already given up so much.

He exhaled out his nose, the sound heavy between them. "Sarah. Can you not?"

That was it! "Can I not what? Stand up for myself? Have an opinion? Or just a brain?"

For a moment she thought he was going to give her anger right back to her, but instead, his shoulders slumped. "Don't make this more difficult than it has to be."

Part of her wanted to give in to the pleading whisper of his voice. But she couldn't let him get the best of her every day for the rest of their lives. They had to have some sort of compromise or she would completely lose herself and who she was.

"I can't sleep in here with you, Jonah."

He shrugged. "Why not? There are two beds. And . . ." He stopped as if gauging his words. "Buddy had to move out of here so you could move in. It was really hard on him."

"So let him move back in."

He shot her a look, but she wasn't giving in without a fight.

"I can move in with Prudy. Or maybe there's an empty bedroom now that Aaron is gone."

"My parents . . ." Jonah shook his head. "I don't think they would understand."

Sarah was about to tell him that she really didn't care what his parents thought, but even inside her head, the words sounded harsh and mean.

"And do you really want everyone in the house to know that . . . that . . ." He stopped as the words failed him. But he didn't need to finish. She knew what he was going to say. Did she really want everyone in the house to know that they weren't even sleeping in the same room? With them sharing space, even if they weren't sharing a bed, at least they could pretend and everyone would have to go along with them.

But where they were sleeping was another matter they hadn't discussed.

"Are you saying we're going to sleep on the two beds?"

A dark red flush started at his collar and worked its way up to his hairline. "We might need to push them together . . ."

That was when she knew. He was as embarrassed as she was. The situation wasn't any easier for him. Even though they were living in his home, even though he was staying on familiar ground, it wasn't any easier for him. And the only way for them to get through this was together. Together meant compromise.

Her resolve slipped even though her anger remained firmly in place. "Okay. Fine." It was only for six months. After that they would either have their own house or move in with her parents. And once they were there, no one would be able to tell her she had to share a bedroom with her husband.

* * *

Jonah could see the exact moment when Sarah caved. Didn't she understand? This was just as much for her as it was for him. She was only making it harder on the both of them.

"Bathroom's through there," he said, pointing out to the hallway. It was directly across from his room . . . theirs.

"Listen . . . I hate this as much as you do. But can you please, for the sake of peace, try not to disagree with everything I say?"

She turned and eyed him coolly. What happened to the bumbling Sarah who was always underfoot? The Sarah who would do anything for a crumb of his attention? Where did this angry woman before him come from?

"Okay, but you can't spring things like this on me and expect me to just accept it like it's nothing."

He shifted uncomfortably. Was that what he had done? Surprised her with their sleeping arrangements and then expected her to just accept it?

This entire situation was beyond him. He had never experienced anything like this. How was he supposed to know what to do?

"Maybe we should set a few ground rules."

She nodded, her expression clearly relaying that she thought it was the first intelligent thing he had said all day. "*Jah*. That would be good."

The sound of a tractor engine floated in through the open screened window.

She stopped, her gaze snagging his.

"I guess everybody's home now." He sent her an apologetic look, then started for the stairs. He could hear her behind him, her lighter footsteps on the wooden staircase.

Buddy was the first one inside, practically sliding on the floor as he hustled in, then came to an abrupt stop.

He grinned as he spotted Jonah. "So you're a married man now."

Jonah dipped his chin. "*Jah.*"

"Do you feel different?"

"No." Jonah didn't have to think about it. Of course he felt different. The entire situation was uncomfortable and strange and completely out of his control. But he couldn't tell Buddy that.

Sarah frowned but didn't say anything, and for that he was grateful. Still, he couldn't shake the nagging feeling that he'd just hurt her in some way.

Jonathan was in next, followed by his *mamm* and *dat*. Most likely, Prudy had stayed outside to play with the new kittens in the barn. His baby sister seemed oblivious to the special events of the day.

"Well now," his mother started. She folded her arms around her ample middle and looked from one of them to the other. "Did you get all settled in?"

"*Jah, danki.*" Sarah's words were barely above a whisper, but she lifted her chin as if in defiance.

Jonah wasn't sure where her spunk came from, but she definitely had it. Had she just developed it, or had it been there all along and he just never noticed?

"*Gut*, *gut*," his mother said.

He knew that his parents were about as happy concerning this marriage as he was. His mother was just making the best of the situation. What more could they do but accept and go on?

"We were just on our way to take a walk," Jonah said. It was almost the truth. How many lies was he going to tell before this was all said and done?

Jonathan rolled his eyes. "Newlyweds." He laughed and moved to the refrigerator to get a drink.

Jonah grabbed Sarah's hand and pulled her from the

kitchen and out onto the back porch. But he didn't stop there. He kept her hand in his and tugged her down the stairs behind him. Her hand felt warm and solid in his. And it hit him that this was the first time they had held hands. They were having a baby together, yet he had never walked with her hand in his.

But he and Sarah never had many interactions until that night. The next few months would be filled with a whole bunch of firsts. He might as well get used to it now. That and the feel of her hand in his.

"Where are we going?" she asked as he continued across the yard.

"The barn," he replied. "We'll have a little privacy there." He could feel his family's eyes on him as he led her across the yard.

One of the horses nickered as he stepped inside.

Sarah followed him. He sat down on a paint bucket while she leaned against the stack of hay in one corner.

"Jonah," Prudy cried, running up to him, carrying a small black kitten in the crook of her arm. "There you are."

He couldn't stop the smile at the sight of his baby sister. "Here I am," he said.

She held the kitten out to him. "Look. I think he's my favorite."

"Did you know the English believe that black cats are bad luck?" he asked.

Prudy frowned and held the kitten closer to her. "How can anybody think that cat would be bad luck?"

"That's the English for you," he replied.

The hay under Sarah rustled as she shifted her position.

"Prudy, can you take the kitty outside and play with him?"

Prudy nodded, oblivious to his discomfort. But that was

just her way. Aside from being only six, she was doted on by everyone in the Miller family. Jonah wasn't sure what favor they were giving her by allowing her these freedoms, but it was a fact all the same.

"*Jah.* Okay." Still clutching the cat to her middle, Prudy made her way out of the barn.

"I'm sorry about getting us into this." Sarah's voice was barely above a whisper.

Jonah jerked his gaze to her. Was she serious? "I hardly think you can take all the blame." There. He'd said it. It was as much his fault as Sarah's. Maybe even more so.

"I think your family might disagree."

Jonah shook his head. "This isn't about my family anymore." Wasn't supposed to be. They had done what was dictated for them to do. They were members of the church. They had served their excommunication. They had gotten married. They had made it right. As far as the Amish church was concerned, they were absolved. Now they just had to figure out how to get through the rest of their lives with each other.

"What are we supposed to do?" Sarah asked.

He didn't have to ask. He knew what she was talking about. What were they supposed to do each day, every day, pretending to be married? How did a person act once they were married? It would have been different if they were in love. But he wasn't in love with Sarah. There was a time when he thought she was in love with him, but he wasn't so sure about that anymore either.

"We just do it," he said. It sounded incredibly simple and yet so complicated. Just do it. "Tomorrow I'll go out with my *dat* and harvest the rest of the corn. You'll stay here and do laundry and such. Isn't that what we're supposed to do?"

"I guess." Sarah looked up from picking a spot on her

pristine white apron. "Is this even going to work?" she asked.

"I don't know." His voice cracked on that last word. He cleared his throat, wondering why suddenly he was so choked up. "It will if we make it that way."

"Make it that way," she echoed, her voice just a mumble in the air between them. She seemed to think about it a moment, then gave a small nod. "*Jah*, I guess so."

"I know so." He smiled with a confidence she didn't reflect. What choice did they have other than to make it work? Amish divorce was as rare as hen's teeth. They could move into separate houses and live apart, but what kind of life was that?

"I'm sorry, Sarah."

That crystal-blue gaze jerked to his. "You are?"

"I handled that night . . . badly." It was an understatement, only a fraction of the truth. "I took advantage of your feelings for me." He shook his head and stared at the ground for a moment before finally meeting her gaze once again. "I only pulled over to give you a ride home and . . ." He spread his hands, an expressive gesture that said nothing at all.

"Maybe if I hadn't been so angry with Sam Troyer." She gave a one-shoulder shrug.

"Maybe I shouldn't have invited you to the pond to talk."

"Maybe I shouldn't have accepted."

But she had been so easy to talk to that night. She had told him all the things he wanted to hear and things that were true about him and Lorie.

As much as he hated to admit it even now, Lorie had been slipping away from him for years. Finding out that her father was English and that he had left a mother and another life behind only pushed her further away. It was only a hop, skip, and a jump from finding an English family to falling in love with another man. An English man.

Jonah still couldn't get his mind wrapped around it. Lorie was gone. Married to another. It still hurt to think about it, but each day that pain got a little smaller. Maybe one day soon it would disappear altogether. But until then he had a wife to care for, a marriage to build. Even if it wasn't based on love. "Can we just try?" he asked.

Her eyes searched his face looking for something, he didn't know what. Deception? Insincerity? Or maybe a weakness she could exploit?

He shook the thought away. If there was one thing he knew about Sarah Yoder, it was that she was a sweet and caring person. He might not be in love with her, but he could have chosen much worse.

"Marriage?" she asked. "Do we have a choice?"

"Yes. We can choose to get along and work at this."

She sighed. "You're right." All the starch went out of her shoulders. "It's just so . . . hard."

They were married. It was beyond unfair. Yet again the whole situation had been increasingly unfair to the both of them. What was that his dad had always said? Fairs were where you got cotton candy. It was time both of them realized it.

He swallowed hard. She looked so sad and vulnerable when she wasn't fighting him with every breath. He wasn't sure he could handle that any better than her animosity. "I know. And . . . I'm sorry."

"You are?"

"I'm sorry we ended up in this place, and I'm sorry that this wasn't what either of us had planned. But the bishop is right. The rest of our story depends on us. We can make it happy or not. Our choice."

"My mother," she said.

"What?" Just when he thought he was making progress . . .

"My mother was the one who said that. Not the bishop."

He nodded. "Whoever said it, it's true. So are you with me?" He stood and reached a hand toward her. As far as offerings went, he couldn't say it was much of one, but it was all he had for now. The promise to work on their marriage, give happiness a try and see where it might lead them.

She looked at his hand for what seemed like forever, then she pushed off the hay bale and wrapped her fingers in his.

Her blue eyes held a glimmer of a smile and his heart gave a small thump of hope. Surely if they just tried, they could make everything right again. Surely they could find their own piece of happiness.

Supper was an awkward affair. Only Buddy and Prudy acted as if everything were normal, as if having a stranger at the table wasn't strange at all.

Then again, was Sarah really a stranger? He looked across the table at his wife. How long had he known her? Years. More years than he could remember. And yet what did he know about her? He knew that once upon a time she fancied herself in love with him, and that her hair was the color of the finest dark chocolate he had ever seen. Her eyes were the clear blue of the sky just above the tree line, and when she laughed the sound was clear and true like a bubbling brook.

But he hadn't heard her laugh in a long time. Not since that night down by the pond.

He pulled that thought in before it started chasing around his head like a runaway horse. That night was the last thing he wanted to think about. It represented all of his failures and all of his shortcomings. And now he only wanted to look to his future.

His wife.

How had it come to this, truly? And what were they going to do about it?

They had made their pact in the barn, but a pact and a promise didn't get them through each day. Now they were sitting across from each other at the supper table for the very first time. And later they would go up to his room and go to bed, for the very first time. He didn't know how to act. He didn't know what to say. If she had been Lorie—

She's not Lorie.

She was nothing like Lorie, and though he had long ago forgiven her, Lorie had deceived him. She told him lies about where she was going and who she was meeting. She hadn't even told him about her secret paintings. Only after she had run away to the English world had he learned of her love for art, of her doubts about joining the church, and that she had never felt a part of their community. Or maybe he had just never asked.

How was he supposed to know? He didn't know any more about the wife sitting across from him than he did the girl he loved for so long. How did he make it different this time? He wasn't sure he knew how. But he had to try. It was his life now, like it or not. And he only had one choice: make the best of it or not. If he chose not, everyone would be miserable. No, the best thing was make the best of it every day, and with any luck what Sarah's mom said would be true for them—that love would come—but he wasn't holding his breath.

Sarah waited until Jonah went into the bathroom upstairs before rushing into their room and shutting the door behind her. She had just a few minutes to change into her nightgown before her husband came back into the room. What an odd thing to think, yet there it was. She wanted to be changed and completely covered up once again before he came back in.

She hurried as best she could, though her fingers grew clumsy in her haste. Knots became impossible to untie and pins grew stubborn. Finally, with her heart beating in her throat, she pulled her nightgown over her head. She threw back the covers on the bed next to the door and tucked them around her legs as she started to unpin her hair. A soft knock sounded on the door, then Jonah let himself in.

She didn't know why he'd knocked, especially since he walked in right after, but she was grateful for the warning all the same.

She worked her hands free from her hair and undid the ponytail, allowing the dark tresses to fall across her shoulders. Her hair grew fast, and now it almost reached the back of her knees. Unlike a lot of Amish women, she trimmed the ends simply because it made it easier to put up in a bob. She'd never told anybody her secret, not even Annie, who was so flighty she didn't notice anyway.

Jonah stopped in his tracks watching her as she took a brush to her dark hair. She saw him, although she wasn't looking directly at him. She was doing everything in her power to ignore the situation, that they were sharing a room. Again, how different would this be if they had been in love? But they weren't in love. They hadn't shared hopes and dreams, just one night beside the pond where they had let themselves go and surrendered to a power they hadn't known existed.

He just stood there. She raised her gaze to his. His expression was blank, though he swallowed hard and moved farther into the room, and the spell was broken.

Sarah ducked her head, continuing to brush her hair as she watched Jonah roam about the room. He'd changed into a pair of pants for sleeping and a T-shirt. He looked cool and casual and handsome, of course. And intimate. She'd never seen him in anything less. She'd better get used to it. Tonight might be their first night married, but it wasn't going to be their last. Every night they would be sharing a room—

She cleared her throat and set the brush to one side. Jonah whirled around. At the startled look on his face, she had to believe he was as uncomfortable and jumpy as she was. Sarah could only hope that would ease with time. She didn't want to spend the rest of her life feeling the way she did right then.

She gathered her hair at the nape of her neck and pulled it across her shoulder, plaiting as she went. Her hair had a tendency to curl, and there were a few snarls already making their way through the strands. But she managed to get it braided enough to keep it out of her face while she slept.

"Your hair is long," Jonah said.

She grabbed the ponytail holder from the nightstand and wrapped it around the end. "It grows fast."

She wasn't sure what was dumber, his question or her response.

Lord, get me through this.

"I don't have an alarm clock," Jonah said. He moved toward the bed and she was thankful to see that he got underneath the covers still fully clothed. She averted her gaze to nothing in particular. Just away from him.

"So we don't have to get up at any particular time in the morning?" she asked.

"Are you ready to turn the light out?"

She nodded.

He reached out and flipped off the lamp between them. The room fell to darkness.

"*Mamm* will wake us up, when it's time."

Just great. That meant they would all know. He hadn't said another word about scooting their beds together and she wasn't about to bring it up now. She'd had enough embarrassment for one day.

She eased beneath the covers and turned onto her side, trying to get comfortable. It was always strange sleeping in a bed that was unfamiliar. But she knew that wasn't the cause for her discomfort. No, she was wound up and nervous due to the man lying across the room from her.

What do you think he's going to do? Jump up and come demand marital rights? Even though the thoughts were in her head, they still brought a blush to her cheeks. Once again she was thankful for the darkness to hide her reaction to him. No, Jonah wasn't like that. Their marriage wasn't like that. Even though—

She lay in the dark and listened to him breathe. She could hear a few other noises stirring around the house, and occasionally she thought she could hear one of the kittens cry from the barn. She did her best to make her breathing shallow and quiet, but even to her own ears it sounded weary and heavy in the darkness. It was just a matter of time, she told herself. That was what they needed: time.

"Good night, Sarah."

At his words her shoulders relaxed a little, and for the first time she felt like she might actually have an opportunity to sleep. "Good night, Jonah."

Chapter Eight

Sarah was not happy.

She eyed the wringer washer, hoping her trepidation didn't show on her face. How long had it been since she had used one of these? Five years? Six? Could be even longer than that.

A while back, her father had given her mother the gift of a propane-generated top-loader washing machine, just like the ones the *Englishers* used. It was a dream. As easy as chocolate pie to use, and so much less effort than the older wringer models required.

"Is anything wrong?" Gertie asked.

Sarah jerked her attention from the antique to her mother-in-law's face. "No. Nothing." Nothing except that she had no idea how to work the machine. But there was something in Gertie's hard stare that said she should. And there was no way Sarah was telling Jonah's mother anything different.

She would just have to figure out how to work the machine. She had used one once upon a time. Surely she could remember. All she needed to do was get started.

She hadn't forgotten everything, and soon she had the machine chugging along. Once the first load had washed, she started it through the wringer. This wasn't so hard, a little more time-consuming than an automatic washer, but she could handle it.

She picked up one of Jonah's shirts and started running it through the wringer. The machine gave a quick cough and a belch, then the shirt somehow tangled in the wringers. Something ground together, then the machine quit, the shirt still wrapped around the wringers.

"No, no, no, no," she said, gently tugging on the shirt, but it was stuck fast in the machine's rollers. She pulled a little harder, but to no avail.

If she remembered correctly, there was a way to release the rollers. Maybe if she pressed on the lever on the top of the wringers . . .

She pressed down, but nothing. Harder and still nothing. Maybe it was stuck. Or maybe the shirt was caught in the mechanism. Whatever it was, she was going to have to rely on manual moves in order to rescue Jonah's shirt.

She tugged again, and this time the sound of ripping fabric met her ears. "Oh, no," she breathed. Whatever she did must have also unstuck whatever was keeping the wringer from working. It started again while she was still holding the ends of Jonah's shirt. Before she knew what happened, there were two pieces, one in her hands and the other plopped on the floor on the other side of the machine.

"Sarah, are you okay in here?" Gertie picked that exact moment to pop in and check on her.

Sarah whirled around, shoving the torn half of shirt behind her back. "Everything is . . . fine."

Gertie looked at her as if she had grown another head.

"Well, maybe not," she admitted.

Gertie spied the remains of the once beautiful shirt, now a wet, ripped heap on the floor. "Is that—"

"Jonah's shirt," Sarah said.

Her mother-in-law tsked. "That was his favorite one too."

Great. Married one day and she had already ruined her husband's favorite shirt. "I'll make him another." She was a much better seamstress than she was a washerwoman. She could whip him out a shirt in no time.

Worse than that was the look on Gertie Miller's face. Somewhere between disgust and resignation.

"I suppose," she said, then shook her head as she walked away.

Somehow, Sarah made it through the pile of laundry without destroying any more clothes. She lugged the basket outside, the Indian summer sun warm on her face as she started to hang the clothes to dry. October in Oklahoma was unpredictable, but today was a beautiful day and she knew the clothes would be dry in no time. Until then, she was sure Gertie would find something else for her to do, but what she really wanted was to take the tractor into town and look for fabric to replace Jonah's shirt.

No, that wasn't exactly true. It wasn't that she wanted to go into town but that she wanted to get out of the house. Today felt like a disaster.

So she might be overreacting a tad when she felt as if she was on shaky ground where the Millers were concerned. Who was she trying to kid? She *was* on shaky ground. Life would have been very different if she and Jonah were in love, but they weren't. And because of that his mother wore a permanent frown and everyone except for Buddy looked at her as if they couldn't believe she was sitting at their table.

Sarah reached for the next garment on the top of the basket. Surely things would get easier. With any luck Jonah's family would come to accept her. If not, she only had six months of this before she could move out and the two of them could have their own place.

Six months.

The thought almost made her knees buckle. Six months was a long, long time. But then compared to the forever of her marriage with Jonah, surely she could make it through that much.

Just after noon, Jonah pulled his mud-caked boots from his feet and let himself in the back door of the house. The field was really too wet to harvest the rest of the corn, but they had to get it out of the field before it started to mildew. That was the worst thing about fall rain. It made everything a rush. But his father had insisted he come in for dinner. Jonah knew it was because he had a new wife waiting for him, and because their marriage wasn't average, he promised his father he would stay only a few minutes and bring back sandwiches for them all to eat. His father had waved away his offer, but to Jonah that was exactly what was going to happen. He had spent all last night staring at her across the table at supper, then all night long in the darkness listening to her breathe. The last thing he wanted to do was see her right now. She was the reason his eyes felt like they had sand in them and his feet felt as heavy, as if he had anvils tied to each one. Surely it would get easier. Surely he would grow accustomed to having a wife, sharing his room with someone other than Buddy. But he wasn't exactly counting on it.

"Jonah? Is that you?" *Mamm*'s voice floated in from the kitchen.

"It is. I came to get sandwiches."

He rounded the corner into the kitchen only to draw up short as he saw Sarah sitting at the table, an assembly line of food in front of her. A stack of sandwiches sat to her right, and his mother sat at the end of the table wrapping them in plastic wrap.

"Are you feeding the entire district?"

"Just my boys."

He always thought it was funny when his mom referred to his *dat* as one of the boys, and he smiled a little to himself.

His parents had a good relationship. They got along fine and had raised six kids together. He could only hope that one day he and Sarah might have something similar. Right now he would settle for a shadow of that companionship and cooperation.

"Get a sack out of the pantry and start loading this up. I know with the rain last night, your father wants to finish up today."

He nodded. It was just proof again, the understanding his parents shared.

His gaze drifted toward Sarah. Her father worked in town and her mother did sewing on the side. She didn't know what it was like to farm the land. Would she survive as a farmer's wife? Would she eventually know all the ins and outs that he took for granted? That his mother and the rest of his family understood?

Sarah stood and moved to the pantry, taking out a sack and loading the sandwiches inside.

"There's lemonade in the refrigerator."

Sarah sighed and moved to the fridge. Her mouth was turned down only slightly at the corners, as if she wanted to frown but yet didn't want to.

"Sarah?"

She shook her head and pulled the recycled milk jug from the icebox. "Here, Jonah."

"Don't forget the chips," his mother reminded her.

Sarah sighed again and moved back to the pantry. "Third shelf on the left."

Jonah watched as she took out the bag of chips and put them in the sack with the sandwiches. Where had her spark gone? Where was the girl with the flashing blue eyes who stood up to him over the smallest detail of their forced marriage?

He didn't know, and he didn't have time to find out. He had a field to clear. He would have to worry about that later.

He could feel her eyes on him as he grabbed the sack and the container of lemonade and headed for the door.

"Can you pass the salt?"

Jonah looked to Sarah. The shaker sat directly in front of her, but he really didn't need it. He just wanted her attention. He wanted her to look up, be a part of the conversation. Laugh, talk, yell, something. It was as if someone had sucked the life out of her and left the shell of her body to walk around without her in it.

She handed it to him without looking at him, without a smile, a glance, an accidental touch.

He shouldn't care, but he did. He hadn't wanted to marry Sarah, but he didn't wish her unhappy either.

He waited until the kitchen was cleaned, the dishes washed and put away, before approaching her. "Will you walk with me, Sarah?"

She whirled around, still drying her hands on a dish towel. She met his gaze for the first time since he had come in to the house to get lunch that afternoon. "You want to walk with me?"

She needn't have sounded so surprised. Okay, maybe she should, since he hadn't acted much like he wanted her around. "*Jah*, of course. You are my wife."

Buddy giggled, and Jonathan slapped him on the back good-naturedly. As long as they were living in his parents' house, he would never be able to live it down.

"I don't know," she said.

"You don't know that we are married?" he teased.

"I don't know about going for a walk. Aren't you tired from your work today?"

"Not so tired that I don't want to walk with you."

He could almost see her surprise, but she hid it so quickly that he wasn't sure if it had been there or it was just his hopeful imagination.

"Let me get my sweater." She moved past him and up the stairs, returning quickly with a dark-colored sweater over her apron and dress.

Buddy and Jonathan were still joking about newlyweds and the lack of need for a sweater, but Jonah ignored them and walked Sarah out the front door and down the porch steps. The days were getting shorter and nighttime had already fallen.

"You don't really want to walk, do you?" She stopped just at the bottom of the steps.

"Of course I do. Why would you say that?"

If he wasn't mistaken, she rolled her eyes at his question. Good. That was more like the Sarah he knew. "I don't know. You never wanted to marry me to begin with."

"That doesn't mean we can't try to get along."

She pulled her sweater a little tighter around her and squarely met his gaze. "Your mother hates me."

He sucked in a breath at her blunt words. "She doesn't hate you."

"I'm going back inside." She started past him, but he stopped her with one hand on her arm.

"My mother can be a little difficult."

"I ruined your dark blue shirt today."

"You ruined it?"

"It got caught in the wringers. Something with the buttons. I don't know. I haven't used a washer like that in years. I almost burned every bit of supper that I touched and I wanted to make you another shirt, but I'm not sure I can use your mother's sewing machine without making every stitch crooked as a river."

"And you think this makes her hate you?"

"She hates me because she knows you don't love me either."

Her words stabbed at him. It shouldn't have bothered him. It was the truth. He didn't love her. But that didn't mean that his mother was against her.

"I want to go home, Jonah."

To his dismay, tears rose in her eyes. During all this time he had never once seen her cry. She had endured so much, shame in front of her family and the church, a *Bann*, and a forced marriage. Now she wanted to cry?

Still, her tears moved him to action. He took two steps toward her and pulled her easily into his arms.

She felt slight, as if she weighed no more than a bird. Sobs racked her thin shoulders. She tucked her face into his neck, her tears wetting his skin. He ran his hands over her back, soothing her as she cried it out. He wondered if it was the stress of the baby getting to her or if perhaps she was merely overwhelmed by all the life changes she had been through.

"I want to go home," she said again, her words muffled, but he could understand them all the same.

"You are home," he said.

She shook her head, smearing her tears against the collar of his shirt. "This is your home. I want to go to my home."

Something in her tone sent his heart plummeting to the soles of his shoes.

"I'll get you a home, Sarah. As soon as I possibly can. I promise you." And he meant every word.

"Can I talk to you for a moment?" Sarah twisted her fingers together as she waited for Jonah's answer.

"*Jah?*" He was on his way out to the field, the last of the harvest before they burned the fodder on the fields to help fertilize next year's crops.

Suddenly the words deserted her. "I . . . uh, about last night . . . I mean, I'm sorry. I didn't mean to go all crazy on you. It's just—"

He held up a hand to stop her words. "It's okay. The last few weeks have been a bit trying."

That was an understatement, but she wasn't about to correct him. He wasn't laughing at her weakness or scoffing at her sobbing. Maybe, just maybe, he really understood how hard this had been on her as well.

"I didn't mean to be a burden."

He shook his head. "You're not a burden. The situation is."

"But we're going to get through it, right?"

"That's the plan."

She smiled at him then, realizing that it might have been the first time she had really smiled since she had moved into the Miller house. "I guess I'll see you at lunch?"

He nodded and she turned to go back into the house. "And, Sarah . . ."

"*Jah?*"

"Why don't we go into town tonight? Maybe get supper at Kauffman's."

"Like a date?" She was almost afraid to say the word.

He seemed to think about it a minute. "Exactly like a date."

"I'd like that."

For a moment she thought he was going to say more, then he turned on one heel and started for his tractor.

And Sarah decided right then, nothing could ruin this day. Tonight she had a date with her husband.

Chapter Nine

"Can I go into town with you?" Buddy stood in the living room next to Jonah as he waited on Sarah to finish getting ready.

"Not tonight, Buddy." Jonah glanced at the staircase. Why was his heart pounding? It was just dinner. With Sarah. But somehow it felt special, this first date with her.

"Aww." Buddy put on his full pout.

"Just not tonight, okay?" He felt sorry for Buddy. The changes had been hard on his brother as well. "Next week maybe we can go to Tulsa to the zoo. Would you like that?"

It was a dumb question. Buddy loved going to look at animals, and the Tulsa Zoo was one of his favorite places in the world. "*Jah. Jah.* Promise?"

"Promise." Movement at the top of the stairs caught his attention. He looked up just in time to see Sarah headed his way.

Her royal-blue dress made her eyes shine. A faint tint of pink stained her cheeks, and for once her dark brown hair lay smooth and tamed, neatly rolled under the sides of her *kapp*.

"Wow, Sarah. You look pretty." Leave it to Buddy to say what Jonah couldn't.

She smiled prettily and the pink in her cheeks deepened. "*Danki*."

"Are you ready?" Jonah cleared his throat.

"*Jah*."

"Sarah, you need a sweater," Buddy advised. "It's getting chilly outside. *Dat* said the weatherman said we might have frost on the pumpkins tonight."

"My sweater is down here."

Jonah spied it lying across the back of his mother's rocking chair. He held it out so Sarah could slip her arms in the sleeves.

"*Danki*," she murmured. She grabbed her purse, and together they headed out the door.

Buddy followed them out onto the porch, waving the entire time. "Bye. Bring me back something. Pie. Bring me back some pie."

Jonah laughed at his brother's antics. It was better by far than examining why it felt so right to be walking next to Sarah. "*Mamm* has pie in the kitchen."

"Not like Kauffman's coconut cream."

"Is that your favorite?" Sarah asked.

"Oh, *jah*." Buddy gave an exaggerated nod.

"Then I'll make sure they give you the biggest piece they have."

"*Danki*, Sarah. *Danki*," Buddy called. He disappeared back into the house as Jonah helped Sarah onto the tractor.

"You're *gut* with him," Jonah said, climbing up behind her.

She settled down behind the seat, but he caught her quick shrug. "I like Buddy."

Jonah started the tractor. Lorie had been good with

Buddy too. Most probably because her own brother, David, had a few problems of his own. David's issues weren't as obvious as Buddy's, but he attended a special school for children with learning problems. "He likes you too."

They rode into town without speaking. Strange, but Jonah didn't feel the need to fill up every second with chatter. It felt good just being with her. The tension was absent. Or maybe it had merely shifted. It had gone from her being uncomfortable around his family to . . . something else.

There were a few tractors parked along Main Street. Jonah found a parking spot and together they made their way into the restaurant.

The few Amish who were eating at the restaurant stopped and stared as they walked in. Jonah supposed that they would get used to seeing the two of them together. Until then, they would just have to endure their looks.

"Hey, Jonah. Sarah." Sadie Kauffman greeted them, two menus in her hand. "Table or a booth?"

"Booth," they said at the same time.

"This way." Sadie led them through the restaurant.

Jonah could feel the gazes following them, but he acted as if there was nothing different about today. As if this were the most natural place in the world for him to be.

"Ezra said you came out to the ranch a while back."

Jonah nodded as he slid into one side of the booth. "You know Buddy. He loves looking at the animals. I need to bring him out again before it gets too cold."

Sadie smiled. "You'll have to take him over to the King place. They have several camels now."

"I had heard something about that. So it's true?"

"*Jah*. Once Titus Lambert got back into town, he bought the camels Ezra had, then a few more. They're milking them, you know."

So the rumors were true. Even as far-fetched as they sounded.

"What can I get you to drink?" Sadie asked.

They ordered and she moved away to get their waters, leaving them to look over the menu and the day's specials.

"The roast beef sounds *gut*," he said.

She wrinkled her nose. "It doesn't taste the same anymore."

He looked up from the menu, snagging her gaze. "What? How can that be?"

She rubbed a hand across her midsection. "The baby, I guess."

It was the first time she had mentioned the baby since she had first told him about the pregnancy. "Being pregnant makes things taste different?"

"Everything is different."

Now that he knew to be true. "Is it . . . bad?"

She shook her head. "Just different, you know? But I hear there are a lot more changes to come."

It was the first time he'd thought about the changes they were facing. Not just with marriage but with their entire lives. They were having a baby. "Have you been to the doctor yet?" Why hadn't he asked this before now?

"Once."

"And you're going again?"

"Next week."

"Do you . . . do you want me to go with you?" The words shocked him. Evidently they had the same effect on her. She drew back, blinking with surprise.

"Do you want to?"

"*Jah*." He didn't even have to think about it. He did want to go with her. He felt far removed from the actual events, but they were having a baby. Soon her body would start to change. The baby would start to show.

A baby.

The thought made his heart pound in his chest. It was exciting. Thrilling, even. They might not have planned this, but the results were still amazing. Perhaps even a miracle.

"Jonah?"

He jerked his attention back to Sarah, only then realizing he had been staring off into nothing thinking about a son he could teach to farm or a daughter to follow him around much like Prudy did with his father.

"Are you ready?" Sadie asked.

Jonah had the feeling it wasn't the first time she had asked. "*Jah*." He turned to Sarah. "You don't mind if I have the roast beef, do you?" He had heard some of his mother's friends talk when they thought no men were around about the many things that could make them sick when they were pregnant. He wasn't sure why he remembered it and why it came to mind now, but he surely didn't want to order a meal that Sarah couldn't stand to have on the table.

She smiled, then it disappeared in a flash. "No. That's fine. Whatever you want."

"Are you sure?"

She nodded. "I don't like to eat it, but that doesn't mean you can't."

Jonah folded his menu back to rights and handed it to Sadie. "I'll have the roast beef, then."

"All righty," Sadie said, tucking her pencil behind one ear. It was strange seeing her without the standard Amish prayer *kapp*, but he was slowly getting used to it. Now that she had married a Mennonite, she wore a small black doily-thing pinned over the bob at the nape of her neck. "I'll have this out in a bit." She moved away, and Jonah looked at Sarah.

"You ordered, right?"

She nodded. "You were a thousand miles away."

Not quite that far. "I was just thinking."

"Jonah," Sarah started.

"If you're going to apologize for my shirt again, it really is okay."

"That's not it."

She had something on her mind—he could see it in her eyes and the way her hands flitted about, fussing with everything from her silverware to the little plastic box on the table containing sugar and sweet substitutes.

"This is going to take time, Sarah." They all needed time. Time to get used to being married, time to get used to such a big change in plans, time to get used to each other.

"I know." She shifted in her seat. "I just wanted to say *danki*."

She caught his gaze with hers, her blue eyes earnest and swimming with thanks. Or were those tears again?

"Sarah?"

She shook her head. "Nothing."

He was about to press the matter when she sucked in a sharp breath, her eyes widening as she stared over his left shoulder. "Oh, my."

Jonah turned in his seat to see what had captured her attention. Lorie Kauffman Calhoun had just walked into the restaurant.

Chapter Ten

"Don't look," Sarah hissed. It was bound to happen. Lorie had family in Wells Landing, after all. She and Zach might've moved to their own house in Tulsa, but of course she would come back to visit her family. And of course she would go to her family's place of business, the one place she had worked for as long as anybody could remember, the Kauffman Family Restaurant.

Sarah didn't think she worked there any longer, but why wouldn't she come on a Thursday night to see her family and maybe eat?

"Why can't I look?"

She studied his face for some hint of his thoughts. He seemed calm enough, as if Lorie's presence hadn't bothered him in the least. But it was bothering Sarah.

"Are you okay?"

She nodded, then shivered as her prayer *kapp* strings tickled her neck. "*Jah*," she said. And she supposed she was. Okay, that was, except she was sitting at the table with Jonah, married and going to have his baby, when his ex-girlfriend came in the door with her new husband. It was beyond awkward. Especially since Sarah and Jonah's marriage had been thrust upon them. "Do you think they saw us?"

Sarah looked to one side as Jonah's maple syrup eyes stared at her intently.

"Why would I care if she sees us?"

Sarah shook her head. She didn't have an answer for that. But she knew that Jonah's reaction was perfectly normal. He had moved on. It might have taken him longer than it had Lorie, but choices had been made, decisions carried through. There was no hope now for him and Lorie. Not only was she married to another, so was he. Yet Sarah couldn't help feeling that stab of guilt, or maybe it was remorse, that things would never go back to the way they were before. Yet this was the one thing she had wanted: Jonah for her very own. And then it hit her—she was worried that Lorie would think, like everyone else, that Sarah had simply gotten pregnant to trap Jonah into marriage. No one could ever understand what happened that night. She'd been there and she wasn't sure she understood it herself. Never before had Jonah paid two ounces of attention to her, and yet he had heaped it upon her that night by the pond. It wasn't an excuse; it was merely the truth.

"Here we go." Sadie slid a steaming plate of roast beef in front of Jonah, then set Sarah's plate of fried chicken and mashed potatoes in front of her. It sounded so good on the menu, crispy fried chicken, mashed potatoes and gravy with a side of green beans seasoned with bacon and lots of black pepper, but now that it was sitting in front of her she wasn't sure she could stomach it at all. Yet she had a feeling it had nothing to do with the baby and everything to do with Lorie Kauffman. Lorie Calhoun.

Jonah grabbed the pepper and began sprinkling it liberally on his meal.

"Y'all need anything else?" Sadie asked.

Sarah shook her head.

"No. *Danki*." Jonah picked up the salt as Sadie moved away.

"Aren't you going to eat?" He took his first bite and sighed with pleasure.

She picked up her fork and made a play at stirring the mashed potatoes. "What if she comes over here?" Sarah couldn't say exactly why it bothered her so much, it just did. What was she supposed to say to Lorie now? What would Lorie say to them? Maybe coming out to eat tonight wasn't such a good idea after all.

"What if?" He took another big bite, and Sarah made a mental note that the next time she was cooking dinner she would make sure to have roast beef on the menu. He seemed to enjoy it so much.

"I just don't want her to think—" She didn't want her to think a lot of things, but Lorie, like the rest of the town, had made up her mind. It didn't matter how big or little the city, there was no stopping the rumor mills and gossips. She had learned that a long time ago and it still held true today. But the thought that Lorie, who had run out to the English world and abandoned all she had known her entire life, would pass judgment on her was almost more than Sarah could stand.

Movement near their table drew Sarah's attention. Her eyes went wide and the bite of bread she just put in her mouth turned to dust. Lorie was on her way to their table.

She looked the same, only different. Her eyes were as bright as ever, her smile as sweet. Though she wore her long, blond hair down now. Sarah could tell that she had cut a great deal of it off, though it still hung halfway down her back. It looked beautiful and shiny, glinting there under the fluorescent lights in the Kauffman Restaurant.

She wore jeans and a sweater, nothing fancy, nothing dressy. Around her neck she wore a thin gold chain, the cross dangling from it catching the light as she moved toward them. Sarah had always liked Lorie, hated the fact that Lorie had the one thing she wanted most. Jonah. But now Sarah had Jonah and Lorie had Zach. The tables were turned, the playing field even, as they say.

"Hi." Lorie stopped at their table, her hands clasped in front of her.

Jonah stopped eating and sat back a little in his booth seat. "Lorie."

She gave them both a quick smile. "I just wanted to come over and give you my congratulations."

"Thank you." Sarah returned her smile.

Jonah merely nodded.

"I wish you all the best." She took Sarah's hand into her own and squeezed her fingers.

Sarah could see the sincerity shining in her eyes. Then Lorie moved away, back toward her husband, who was sitting across the restaurant.

"That was—"

"Weird," Jonah finished for her.

"I was going to say sweet."

His forehead wrinkled as if he hadn't thought of that possibility at all. "I guess."

"It is. She didn't have to come over here and say anything at all. And yet she wanted to wish us well."

"I suppose." He tucked his head over his plate once again.

"When are you going to forgive her?"

He jerked his chin up and pinned her with his gaze. "I forgave her long ago."

She shook her head. "No, you didn't."

He opened his mouth, presumably to protest, then shut

it again. He grunted, not much of a response, and tucked into his food once again.

Sarah picked up her own fork, her appetite returning full force after the first bite. But Jonah, it seemed, had a lot more on his mind.

"You're right," he said once they had paid their bill, climbed back onto the tractor, and driven halfway back home.

"*Jah?*"

"About Lorie. I haven't forgiven her." His voice was barely audible over the tractor engine.

"You two were together for a long time." She didn't add that she had known, everyone had known, that the two of them had plans. Then Lorie up and destroyed all of that. Of course it would take a while to get his feelings back in order, to understand what had happened and why.

"I shouldn't be angry with her."

"It's understandable if you are."

He shook his head. "It was better that she discover all this before the wedding." He sighed. "I'm not sure there was ever a true hope for us, you know. She hadn't even joined the church. It was as if she knew all along that she was destined for other things."

"Maybe," Sarah murmured. What else could she say?

Jonah grew quiet, thoughtful, and she wondered what was going through his handsome head. Was he thinking about what it would take to forgive Lorie, or was he simply lamenting the fact that he was married to her?

"Sarah." Her mother met her at the door with a smile on her face. "What brings you out today?"

She didn't think it would be acceptable to say that she needed to see a friendly face. "I thought it would be a *gut* day to come visit," she said instead. "And make a new shirt for Jonah."

Since Sunday wasn't a church day, she hadn't seen her mother since just after the wedding. It took everything Sarah had not to fling herself into her mother's arms and hold her close.

Her mother's smile deepened. "A new shirt, huh?"

Sarah held up the bag of dark blue fabric she'd brought with her.

"You don't want to use Gertie Miller's machine?"

"It's a little different than yours." That was an understatement. The old-fashioned foot pedal machine looked like something from a museum instead of a modern Amish house. But "modern Amish" was not a term Sarah would apply to her mother-in-law.

She didn't need to say any more for her mother to understand. She knew that sometimes the familiar was just what a bride needed.

"I heard you and Jonah went out to eat the other night."

"Did you also hear that we saw Lorie Kauffman?" She started clearing the table so she could lay out the fabric to cut the pattern for Jonah's shirt.

"That I didn't know."

Sarah shrugged and started spreading the fabric flat. "Did you mean what you said before I got married?"

"I said a lot of things."

"About finding love. Even after the vows are said."

"I did."

Sarah nodded. "I got one of Jonah's shirts caught in the wringer washer."

"A dark blue one," her mother guessed.

Sarah straightened and sighed. "All my life I was raised

to get married and take care of my husband. Now everything I touch falls apart. I burned supper, ruined his favorite shirt."

Her mother moved to sit in one of the chairs, pulling Sarah down into the seat next to her. "You never had problems like this before."

She never had, but then she had never been forced to cook on a wood-burning stove or wash clothes in a wringer washer. "It's just different." It wasn't Gertie Miller's fault that she didn't have all the fancy appliances Sarah's *mamm* had. And despite her mother-in-law's obvious dislike of her, she saw no reason to shame her over things that were beyond her control.

"You know what I think? I think you're trying too hard."

"Trying too hard?"

"I told you that love would come. But you can't rush it. Making Jonah the perfect supper or doing his laundry better than anyone else is not going to make him fall in love with you any faster than God intended."

Sarah blinked back tears. Leave it to her mother to get right to the heart of the matter.

"Oh, sweetie, I didn't mean to make you sad."

Sarah shook her head and dried her eyes on her apron. "I'm just tired, I guess."

Her mother smiled and patted her hand. "That's the baby taking a toll. It'll get better."

Encouraging words. At least one thing was going to get better. "So what do I do about Jonah?"

"Just be yourself and let God take care of the rest."

Be herself, that was one thing she knew she could do.

"Sarah Miller."

It took a moment for Sarah to realize that the nurse was

calling her. Only because no one else moved did she stir into action. She hadn't gotten used to her married name, especially since she rarely used it.

She stood and made her way to the door leading to the exam rooms.

"How are you feeling today?" the nurse asked.

"Fine, thank you."

"Good, good." She led the way to a scale and took Sarah's weight, then motioned for her to sit in a nearby chair so she could take her blood pressure.

It was probably sky-high. She had waited for Jonah as long as she could, then left without him. She had hired a driver to take her into Pryor to the doctor's office. Jonah had said he wanted to go to the appointment with her, and she had been ecstatic. Then he hadn't shown up. The only answer was that he had forgotten, but it all boiled down to one thing: it wasn't important enough to him to remember.

Their marriage, the baby. Everything.

Her mother said to be patient and she would; what choice did she have really? She had forever to wait. She just hoped that it didn't take that long before Jonah fell in love with her.

His tractor was parked in front of the house when the driver pulled his car into the drive. She wasn't going to get mad, she told herself. She would allow him time to explain. And then she would forgive him, but she would protect her heart.

She paid the man, then made her way up the steps to the front porch.

She had made it up only two of them before the door opened and Jonah stepped out. "Sarah." He wore a smile, but it fell as he caught sight of her expression. Could it be that she wasn't as adept at hiding her emotions as she thought?

"I can explain," he said.

She brushed past him and started into the house. "There's no need."

Jonah followed behind her. "There is. And I'm sorry."

"It's okay, Jonah."

"Hi, Sarah." Buddy rose from the table, that sweet grin on his face.

"Hi, Buddy."

"Buddy, can you go upstairs? I need to talk to Sarah alone."

"There's no need for that, Buddy. You stay down here and finish your snack."

Buddy's attention swung from his brother to her, then back again.

"Fine," Jonah said. "I had an appointment today and it ran late. By the time I got back here, you were already gone."

"What did you expect me to do? I didn't want to be late, and I had no idea where you had gone." She hadn't meant it to sound so accusing, but it did.

She had been looking forward to going to the doctor with Jonah. It was still too early to hear the baby's heartbeat. But she wanted to share the experience with him. She wanted, hoped, and prayed that it would bring them closer together.

"Buddy." Jonah's voice was half pleading, half growl.

"I'm going." Buddy trudged toward the stairs.

Sarah wanted to call him back, but she knew their argument would only confuse him.

"If you'll just let me explain." Jonah reached for her hand, and Sarah was helpless to stop him. In all honesty she didn't want to be angry with him. Anger just kept people apart, and that was the last thing she wanted when it came to Jonah.

"You don't have to explain. You've made your stance in this marriage clear and—"

Her words ended as he tugged her toward the door.

"Where are you taking me?"

"Somewhere," he said, his attention centered on the door.

It opened and his mother stepped into the house. "Jonah?"

"We're going out, *Mamm*. We might not be back for supper."

And that was something Sarah couldn't argue with. One less meal surrounded by accusing faces.

"Isn't this a little like kidnapping," Sarah asked as he pulled her down the stairs.

"You're going willingly."

"I am?" Despite all her anger and confusion, she bit back a smile. She had never seen Jonah like this. This take-charge man who had a purpose. Ever since they had gotten married he had let his family dictate his every move. Even before, when his father had said he needed Jonah at the farm and therefore they needed to move in with the Millers after the wedding.

"That's right." Without asking, he boosted her up onto his tractor and climbed on behind her.

His expression was so intent, his mouth a thin line of determination. He was so focused on what he was doing or where he was taking her that Sarah had to grip her anger with both hands. It wouldn't do for her to give in so easily. She had to hold her ground or she would be swallowed up, never to be heard from again. She had made her mistakes, she had sinned and been forgiven. She wouldn't pay for her transgressions for the rest of her life.

He didn't say a word as he drove along. Sarah used the sound of the engine as an excuse not to speak, but the truth was she wasn't ready to talk. She wasn't ready to forgive him for missing the appointment. She would, of course. Just not yet.

Twenty minutes later, Jonah pulled the tractor down the driveway, their destination hidden by trees on either side. Power lines soared overhead and told her that they were on their way to an English destination. Most probably a house. Sarah didn't have time to wonder about the reasons. He pulled to a stop and killed the engine, hopping down and reaching for her before she even had time to form the questions swirling around in her head.

"Jonah," she started, not sure of what she would say next, but unable to remain silent any longer.

"Just give me a minute, Sarah." He released her hand to march across the yard. A FOR RENT sign sat in the middle of the browning grass. He jerked it up and tossed it to one side.

"Uh, I don't think the owners are going to appreciate that very much." Maybe the dumbest thing she had said this entire argument, but she was at a loss. Why had he dragged her out here? And what did this house have to do with him forgetting about her doctor's appointment?

He propped his hands on his hips and exhaled through his nose. She had never seen him so wound up. "I didn't forget to come to the appointment. I was here, working out a deal for this house."

Sarah stared at him perplexed. Then everything clicked in, the house, the sign. "Did you . . . did you rent this house?" It was an English house, but that didn't mean they couldn't live in it.

He shook his head. “No, I didn’t rent it.”

Her growing excitement deflated in a hurry. “Oh.”

“I bought it.”

It seemed to take hours to sink in, but it could have only been seconds. “You bought it?”

He nodded, though he looked miserable. “I wanted it to be a surprise. I was going to tell you this afternoon, on the way to the doctor, but when the owner came, he started talking about rent to own. That changed the agreement and made me late.”

Her heart filled to bursting. He hadn’t forgotten. And not only had he been working to get her a temporary home away from his family, he had found her a permanent one.

“Jonah.” She rushed across the short expanse of grass that separated them. In a heartbeat she threw herself at him, wrapping her arms around him even as tears filled her eyes. “No one has ever done anything like this for me. Never.”

“I’m your husband,” he said. His arms came around her. “I’m supposed to do things like this.”

It felt more than wonderful to be in his arms again. She felt warm and secure, and with the edition of the house, she was beginning to feel important to him. Almost loved.

But the longer she stayed in his embrace . . .

The moment turned from joyous to something else.

Sarah’s breath hitched in her throat. She needed to move away. They might be married, but the situation she found herself in now seemed too intimate by far. Never mind that they were having a baby. That night seemed to be part of a different world. This was now, in the light of day, real.

“Um . . .” She moved her arms from around his neck,

her fingers trailing over his shoulders as if they had a mind of their own.

"Sarah." Her name was a whisper on his lips. And it stopped her in her place, hands on his shoulders, body still pressed so close to his.

She looked into those amber-colored eyes and the world stopped.

Her lashes fluttered shut as he lowered his lips to hers.

The kiss was all she remembered and more. All she could have asked for.

Jonah's arms tightened, pulling her even closer. Sarah melted into him, the potential for the future wrapped up in that one kiss. His lips moved over hers and tasted of promise. Maybe they did have a chance.

Then the kiss ended. He released her and stepped back. The expression in his eyes was unreadable.

"Jonah?"

He grabbed her hand and led her toward the porch. "Let me show you the house."

Jonah wondered if she could feel the trembling of his hand as he escorted her into the house. Surely she couldn't hear the pounding of his heart. Though it sounded on his ears, blocking out most other noises around them.

Why had he kissed her?

Why hadn't he kissed her before now?

He dropped her hand, and she moved farther into the living room. There was a big bay window overlooking the front yard, and a separate dining area and a large, recently remodeled kitchen.

"This is really ours?"

He nodded, words not able to get past the lump in his throat.

"I don't know what to say. When can we move in?"

He found his voice and chuckled. "We have to disconnect the electricity and pack our things."

"By the end of the week?"

He knew that life in the Miller household hadn't been easy for her, but he hadn't understood how hard it had been for her until now.

"We won't have much furniture for a while," he warned. He could take a bed or two from his parents' house and there was an extra couch on the screened-in back porch.

She spun around, the joy in her eyes sending his heart soaring. "That doesn't matter."

"And soon we can get baby furniture."

At the mention of a nursery she rushed down the hallway looking into each room before hurrying to the next one. At the end of the hall, she turned around and headed back toward him. He chocked himself for another embrace, but sadly she stopped short of actually hugging him.

"I love it," she said. "It's beautiful."

Her eyes were shining like the blue jewels the Littles kept in their jewelry store window in town. And he had put that sparkle there. Pride had him nearly busting his shirt buttons. Now he understood why the elders always preached against the dangers pride could bring.

"Can we start packing tomorrow?" she asked.

"Whatever you want," he replied.

"You did what?" Gertie couldn't believe her ears.

"I bought a house today." Her son said the words, but once again she felt as if something was amiss with her hearing. "Sarah and I are going to start packing our things tomorrow."

Gertie laid down her fork, her appetite fleeing with his words. "You don't have to move out. We love having you here."

Jonah cleared his throat and shifted in his seat. "We're starting a family. And we'll need more room soon."

She had put him up to this. Baby or not, Gertie wished there was another way. Jonah deserved a better wife than Sarah Yoder. She was fancy Amish and didn't know the basics of running a regular house. Now she had talked him into buying her a house and moving out.

First Hannah, then Aaron. Now Jonah. She was losing her children one by one. Oh, she understood that was the point in life. A woman married and had children, then sent them out into the world. But no one had told her how hard that would be. At least she still had Jonathan, Buddy, and Prudy. All but Buddy would up and leave her one day. After that, she would only have Buddy and a big empty house.

"You can't pack tomorrow. We'll need to clean the house *gut* first. From top to bottom." She sat back with a self-satisfied sigh. She might not be able to keep her children from growing up, but she could definitely take care of them even after. "I know. We'll have a sisters' day. And everyone can come help. I'll arrange it for Saturday. After that, you can move in."

"That would be *gut*, *Mamm*." Jonah nodded and Gertie noticed that he didn't look toward Sarah. She might protest, but her Jonah knew a good thing when it came to him.

Chapter Eleven

"You don't want to use regular ol' cleaner on that. You need bleach. I'll get it for you."

Sarah pasted on a grateful smile as her mother-in-law moved toward the box of cleaners they had stashed by the door. Sarah had lost count of how many nuggets of advice Gertie had imparted to her today. Thankfully the house was equipped with hardwood floors, with tile in the kitchen and bathrooms. If carpet had been in the rooms, they would have had to pull it up, but it was fine for them as it was.

Jonah had called an electrician out the day before to unhook the house from the English electricity. They had taken the fancy curtains down first thing and replaced them with plain sheers for a measure of privacy. Then the cleaning began.

"Here you go." Gertie handed her the gallon bottle of bleach. "Don't forget to mix it with water. Three parts water, one part bleach."

"*Danki.*"

Sarah moved to the bathroom with the bleach. Anything

was preferable to being in the same room with Jonah's mother.

She didn't know what she'd done, aside from accidentally getting pregnant and having Jonah marry her. After the trouble with Lorie, Sarah would have thought Gertie Miller would be glad to see her son married. But unlike her mother, Gertie must not have believed that love would come to them. But Sarah had hope. These days that was about all she had.

Along with Jonah and this house.

Next week they would move in, and the week after that was Thanksgiving. Soon everything would be great. She just had to be patient.

"It's a shame really."

Sarah turned off the water, the newly familiar voice ringing through the air vents. It was Ellie, Gertie's sister. Sarah had never met her before, as she lived in Clarita. But she gave Sarah the same disapproving looks as Jonah's mother did.

"I'm trying hard to be grateful for God's plan, but I wanted better for him."

"We all wanted better for him."

"But with a baby on the way . . ." She could almost see Gertie shrug.

"I didn't know Jonah had started dating anyone else."

"That's just the thing. He wasn't."

"Then how—"

"I don't know. And I didn't ask."

"Maybe this truly is God's plan for them."

Gertie scoffed. "I suppose it is now, but I know that she somehow tricked Jonah into . . . well, she tricked him and now they're married."

It was one thing to know that his mother felt that way.

It was quite another hearing her talk about it with someone else, actually saying the words out loud.

Maybe she should have taken her mother and Annie up on the offer to help today, but she had felt it best to keep the families apart right now. It seemed to be the best decision. Now she could have used the support.

The words cut like a knife through her heart. No one but her and Jonah knew what had happened that night. Everyone had just come up with their own explanation. She was never allowed an opportunity to give her side. Even then no one would have believed her, but she wished she had at least had the chance. Maybe then, Gertie Miller wouldn't resent her marriage to Jonah so much.

But she wasn't going to let Gertie get to her. She and Jonah might not be in love, but they were trying to make this marriage work. They might be sleeping in separate rooms or separate beds, but eventually . . .

Well, she could hope.

She stopped scrubbing the toilet to rest her back. She and Jonah hadn't talked about where they were going to sleep. Sarah could get her bed from her parents' house, but it was a full bed. Jonah had two twins. Plenty enough room for them to not have to share, beds or rooms. But they hadn't talked about it.

Just one more thing to work out between them. But she was confident they could work it out, once they got away from Gertie Miller.

It took two days to get completely settled into the house. Sarah was grateful for her mother's help setting up the kitchen. Anything that Sarah hadn't already collected for her future, *Mamm* put on a list and picked it all up in town. But best of all, her father furnished the house with all-new propane-compatible appliances. Now she could truly become the wife she had been taught to be.

Those first two days they had eaten casseroles and snacks that family members had brought over to help out. But today was day three. Jonah had gone over to the farm to help his father with winter wheat planting, and Sarah was putting the finishing touches on making their home, including having supper waiting for him when he walked through the door. She had put a roast on to cook a couple of hours before, turning it down low so it would be good and tender.

She had a Mason jar on the table, one of those purple ones that Libby was so opposed to, and had filled it with the three remaining sunflowers from the garden out back. The table had been a wedding present from Jonah's parents, and Sarah couldn't help but believe that Eli was responsible. It was a beautiful dark wood, shined and polished by Abe Fitch himself.

Jonah had set up her full bed in the master room and moved his own twin beds into the room across the hall. Sarah wasn't sure if she was relieved or disappointed. They needed time to get their relationship square, but there were times when she felt like things would never change between them. All she could do was hope and pray and have faith that God knew what he was doing bringing them together. Regardless of what her mother-in-law thought, she knew there was a reason she and Jonah were married. One day they would discover that reason, but until then . . .

She propped her hands on her hips and surveyed her new house. They had a secondhand couch from Jonah's parents, two end tables from her room, and a lamp they had picked up in town. Sarah could just see it next to a big wooden rocker where she would rock the baby to sleep every night. She had seen some inspirational sayings and Bible verses at the gift shop in town that were supposed to go on the wall by way of decoration. But those things would have to wait, as would the nursery. The most important thing right now was to make the house a home that she and Jonah could grow in, and hopefully soon, they could have more than a necessary marriage.

Jonah pulled his tractor to a stop in the driveway of the new house and wiped a hand across his forehead. It might be November, but the sun had been hot today. Indian summer seemed to want to hang on as long as possible, but he knew soon the weather would turn cold and the fields would go dormant until spring.

Now he just wanted to get in and take a shower, then sit down and relax. He had a new book about Oklahoma's part in the Civil War that he couldn't wait to start. And that secondhand couch his parents had given them was calling his name.

It wasn't that the work was so tiring right now, but his parents were. He wasn't sure what they wanted from him, and aside from coming right out and asking, he had no plan on figuring it out. Not that asking would do any good. He couldn't accuse his parents of trying to manipulate his marriage, no, his entire relationship with Sarah.

He shook his head and hopped down from the tractor. His relationship with Sarah. Did they even have a relationship? He supposed they did by default, but what he would call it was another matter. They weren't exactly friends and they certainly weren't more. And yet in a few more months they would have a baby. They were married, bound for life, and yet . . . what he knew about her would fit in the palm of his hand.

Time. That was what his father kept saying, all things change with time. But that was a farmer's mentality. With time, seeds became plants, and plants became more. With time the seasons changed. All things with time.

He let himself into the house and took off his hat, hanging it on the wall hook that he'd hung just inside the door.

The smell of something delicious filled the air and his stomach grumbled in response. "Sarah?" He unbuttoned his coat and hung it next to his hat.

"Jonah?" She came bustling out of the kitchen, her cheeks pink from the heat of whatever it was she had cooking.

"Something smells good."

She smiled. Why had he never noticed how pretty her smile was? "I cooked you a roast."

He managed to keep the pleasant look on his face. Sarah had tried to cook before at his parents' house with less-than-satisfying results. Face it, not every Amish woman was a whiz in the kitchen. But it sure smelled good. He had been hoping it was another heat-up meal from some kind soul in the district. But tonight he would have to eat his wife's cooking.

Time. Just what his father had said. Maybe with time Sarah would learn the ins and outs of her kitchen duties. Until then he would just keep smiling.

"Go ahead and wash your hands. It's ready to eat as soon as we get to the table."

He nodded and moved toward the bathroom in the hall. He had taken it over as his own, left his shaving kit and toothbrush in there while Sarah had the one off the main bedroom. He washed his hands and face, then returned to the dining area just as she set down the basket of bread and peanut butter spread. In the middle of the table sat a large glass cooking dish filled with juicy-looking meat surrounded by potatoes, carrots, and onions all in a thin brown gravy.

"This looks incredible." He hoped she couldn't hear the surprise in his voice, but everything she had prepared at his parents' came out overcooked and dry. And this was not.

"*Danki*." She shot him that sweet smile, then sat in the chair on his right.

Jonah slid into the seat at the head of the table and bowed his head.

He had so much to be thankful for. Not just the food in front of him, but the house, the roof over their heads, and the baby on the way. Yes, he was thankful for the baby. It might not have been planned, but that didn't mean he didn't want it. The baby was a new start. He hadn't realized it until this moment. After Lorie left he had stopped, but now he couldn't do that. He had a family to think about. He had to start living again.

Danki, Lord.

This baby had taken him away from the self-destruction he was heading toward in the English world. It saved him. Sarah had saved him.

He lifted his head and blinked back sudden tears.

Sarah lifted her head and smiled. And he was thankful that she didn't notice the misty sheen in his eyes.

The food tasted even better than it smelled. The meat was moist, the potatoes cooked just right. He wanted to ask what had happened that had so drastically improved her cooking skills, but he didn't want to hurt her feelings. She had been trying so hard to be a good wife to him, even under his *mamm*'s critical eye.

He reached for the spoon to scoop up another helping of roast and potatoes.

"Save room for dessert," she cautioned.

And he knew why. She had never seen him eat this much at one time. He stopped mid-serve. "What's for dessert?" If the main meal was this good, then dessert might just be out of this world.

"Peanut butter pie."

Jonah returned the spoon to its resting place. "That's my favorite."

She smiled. "I know."

"How? I mean, who told you?"

"Buddy."

Bless his heart. He owed him one. A big one. Especially if her peanut butter pie was as good as her roast.

"I just wanted tonight to be special for you."

So she had made the roast like he had enjoyed at Kauffman's and his favorite dessert. "It is special." *Because I'm with you* almost fell from his lips, but he managed to keep it in. The thought surprised him. Even more so because he was beginning to suspect that it was true.

The satisfied look on Jonah's face as he took that first bite of pie was worth a fortune as far as she was concerned. All her past mistakes were corrected. And she could finally see a true glimmer of hope for the future. She pressed her hand to her stomach. A future for them all.

"Saturday night there's a Rook game brewing," Jonah said in between bites of pie. "I saw Hannah today, and she wanted to know if we would come."

They had been invited someplace? Never mind that the invitation was from Jonah's sister. It was one step closer to being accepted as a real couple. "What did you tell her?"

"That I had to ask you."

It was up to her? "Can we go?"

He nodded. "If you want to."

"I want to." Sarah was so excited she almost bounced in her seat.

"Have you given any thought to Thanksgiving?"

She shook her head. "There's not a wedding that day, is there?"

"Not that I know of."

Which would mean they would have to decide which family to eat the meal with. The last thing she wanted to do was spend Thanksgiving with her mother-in-law, but the evening was going so well she didn't want to ruin it by saying as much.

"Hannah's hosting the dinner this year."

So if they went to her parents' house, they would actually be taking some pressure off the newly wedded Will and Hannah. "We could have supper with my *eldra* and then pie and coffee at Hannah's?" Her voice turned up on the last word, making it more of a question than a suggestion.

Jonah scraped the last bite off his plate and licked his fork. "I think that's a great idea, Sarah."

"You do?" She had been prepared with an argument, but he merely smiled.

"That way we can visit with both."

"And Christmas?"

"I would like to spend more of Christmas with Buddy and Prudy. Are you okay with that?"

The young and the young at heart. "I think that sounds like a fine idea."

"So we'll do the opposite for Christmas. Dinner with my family and pie with yours?"

"What about Second Christmas?"

"Maybe we could spend that with your family."

She returned his smile. "That sounds perfect."

* * *

"Can I ask you something?" After the dishes were washed and put away, Sarah joined Jonah in the living room. He had settled down on the couch to read a new book he'd gotten earlier in the week.

He stuck one finger between the pages to hold his place. "What's that?"

She nodded toward the wall clock just visible through the doorway to the kitchen. "It's almost time for bed, and I . . ." She faltered a bit, losing her confidence. She wanted this so very badly. What if he refused? She knew that he had been looking forward to reading his history book all week, and now she was going to make more demands on his time. "I was hoping that we could start the tradition of reading the Bible together each night."

He tilted his head to one side as if thinking about the suggestion. "Is this something you did in your family?"

She moved closer, perching next to him on the opposite end of the sofa. "Every night. *Dat* would get the Bible out and pick a verse to read, then we would all sit around and talk about it and what it meant to us." She cast him a hesitant smile. "It's amazing how you can read a verse and it means one thing to you now, then read it in a couple of months and it takes on a whole different meaning."

He nodded. "I like this tradition."

She nearly wilted in relief. Establishing a family tradition would be good for their marriage. Any bond to hold them together. "Can we start tonight? I mean, I know you wanted to read your new book and—"

He marked his place with a business card from Abe Fitch's furniture store, then set the book on the end table. "Where did you stash the Bibles?"

She got out the closest, the one she had stored in the bottom of the coffee table so it was always handy but never in danger of getting something spilled on it. "Will you read?" She meant for her words to come out strong and sure, but instead they were barely more than a whisper.

His expression was unreadable as he took the book from her.

Sarah did her best to settle back and look normal. She wanted to act as if starting a new tradition with Jonah was no big thing. But it was. Somehow their entire marriage rested on whether or not they got this right. This was their first night in the new house acting as if they were truly one and happy to be married. She had made him a fine supper and his favorite dessert. She had wanted everything to be perfect. But it all came down to this. How could they work together, how could they build a life, build traditions together that they would pass down to their children?

Sarah pressed a hand to her belly as Jonah opened the Bible.

"Does it matter where I start?"

She shook her head. "*Dat* always opened the book to where it wanted to open. I guess you could say he left it up to God and what He wanted us to hear."

"All right, then." Jonah cleared his throat and started to read. "Charity suffereth long, and is kind; charity envieth not; charity vaunteth not itself, is not puffed up, Doth not behave itself unseemly, seeketh not her own, is not easily provoked, thinketh no evil; Rejoiceth not in iniquity, but rejoiceth in the truth; Beareth all things, believeth all things, hopeth all things, endureth all things."

He stopped abruptly as if he had wanted to read more, but was unable to go on.

"Jonah?"

"I heard an English preacher talk about this verse once."

"An English preacher where?"

He shook his head, and she wondered if she might not want to know.

"People have stopped saying 'charity' and have replaced it with 'love.'" He stood. "Where's my Bible?"

"In the bookshelf."

Flanking the windows on the opposite side of the room, a bookcase held a variety of books, plus games and a couple of knickknacks. It was a little sparse right now, but one day soon . . .

Jonah grabbed his Bible from the shelf and thumbed through it. It fell open to a spot where a small card had been placed.

"Love is patient, love is kind," he read. "It does not envy, it does not boast, it is not proud. It does not dishonor others, it is not self-seeking, it is not easily angered, it keeps no record of wrongs. Love does not delight in evil but rejoices with the truth. It always protects, always trusts, always hopes, always perseveres."

The verses took on a whole new meaning for her. "That makes it a little easier to understand." She forced a laugh, but it sounded a little like she was choking.

Jonah stared at the card he held in his hands. "*Jah*," he said absently, not bothering to look up. It was as if his thoughts had been captured by the verses he had read.

"Where did you get that?" She nodded toward the card.

"I, uh . . . I went to an English church once. They were handing these out at the door."

"You went to an English church?" Suddenly the verses took a backseat to the fact that Jonah had been to an English church. She had heard about all the parties he had gone to, though she was certain the tales had been embellished as they were retold. But no one had ever said anything about him attending a church.

"I, uh . . ." He cleared his throat. "I wanted to know what Lorie saw in the English world."

"And that meant experiencing all of it." Not just the parties, drinking, dancing, and wearing English clothes. But even church.

"*Jah*."

Sarah didn't know what to say. The verse he read had been almost enough of a coincidence to set her back a bit. But to know that he had followed Lorie and gone to church to see what she saw in the English world was almost more than she could comprehend. No wonder he looked so sad all the time. No wonder he walked around in a daze. Jonah Miller was a good Amish man. He had been baptized longer than any in their group. There was no way he could understand what drew Lorie away. There was nothing there for him. Nothing at all.

"I'm sorry," she finally managed to say.

He frowned. "For what?"

"I'm sorry that Lorie treated you so poorly, but I'm mostly sorry that you tried to understand what took her away and weren't able to understand. And I'm sorry. I've thought all along that you might have taken advantage of my feelings for you. But that night . . . you were down and sad. I never meant to take advantage of you." She moved past him and into her room. "*Gut* night, Jonah."

Chapter Twelve

Jonah turned onto his side and fluffed his pillow for the third time in as many minutes. Sarah's words kept repeating in his head, over and over. What God wanted them to hear.

Had God wanted him to hear a lesson of love?

When he had gotten the card from the ushers at the English church, he had thought it was a message that he needed to be patient and kind. He needed to keep his faith that Lorie would come back to him, and so he had kept the card. And waited.

Now he was wondering if God was trying to tell him that Lorie might be gone, yet Sarah was still waiting.

Except that night by the pond. She had told him that she had given up on him ever loving her. But those were the words that intrigued him the most. When she was constantly and completely at his beck and call, he hadn't wanted her. But once she had removed herself from him, he had become intrigued. More than intrigued.

And look where it had landed them.

Now she was his. His wife. His life mate.

And once again the card had come to light.

Would her love for him come back? Was that what God was trying to tell him?

Love is patient, love is kind.

Sarah was both of those things.

It does not envy, it does not boast, it is not proud.

There was not a more humble soul than Sarah Yoder.

It does not dishonor others, it is not self-seeking, it is not easily angered, it keeps no record of wrongs.

He had never heard her say an unkind word about anyone. Not even his mother when she was nitpicking Sarah's every move.

Love does not delight in evil but rejoices with the truth.

Sarah was pure of heart, of that he was certain.

It always protects, always trusts, always hopes, always perseveres.

That was his job, to protect her and the baby. Keep them safe. Care for them. Maybe her mother was right. Maybe love would come to them, but only because Sarah was the most loving person he had ever met.

Jonah flipped onto his other side. Sarah was all these things and more. She had loved him once. Perhaps it wouldn't be impossible to make her love him again. And he fell asleep thinking of all the ways he could make his wife fall in love with him once more.

Jonah examined the wood and counted out the lumber. The only bad part about buying an English house was that there was no barn. Since they had to drive a horse and a buggy on Sundays, a barn was an Amish necessity.

His father and brothers had promised to come over after the holiday and help him put one up. Nothing fancy. Two stalls and a roof. That was all they needed for now.

Maybe later, after they had more children, they would need room for more horses and buggies.

"I think we should put a metal roof on it." His father came up, slapping his work gloves against his thigh. "You won't have to replace it for thirty years or more."

It would be more expensive, but worth it for the future.

"I mean, you are planning on staying there for a while, right?"

Jonah frowned. "What's that supposed to mean?"

His *dat* shrugged. "Your mother seems to believe that you might be unhappy."

"Unhappy?" He was the furthest from unhappy that he had been in a long time. He might even go out on a limb and say that he could very well be happy. Honestly happy. How long had it been since he could say that? Longer than he cared to remember. But actually admitting that . . . well, that was more than he could think about right now. "We're taking it one day at a time."

His father nodded. "Sometimes that's all you can do. Then one day you wake up and you're in love."

Was that how it would happen? One day he would wake up and the pain of losing Lorie would be gone, replaced by a new fledgling love for Sarah?

He could deal with that. Welcomed it, even. "Are you ready to go?" he asked his father.

Dat nodded. "As soon as you decide what kind of roof you want."

"Metal sounds fine." Metal that would last a good long while. Long enough that it would still be there when he woke up and found himself in love.

* * *

Love. The word knocked around his head all afternoon as they loaded up the trailer, picked out nails and a new hammer, and drove everything back to the new house.

The house had a separate garage with plenty of room for their tractor, their buggy, and all the materials they had bought that afternoon. Jonah and his father stacked all the lumber inside.

"You want to come inside and get something to drink? Look at the house?"

His *dat* glanced at the door, then back to Jonah. "Not tonight. Maybe when we come to put up the barn, *jah*?" He clapped Jonah on the back, then climbed on his tractor and drove away with a small wave.

The whole thing happened so fast, Jonah was still staring at the cloud of dust behind the tractor when Sarah opened the back door.

"Jonah? What are you doing out there?"

"Seeing *Dat* off" didn't sound quite right since his father was long gone. "Thinking" would only bring about more questions. "I'm coming." He reached behind the seat on his tractor and pulled out the surprise that he had picked up for Sarah in town.

The wonderful smell of fried chicken wafted around him as he entered through the kitchen. The room was warm, brightly lit and welcoming. And walking inside felt like coming home.

"Supper's almost ready," she said, turning back to the stove and stirring a pot filled with something steaming and tasty smelling.

Suddenly he was overcome with the urge to take her into his arms and kiss her silly. Was it the inviting smells of the kitchen mixed with his rumbling stomach? Or was it the becoming pink flush that had stolen into her cheeks? Or maybe it was all the talk about love. Whatever it was, he squelched it and moved into the living room to hang his coat and hat by the front door.

"What's in the sack?" Sarah set the platter of chicken on the hot pad in the center of the table.

"A present for you." He held it up but made no move to give it to her.

She stopped, a hint of a smile toying with the corners of her mouth. "You bought me a present?"

He nodded.

"Are you saving it for Christmas?" Her blue eyes held a sparkle of excitement. Even if he had wanted to, he wouldn't have been able to keep the gift from her after seeing her joyous expression.

"No." He sat the sack on the table and stood back. "I didn't have time to wrap it."

The happiness on her face said she didn't care about wrapping. She opened the sack and gasped as she pulled out the fall centerpiece. "Oh, Jonah," she gasped. "It's beautiful."

He wasn't sure about that, but he thought it was nice. Big sunflowers and chocolate-brown candles mixed with strands of ivy and other flowers in burgundy and dark orange.

"I saw it in the window at the florist's." He shrugged, not really knowing what to say. It was something his mother would have liked, and he thought Sarah might too. It was their first Thanksgiving in this house and it deserved something special. Or maybe he should just tell her that he saw it and wanted her to have it.

"I'm only sad that it's real and will eventually die." She sat the piece on the end of the table since their supper was taking up most of the room.

"How about next week I take you in to the craft store

and you can pick up what you need to make a silk one that will last forever."

She smiled. "I would like that very much. *Danki*, Jonah."

It seemed that he should say more, but the moment just hung suspended between them.

She moved first, motioning toward the kitchen with one flighty flick of her hand. "I'll just go get the rest of supper."

Her words set his feet in motion. "I'll wash up."

Sarah maintained that warm feeling all through supper, their Bible reading, and clear into when she slipped beneath the covers.

Friday morning dawned cold and bright. If Jonah and his father and brothers were going to build the barn, they better get on it. She knew they had plans to work on it after Thanksgiving Day, but Sarah had heard talk that it was going to be a snowy winter.

Oklahomans never knew what the winter would bring. Sometimes it wouldn't snow at all, barely frost, which would make the bugs unbearable come the spring. Other times they'd have a blizzard, a literal blizzard. They'd had ice storms that knocked out the English power lines and total snowfall that could be measured in feet rather than inches. Apparently this was to be one of those white years.

Sarah threw another log on the fire and moved back to the kitchen to clean up the breakfast mess. Tomorrow was Saturday, and Gertie was hosting a sisters' day to can chicken thighs for the winter. Canning meat was a lot different than making pickles or putting up jelly, and Sarah would have loved the chance to go and observe, but she hadn't been invited. She told herself it was because it was a sisters' day, but she knew that Hannah, Jonah's sister, had been invited. She wasn't Gertie's sister, but she was playing a part in the day.

Sarah sighed and wiped her hands on a dish towel. She had to have faith that one day Gertie would accept her as Jonah's wife. Maybe when the baby came. She ran a hand over her unchanged belly. Soon. Soon she would start to show. The baby would start to move. They would be able to hear the heartbeat. Maybe then it would feel real to her. Right now she almost felt like a fraud, like she had been going through the motions without the truth behind her. She was sure Gertie felt the same way. The woman never said as much, but she didn't have to. Sarah could tell every time she was around Jonah's mother. But Jonah was about to give his parents their first grandchild. Hopefully then Gertie's heart would thaw when she saw Jonah's child for the first time.

Until then, she would just have to not worry so much about Gertie and her opinions. Jonah seemed to think she was pretty special, and that meant everything in the world.

Saturday night Sarah took extra care with her appearance. She had made herself a dress out of the dark blue material that she had used for Jonah's replacement shirt. The color reflected in her eyes and made them look twice as big as they normally did.

Other than church, this would be their first outing as a married couple, and she wanted everything to be perfect. She smoothed another dab of baby lotion over the small rolls of hair at each side of her face and picked up her prayer *kapp*. She was as ready as she'd ever be. She pinned her *kapp* in place, critically studying her reflection. She wasn't tall and thin and blond like Lorie, but she was not ugly to look at. Her teeth were strong and white, her skin clear. So her hair was a little unruly at times; all in all, she wasn't an unattractive person.

She ran her hands down her dress and apron, then grabbed her coat. It was time to go. Now or never. They were headed on a date.

Jonah nearly took her breath away when she caught sight of him. His beard was growing in nicely. It had a rusty tint to it that she liked. How much longer before it would be a full-fledged beard? Not long. And her husband would have the mark of a married man.

"Are you ready to go?" he asked. He had put on the shirt she had made him. She might not be able to cook on a wood-burning stove or do laundry in a wringer washer, but she could sew. Every little stitch near perfect. She shouldn't be proud, but with all the shortcomings she had suffered lately, she would take whatever confidence she could get.

"*Jah*."

He handed her a scarf and her bonnet. "It's supposed to get down near freezing tonight by the time we head back."

"*Danki*." Had he always been this thoughtful?

A car horn sounded outside and she jerked her gaze to his. He gave her a secret smile, then opened the front door for her to precede him outside.

In their grass-and-dirt driveway sat an English car, the lights on and the engine running.

"Is that a driver?"

For a moment she thought he was about to grin, but he managed to contain the motion. "Since we moved out here it's really far over to Will and Hannah's. I don't want us to get cold."

It was the sweetest thing, she thought as she made her

way toward the car. He locked the door and they got inside with the driver.

"All this for card night?" It was almost too good to be true. Or maybe he was too good to be true. But that didn't mean she wasn't going to enjoy it. With a slow progression, things were changing between them, and she was grateful.

He shrugged. "It's important. Even if it is just card night."

In the dark interior of the car, Sarah smiled. They just might make it after all.

Will and Hannah's house sat on the opposite side of the district. A few more feet and they would've been completely out of Bishop Ebersol's district, but as it was, they all still went to the same church.

The house was warm and inviting and built more like an Amish house usually was, with an upstairs and no previous wiring for electricity. But that wasn't to say that Jonah wasn't enjoying the house he and Sarah shared. It was just different was all.

"Sarah, help me get these to the table," Hannah requested.

Sarah took off her coat and hung it in the front closet and followed Hannah to the kitchen. Jonah stared after her. As strange as it seemed, there was so little he knew about his wife. And he had known her most of his life. How was that possible?

"I brought sausage balls," Sarah said, handing the foil-covered platter to Hannah. "My mother's recipe."

Had he ever eaten those at any other meetings? He couldn't remember. He watched her disappear with a swish of her skirts, wondering when they would be to the point where they finished each other's sentences and knew everything there was to know. Would they ever get to that point?

"*Gut* to see you out tonight, Jonah." Andrew Fitch clapped him on the back, his bright smile shaking Jonah out of his deep thoughts.

"We wouldn't miss it. Anything to get out and see how my sister's living."

Andrew looked around him with admiring eyes. "It's a nice house." And it was. Somewhere between fancy and plain. The walls were warm yellow and white, and wood trim seemed to grace each room, adding to the warmth. He should do that for Sarah. Add some wood trim, maybe paint the walls a deeper color. Overall he liked the feel of walking into sunshine even though he was indoors and it was dead of winter. He was sure his mother would classify the whole setup as "fancy Amish," though he saw no problems with that. Having a nice place to live didn't damage someone's faith.

"I think the bishop helped."

Cephas Ebersol was a dairy farmer by trade, but a closet carpenter. He loved woodworking almost as much as Abe Fitch. Jonah had heard his parents talk about all the help Cephas had given Will and Hannah in the construction of the house. That was just the kind of man he was. Maybe he should ask for a little assistance of his own. Though he was sure Cephas had more on his plate right now, what with Mary just marrying Aaron. Jonah's brother had said as much, but Jonah knew that Aaron was looking for a house for his new bride. When the papers were signed, Jonah was sure that all of Cephas's time would be spent improving Mary's house, but it wouldn't hurt to ask.

A deep gong sounded throughout the rooms.

"Is that it?" one of the girls squealed, her voice carrying in from the kitchen.

"Yes." He recognized the gush of a word as belonging to his sister.

The girls rushed through the foyer where the men were standing and into the dining room. Jonah followed, hoping to get a look at whatever had caught their attention.

He peered into the sunshine yellow room to find the women all clustered around the huge grandfather clock nestled in one corner. He couldn't see much of it since the girls were all gathered around, but he caught a glimpse of the top and the golden clock face. It was beautiful.

"I have it set to play 'Amazing Grace' at the top of each hour. It chimes at the quarter hour and gongs at the half hour. And when it's closer to Christmas I can make it play 'What Child Is This.'" His sister was beaming with joy.

The other women oohed and aahed over the beauty of the clock and its size, and he thought he even heard a few whispers about the cost.

Was it really that special?

"I got Caroline a grandfather clock when we got married," Andrew said, draining the last of his punch. "But it was nothing compared to that one."

Jonah shook his head. He had seen the love that flowed between them. "I bet she loves it just as much."

Andrew smiled. "I think you're right."

But Jonah hadn't gotten Sarah a grandfather clock when they had married. He'd been too wrapped up in hating the fact that he was getting married to worry overly much about the etiquette of marriage. He hadn't bought her anything.

Just a house.

That was something. Wasn't it?

But Will had bought Hannah a house and a clock.

Andrew had done the same. Emily and Elam had moved in with his parents to help take care of his father, but that didn't mean Emily didn't add a huge grandfather clock to her list of earthly possessions. He looked around at this circle of friends. Was he the only one who had forgotten such a time-honored tradition? Was it even that important?

He looked back to where the girls stood, all still gazing at the clock as if it had been made of solid gold.

Evidently it was.

Sarah could feel the gazes fall on her when no one thought she was looking. Men and women alike, everyone in their group seemed to turn their attention on her at some time during the evening.

After they had checked out Hannah's new clock, the group had gathered in the family room. Four card tables had been set up for their tournament.

"The rules are simple," Will said. "The winner from table one will play the winner of table two. Same thing with three and four. Then those winners will play each other for the championship."

"What do we win?" someone called. Sarah wasn't sure who.

Will smiled. "Bragging rights." He glanced around the room once again. "Any questions?"

"When do we eat?" She wasn't sure but she thought Obie asked. It made sense. He was always hungry.

"When you lose," Andrew returned.

Everyone laughed and started for their chairs.

Will and Hannah along with Emily and Elam sat at the first table. Clara Rose and Obie sat down with Ezra and Sadie while Caroline and Andrew and Mark and Ruthie sat at the next one. Sarah and Jonah gathered around table four with Titus and Abbie.

Jonah had the first shuffle, and she took the time to study her husband. Why did he seem so different tonight? His hair looked the same as it always did. Maybe a bit longer than normal. His beard was starting to grow in nicely, now rivaling that of the other men at the tournament.

His blue shirt was the one she had made him after ruining his favorite one in the wringer washer. Nothing was out of place. Nothing out of the ordinary. So why . . . ?

He dealt the cards and everyone placed their bids.

"Sarah?"

She started. "Sorry. What?"

"It's your turn," Jonah said, a perplexed look on his face.

"Right." But her concentration was shot and they lost the first hand.

"Are you okay?" Jonah captured her gaze.

She nodded. What was wrong with her? It was as if she couldn't focus at all.

"Pregnancy brain." Caroline leaned close so only she could hear.

After two children, she would know. "It's like your brain can't handle thinking about the baby and something else at the same time."

"So it chooses the . . . baby?" It was the first time she had talked about the pregnancy with anyone since their church confession.

"Exactly." Caroline nodded.

Great. That was exactly what she *didn't* need. Something else to distract her for the next seven or so months.

Titus clapped Jonah on the shoulder sympathetically.

"Good luck, my friend," he said, and Sarah wondered if they had been eavesdropping on her conversation.

"How is the camel business?" Elam asked, effectively changing the subject. "Are they ready to milk yet?"

"Don't make fun," Titus warned. "Camel's milk is the wave of the future."

Thankfully the conversation switched to the merits of camel's milk over cow's milk as the two very different dairy farmers touted their own product.

Sarah just smiled to herself, thankful to be let off the hook. Now to dig in and concentrate on the game at hand.

Despite all her efforts at trying to concentrate, she and Jonah lost to Titus and Abbie, who in turn had to play Caroline and Andrew. The second table hosted Emily and Elam versus Ezra and Sadie.

"Come on," Hannah said, motioning the women into the kitchen. "I have a project."

Ruthie eyed her skeptically. "This doesn't involve painting, does it?"

Hannah laughed. "You'll have to trust me enough to come see."

Ruthie, Sarah, and Clara Rose all followed Hannah into her newly remodeled kitchen.

"You have such a lovely home," Sarah said, looking around at the pristine floors and Formica countertops. Hannah's kitchen was a great deal larger than Sarah's, though she thought it might appear that way since there was no kitchen table to break things up. Sarah sort of liked having the table right there. Did everyone say the kitchen was the heart of the house?

"I hear your house is coming along." Hannah shot her a sly look as she pulled a huge bag of cheese from the fridge. She set it on the island worktop, then went back for more.

"We moved in so quick it seems like it's taking forever," Sarah said. And it did. She wanted Jonah's home to be perfect. Now. She wanted him to come home every day from working with his father and know that the house she had built for the two of them would rival anything anyone else in the district might have.

Of course she would have to say a quick prayer about that tonight. She shouldn't be overly proud of her house. There was a reason why pride was considered a sin.

But Jonah had bought them a fixer-upper. It might not be as large as Hannah and Will's place, but there was a little land where they could add on, a place for them to build a barn and the detached garage where they could store their tractor and buggy. All in all, she was happy with her home. Happy with Jonah.

She stopped and pressed a hand to her belly. She was happy with Jonah. She inhaled sharply.

"Sarah? Are you okay? What's wrong?" Ruthie moved close as Hannah continued to grab things out of cabinets for the big project.

"Is it the baby?" Hannah asked.

Sarah shook her head. "I'm fine."

"You don't look fine," Clara Rose said. Her blue eyes were filled with concern.

"*Danki*," Sarah quipped.

"You are pale," Hannah said.

Sarah shook her head again. "Really. I'm fine. Just a touch of indigestion."

"I told Mark those meatballs were too spicy."

Sarah didn't bother to tell her that the meatballs had nothing to do with it. But if she said that she would have to explain. How did a person tell their friends that she thought she was happy in her marriage? How ridiculous. "Maybe," was all she said.

Let them believe that Mark's meatballs were too spicy for her pregnant constitution. It was better than letting them know that she might have fallen in love with her husband. For real this time.

Chapter Thirteen

They had just gotten everything measured and into the large mixing bowl when Abbie and Sadie joined them in the kitchen.

"I guess it's between Caroline and Emily."

Andrew and Elam were lumped in with their wives, most probably because Caroline and Emily had been best friends since Caroline had come to town three years ago.

"Maybe we should go watch." Clara Rose glanced toward the doorway that led back into the family room.

"Oh, no," Hannah said, with the quick shake of her head. "I'm not going to be the only one mixing this mess."

Sarah looked into the very large bowl Hannah had placed on the counter. Everything fit neatly inside. But there was only one way to mix the varied ingredients.

Hannah washed her hands, then dried them on a paper towel. "Whoever is going next better wash up."

Clara Rose glanced back toward the family room and gave a quick shrug. "I mean, you're already elbows deep in it. Why should we get our hands all covered in . . . cheese?"

"Because if you don't help, you don't get to take any home."

"Fair enough." Clara Rose moved to the sink and lathered up her hands as everyone laughed.

"Are you sure this is going to be enough?" Sadie asked.

Hannah rubbed her nose on the sleeve of her dress, her hands still buried in the cheese ball mixture. "I tripled it. So maybe."

"I was being sarcastic." Sadie laughed. "That's a lot of cheese ball."

"I wanted everyone to have one for the holidays. You can either take it with you if you are visiting or have it at home for a snack later in the day."

"It's a wonderful gesture, Hannah," Sarah said. "I really appreciate it."

A chorus of agreement went up around the room.

"We do thank you," Sadie added.

Clara Rose sidled up next to her and bumped her from in front of the bowl. "Now clear out. It's my turn to mix."

Caroline and Andrew ended up winning the tournament with the promise of a pre-Christmas rematch from Emily and Elam. The grand prize was an edible fruit arrangement that Hannah had learned to make at the community center.

Sarah had been friends with Hannah for years and never known her to be so obsessed with kitchen chores. But since she had gotten married, that seemed to have changed. Sarah was happy that her friend had found something that suited her so well.

The other part of the prize was a cheese ball without having to do any of the work. Not that it was that hard, just time-consuming and a little messy to get everything mixed up properly.

Sarah took her turn forming the mixture into softball-sized lumps and plopping them into the to-go containers. Tripling the recipe was more than enough. Each couple had two cheese balls to take home as well as a fun evening of friends and fellowship.

It was after ten when the driver came to pick up Sarah and Jonah. All in all, it was the best evening she'd had in a long while. Her mother had said that it would take time for everyone to come around. It helped that Jonah was treating her more like a wife than a liability. She could barely tell any differences in her friends' marriages and her own. Except tonight when she and Jonah got home, they would go to separate rooms. But perhaps one day . . .

They pulled into the driveway and Sarah got out, unlocking the door while Jonah paid the driver. The house would be cool and they would need to get a fire started soon in order to warm it back up.

"Brrrr . . ." Jonah was on the porch behind her almost before she could get the door open.

He moved toward the woodstove while she went to the kitchen to put the cheese balls in the fridge.

"It was a fun night, *jah*?" Jonah asked as she moved back into the family room.

"It would have been even more fun if I could have concentrated more." Sadie had done better than she had, and Sadie was much further along than Sarah.

Jonah smiled. "We'll get 'em next time."

Her heart soared. Next time. She loved the sound of that. Next time meant they would go out as a married couple again. They would have a good time, talk with friends, play Rook, and make cheese balls. Live their life together. But she only nodded. "Next time," she managed to say without grinning from ear to ear. It wouldn't do to have him know how exciting the prospect was to her. It wouldn't do at all.

"Do you think it's going to snow?" Andrew looked out the barn door and up at the cloud-heavy sky as he asked the question.

It was all anyone could talk about today. Church was being held at Caroline and Andrew's house. Thankfully, they had a large barn where they could set up the benches into tables for the after-church meal. And the thick wooden walls kept out the chilly Oklahoma wind.

"They're not calling for it," Jonah said. And he hoped it held off until after the next weekend. Thanksgiving was Thursday, and starting on Friday, he and his father and brothers were building the new barn.

"The girls are already talking rematch," Andrew said. Jonah realized he'd missed the first part of what his friend had said, but it only took a minute for him to catch up. He was referring to the card game from the night before.

"*Jah?*"

"Week after next. Are you two up for it?"

"I'll have to get with Sarah, but I don't see why not."

Andrew stared at him as if he'd suddenly sprouted tulips out his ears.

"What?"

Andrew shook his head. "Nothing. It just seems married life agrees with you."

"Agrees with who?" Elam Riehl picked that moment to saunter up.

"With our friend here." Andrew used his coffee cup to indicate Jonah.

"Happens to the best of us." Elam chuckled.

"Why wouldn't it?" Jonah asked. He hadn't meant for his tone to be so stern, but that was exactly how it came out.

Andrew and Elam shared a look and Jonah knew what they were thinking. He had been forced to marry Sarah and he hadn't exactly kept it a secret that he wanted nothing to do with her. But that was before he had gotten to know her. She was just about the hardest-working person he knew. She had gotten their house together in record time. Even when he could tell she was about to fall asleep on her feet, she kept going. She hadn't complained at all about his mother's interfering and she got excited over the smallest gift from him. And when she got excited . . . her eyes sparkled like gems, her sweet lips curled upward into a smile, and he felt like the best man on earth.

So, yes, maybe being married agreed with him. But it was more than that. It was being married to Sarah.

There. He had admitted it. He was starting to fall for Sarah. But wasn't that supposed to happen? Falling in love was best for all involved. He, Sarah, the community, the baby. Everyone.

"There you are." Buddy picked that moment to rush up in true Buddy fashion.

Jonah was grateful because it kept him from having to answer. "What's up, Buddy?"

"*Mamm* and *Dat* are about to leave. They wanted me to come get you."

Jonah frowned. "Is everything okay?"

Buddy nodded. "*Jah*. I think *Mamm* has something she wants to give you, and I heard them say something about Thanksgiving."

He nodded toward Andrew and Elam and moved away with this brother.

His parents were waiting for him in the buggy.

"Buddy said you wanted me?"

His mother cleared her throat. "About Thursday. Dinner is at one."

"About that," Jonah started. He rubbed the back of his neck, wishing he had put on his scarf before coming out here to talk with his *eldra*. This wasn't going to go easy, and it was cold. "Sarah and I talked, and we're having the meal with her folks. Then we'll be over later for pie and coffee."

His mother's cheeks reddened until they were nearly the color of pickled beets. "When did you decide this?"

Jonah shook his head. "It's . . . the other day. See, we've spent more time with my family. We thought this was only fair."

His mother harrumphed.

He knew she wasn't going to like the decision. His plan had been to tell her the day of. Once the holiday was upon them, she wouldn't be nearly as quick to get angry as she was right now.

"We're still coming by for pie."

"So you said."

The last thing he wanted to do was hurt his family, but there seemed to be no other way. He wondered what his other married friends did to balance the holidays between families. He had never thought to ask.

"We're planning on coming at Christmas, though."

Her eyes brightened, but only a little. "For the meal?"

"Yes, *Mamm*."

She stiffened her spine, but he thought he saw a smile play at her lips. "Very well, then. See you on Thursday for pie."

Jonah stepped back and gave his mother a small wave. This marriage thing was turning out to be a lot trickier than he had planned.

* * *

Gertie sat back in her seat as Eli set the buggy into motion.

"What's on your mind, *Mudder*?"

She inhaled, trying to get a grip on her raging emotions. Jonah had been forced to marry Sarah Yoder, and Gertie was doing her best to accept that. But she would have much rather he married someone more down-to-earth. Some of those fancy Amish might as well be English with all their gadgets and trinkets.

"I worry about him," she finally said.

Eli clicked his tongue like he did when he was thinking. "I think he's doing just fine."

Gertie harrumphed. It seemed she made that noise far too much these days. "How can he be fine when his wife can't even run a wringer washer?"

Eli paused, and she knew her quiet husband was measuring his words carefully. "It doesn't really matter if she doesn't have one."

"That's just it. I worry that he married into fancy Amish." She shook her head. "They are going to be the downfall of our district. Those Yoders and the Lapps." Thomas Lapp's family was the worst, driving around town in a tractor that had never met a field.

Eli cleared his throat. "Seems to me that Hannah married pretty fancy."

She folded her hands in her lap as they rode along. "That's different."

"How so?" Her husband took one hand from the reins and scratched his chin whiskers.

"It just is. Hannah was raised right. She can cook on a woodstove and run a wringer washer. She doesn't have to have fancy appliances in order to cook a meal."

"But her house is fancier than the one Jonah bought Sarah."

She turned in her seat to get a better look at his expression. Was he serious? Could he not see the dangers that had befallen their eldest son? "You just wait. By this time next year, it'll be fancier than anything we've ever seen. Just wait. Why, I wouldn't be surprised if she wasn't using the electricity from the outlets."

Eli sighed, and she hated the sound. It meant he disagreed with her no matter what words followed it. "You don't really mean that."

"I do." She folded her hands in her lap once again, her piece being said.

He pressed his lips together, then gave his head a small shake. "If you feel this strongly about it, then I guess all we can do is pray."

Thanksgiving dawned bright and cold. Sarah looked out at the blue sky and knew today was one of those deceptive days. From inside the house, the weather looked like a pretty summer day, but if she touched the window she could feel how cold it really was.

"Are you ready to go?" Jonah came up behind her, his coat already on.

Sarah nodded. "Let me get the food." She had a box of offerings for dinner at her mother's house, including cinnamon pudding and sausage and noodles. She had packed a peanut butter pie to take to Jonah's family. She figured it could stay out with the tractor while they were at her parents' house and be nice and cold by the afternoon.

They would have to take the tractor since it was a holiday and there weren't many drivers willing to take time away from their family in order to cart the Amish around, but

Sarah didn't mind. Yes, it was cold and the wind stung her cheeks, but it felt good to ride along beside Jonah.

Their relationship was changing. She could feel it. They were becoming increasingly comfortable around each other. The simple fact gave her hope that one day they might even have a normal marriage.

There were no other tractors parked outside her parents' house when they pulled up. Sarah had two older brothers, but it seemed that they were spending the holiday with their wives' families.

Jonah parked the tractor and hopped down, pulling the box from its storage place behind the seat. He had rigged up a wooden crate and a bungee cord to provide a stable place to haul small items.

"Leave the peanut butter pie here," Sarah instructed.

"Are you saying I have to wait until this afternoon before I get to eat any of it?" His eyes twinkled as he said the words.

Sarah smiled, happy that he liked her kitchen efforts. "You can have some cinnamon pudding."

He made a face. "Not even close."

Sarah laughed. "Sorry."

"You're not. I think you did this just to torture me."

"Hey! I made the pie, didn't I?"

He nodded. "Okay. I'll give you that. But next time, let's have it for breakfast."

Sarah laughed and followed her husband inside.

The Yoder family Thanksgiving celebration was warm and inviting, if not extremely traditional. Bowls and platters covered the long dining table. Chicken and filling, rolls and beans.

Jonah felt blessed to be a part of such a celebration.

Plus, it was a little quieter. Only Annie, Hilde, and Otto had joined him and Sarah at the table.

"Would you like more corn, Jonah?"

Jonah sat back and patted his stomach. "*Danki*, Hilde, but I couldn't hold another bite."

"I hear your *dat* and brothers are building you a barn tomorrow," Otto said.

"*Jah.* We're starting one. Since the house belonged to the English, there's not a place for us to keep the horse out of the weather."

Otto nodded. "If you need more help, let me know. I'd be happy to lend a hand."

"*Danki*."

"Coffee, anyone?" Annie came back in from the kitchen with a large coffeepot.

Jonah turned his cup over near his plate and leaned back so Annie could pour him a portion. "*Danki*."

Sarah and Hilde got up and went into the kitchen only to return with the cinnamon pudding Sarah had made and a pecan pie.

"Dessert," Sarah said. "Which one would you like?" She smiled prettily at Jonah, and he felt like a king.

"What? No pumpkin?"

Hilde laughed as Annie came up from behind cradling a beautiful pumpkin pie in her hands.

"A slice of each?" Sarah asked.

"Oh, no." Jonah shook his head. There was no way he could eat that much, then turn around and eat more at his parents' house.

"Just a little one," Annie said in a singsong voice.

"Pecan," he said, feeling quite spoiled by the Yoder women.

Their household was so calm and loving. Dinner had

been a quiet affair, giving everyone a chance to reflect on all the things they were thankful for.

He was thankful for so much. No, the year hadn't turned out exactly like he thought it would. Nowhere near, actually. But he had a fresh start. He could have gotten into so much trouble in the English world, and yet God had looked out for him. He hadn't discovered what Lorie had found there and he might not ever, but he had found Sarah instead. He couldn't say that she would have been his first choice in a wife, but he was thankful for her all the same. She had been a good wife to him in the weeks since they had married. And they were having a baby. He was about to start a family. For that he was doubly grateful. They had a nice house and supportive families. Two people couldn't ask for much else. All that was left to do was to praise God for their blessings.

Hilde served him a way-too-big piece of pecan pie, then offered ice cream. Despite his protests, he ended up with a large scoop at the side of his pie. It was delicious, but he was sure if he ate one more bite they would have to roll him out to the tractor when it was time to go.

"When are you going to start decorating the nursery?" Annie asked as she devoured a large bowl of cinnamon pudding.

Sarah's gaze jerked to his. They hadn't really talked about it. In fact, it seemed as if they constantly avoided discussing the baby at all. Which was strange considering that it was the very reason why they got married.

"We haven't talked about it," Sarah finally answered.

"We have the cutest fabric in at the store. I think it would make the sweetest sheets and blanket. It's yellow with little giraffes on it. Adorable."

Annie chattered on in that Annie way of hers while Sarah and Jonah continued to simply look at one another.

He had put it off long enough. They needed to get to the store and start gathering things for their new arrival. Up until now, he'd sort of ignored the fact that they were having a baby. It was ridiculous, he knew. He needed to take her to buy material to sew curtains and bedding. Everyone said the time flew by. How many of his friends had gotten married, then had a baby, stating that time seemed to fly by? All of them, as a matter of fact.

Jonah ducked his head over his pie and picked at the crust as if his life depended on it. He had been in denial too long. It was time to grow up and acknowledge what they had done and acknowledge that like it or not, their baby would arrive soon, and the little Miller needed them both.

Hilde watched Sarah and Jonah exchange an intimate look. Except for church, this was the first time she had seen them together. Her daughter seemed happy, and Hilde wanted to ask but refrained. Marriages weren't always about happiness and love, though she wanted both for her daughter. Both her daughters.

Then Jonah looked away and the moment between them was broken.

Hilde turned back to her dessert. She was so thankful to have Annie, Sarah, and Jonah here with them today. Tonight Melvin and Wayne, Sarah's brothers, would bring their families by and they would celebrate with them. So much to be thankful for.

She looked to Otto and smiled. And a grandchild on the way. The baby might not have come about in a traditional manner, but as she had told Sarah, there were so many women who had problems conceiving that they had to look at this as a blessing. They might not understand it now, but they would. One day. There would be a time when they would be able to say, this is what happened. She didn't know when or where that would happen. Only that it would. That God would reveal His plan to them all and the mystery would be cleared.

Until then, it was best just to praise His name and accept His will. And thank Him for all that they had.

Just after three, Jonah and Sarah piled back onto the tractor and headed for his parents' house. He was looking forward to seeing Buddy and Prudy. And Jonathan too, though Jonathan was different. His age and mental state made him more independent. Jonah was ready to see his siblings.

That was the worst part of being married. He didn't get to see Prudy and Buddy nearly as much as he wanted to, even if he saw them a little each day as he went over to the farm to work with his *dat*.

He pulled the tractor down the drive at his parents' house, for the first time noticing the subtle differences between Sarah's parents' house and his. Both had mums on the porch and wind chimes to catch the Oklahoma breeze, but there was definitely something different about the Yoder house. He knew his mother would have called it fancy Amish, but for the first time he was beginning to really understand what she meant.

What still perplexed him was why it bothered her so. His only explanation was pride. Gertie Miller had her own measure of pride, and everything that was associated with the fancier houses had to do with envy. The haves and the have-nots.

But he knew it was a little more than that. A house didn't need solid oak trim or high-grade linoleum floors to raise good Amish children. They didn't need a modern, propane-powered washer or a battery-powered sewing machine to keep clothes nice. Those things were extra. But was it a sin to have them?

He hopped down from the tractor and helped Sarah to the ground beside him. "Want me to take the pie?"

"I've got it." She reached into the wooden crate and retrieved the covered dish.

Side by side they walked to the porch and into the house.

Unlike the Yoders', the Miller house was a bevy of activity and noise. Since they had eaten at Hannah's there was no mess on the kitchen table, which was perhaps the only unusual thing about this Thanksgiving.

His father was asleep in the recliner, though how he could nap while Prudy read books aloud, one doll tucked beneath her arm, Jonah couldn't imagine. Buddy and Jonathan were playing checkers, with Buddy loudly complaining that Jonathan was taking all his men.

His father let out a raucous snore, then settled a little deeper into the chair.

"Jonah?" his mother called from the kitchen.

"*Jah, Mamm?*"

She came bustling out of the kitchen wiping her hands on a dish towel. Her face was slightly flushed and her eyes sparkled like she hadn't seen him in months instead of just yesterday. "Jonah."

"Happy Thanksgiving."

She leaned up to kiss his cheek. "I'm so glad you're here."

"Me too."

She took a step back and glanced at Sarah. "How are you, Sarah?"

His wife smiled prettily, though Jonah noticed that it didn't reach her eyes. "I'm fine, *danki*."

She had told him that his mother held animosity toward her, but he hadn't believed it until now. What made today different? What was he seeing today that he hadn't noticed before?

His mother turned away and headed back into the kitchen. "I'll get the coffee," she threw over her shoulder.

"I brought a pie," Sarah said. "Peanut butter."

Mamm stopped, then turned around slowly. "I made a peanut butter pie. It's Jonah's favorite."

Oh, no.

"I, uh . . ." Sarah stammered. "I guess we can just take ours back home."

His mother cast her a sly smile. "That would be *gut*, dear."

Jonah blinked. "*Mamm*, Sarah worked hard on her pie. I think we should eat it."

The look on her face was pure betrayal. He had picked Sarah over his mother, and she wasn't about to forget it. She sniffed. "If that's what you want."

He swallowed hard and nodded. "It is."

But he knew the line had been drawn.

Chapter Fourteen

"I almost died when I was little. Did you know that?"

Sarah blinked, trying to decipher the words Jonah had just said. "You did?"

He nodded.

They were halfway back to their house and Sarah couldn't figure out why he wanted to talk about this now. The weather had remained steady, a first for Oklahoma. It was still sunny and cold, but somehow it seemed to fit the day. Jonah had taken up for her against his mother. She wasn't sure what it meant, but it warmed her more than her thick woolen coat.

"What happened?"

"We were living in a different house, one on the other side of town."

"How old were you?"

"Three or four." He shrugged. "I don't remember much about it. I was playing outside, I think it was about this time of year, and I fell in an abandoned oil well site."

"Those are dangerous."

"Tell me about it. I don't remember much. I was too young, but the point is . . . my mother." He pulled the tractor to a stop in front of the house, but Sarah couldn't move.

"Your mother what?"

"My mother is a little protective of me because of that. At least, that's what I think it is."

Sarah studied him, cold, but unwilling to move until she heard everything he needed to say.

"So don't take it personally."

"It's hard not to." She couldn't hold back her derisive laugh.

"You shouldn't. It wouldn't matter who I married or for what reason. Today would have happened just the same."

"If they had brought a peanut butter pie?"

"Any kind of pie or cake. But I'm glad you made me a peanut butter pie."

The words warmed her from the inside out. "*Jah?*"

"It is my favorite, after all."

"Whose recipe?" She held up a hand before he could say a word. "Don't answer that. I don't want to know."

Something had definitely shifted between them, but Sarah was hesitant to give it a name. It was too fragile for that, too new, too vulnerable.

They ate leftovers that her mother had packed for them for supper. Then they read the Bible together, as had become their routine.

At ten o'clock, they got up to get to their separate rooms just as they always did.

But Sarah's mind was going in so many different directions. The thoughts made her anxious and uneasy, even a bit nauseous. She pressed a hand to her belly and curled up on one side in her bed.

She woke sometime in the middle of the night, unsure of what disturbed her sleep. She lay there in the darkness listening for a noise, the sound of Jonah padding to the kitchen to get a drink, or the neighbor's dog barking at strange shadows.

Then the pain struck. It seared across her midsection, doubling her in two. It stole her breath and left her panting, wondering what had happened. What was happening?

It had to be the baby, but this couldn't be right. She had never heard of any of her friends talk about crazy pains that woke them up in the middle of the night.

The pain stopped, but left behind little quakes that didn't quite subside as the next one hit. Her body was being ripped in half.

Then the realization hit her as sharp and searing as the pains through her body. She was losing the baby.

Helplessness washed over her. Her mouth tasted bitter and tears burned at the back of her throat. The baby that no one wanted, the aftereffect of one sinful night.

But she wanted the baby. In that moment she realized how much the tiny unseen creature meant to her. She wanted that baby with every fiber of her being, yet it was being ripped from her and there was nothing she could do to stop it.

She rolled to the side of her bed and managed to stand. She had to wait until the next pain hit and subsided before she managed to shuffle toward the bathroom.

She should get Jonah, but she couldn't. She was embarrassed, devastated. Getting Jonah would change nothing. He couldn't stop what was happening to her any more than she could. She was alone in this pain, so very alone.

She finally made it to the bathroom. She shut the door behind her and slid onto the floor as another pain overtook her body.

* * *

She splashed water on her face and stared at her reflection in the mirror. Morning had come. She was numb, but it was better than the pain, both physical and emotional. The baby that had brought her and Jonah together was gone. The reason for their marriage. It was all gone.

But she looked no different. Maybe just a sadness in her eyes and the downward turn at the corners of her mouth. She surely didn't look as if her life had been forever altered.

She had taken a shower late in the night, then wrapped herself in warm pajamas and somehow managed a fitful sleep.

But now it was morning and she had to face the awful truth. And the terrible task of telling her husband.

She shuffled to the kitchen and started coffee on the stove. He would be up soon. Might already be. Shouts and laughter followed by the grind of a saw swung her attention to the window overlooking the backyard.

She sighed. They were building the barn today. She spied Jonah's dad along with Jonah, Aaron, Jonathan, and Buddy. They were all there, the whole of the Miller men. They would be expecting breakfast soon, she supposed. Her gaze shot to the clock. It was just after ten in the morning. How had she slept so long? And why did it feel like she had barely slept at all?

Why didn't he wake her?

She knew, but didn't want to face the answer to that. He didn't wake her because he knew on some level that he couldn't depend on her to get up and have breakfast ready for him. How could he? She couldn't even do the most basic of womanly functions. She couldn't even carry a baby.

Tears stung her eyes and a lump filled her throat,

making it nearly impossible to swallow. The baby was gone. The numbness had subsided, and now raw pain seeped into every crevice of her being. She lunged for the table and collapsed into one of the chairs. Gone, gone, gone. The baby was gone, and yet she was supposed to pick up and go on. Act like nothing had happened. Like nothing earth-shattering had occurred. How did she do that? How?

She folded her arms on the table and laid her head on them as heavy sobs tore through her.

But crying didn't help. It didn't take away the pain of her loss. She wiped her eyes and stood. Regardless of how she felt the day would go on, things would move, ebb and flow. She washed her face once again and got dressed.

She needed to tell Jonah, but she couldn't find the words with all his family around. What was she supposed to do? March out there and declare the loss in front of everyone? She should have woken him last night. The experience was bad enough, but now she had to live it again by telling him, her mother, her sister . . .

The back door opened and she spun around, mixed emotions scorching through her. Glad it wasn't Buddy or Eli, shamed that it was her husband.

"Are you okay?"

She could only fight back tears and shake her head.

"Sarah?" He started toward her, but she held him off with one hand. It was the perfect opportunity to tell him and yet the words fled.

"I—I think I ate something bad."

A concerned frown wrinkled his forehead. "You've eaten what I've eaten."

She shook her head. "Then it must be a stomach virus. You might want to stay away. It could be contagious." The lies were falling from her lips. She would pray about it later, but for now they were self-preservation.

For a moment he looked unconvinced, then he gave a quick nod. "*Jah.* Okay. But I think you should rest. Will you go back to bed?"

The idea sounded heavenly. But if she allowed herself time to lie around, the thoughts might overcome her and then who would she be? "Maybe."

The concern on his face was almost more than she could handle. It seemed to have taken up residence on his face with something that looked a lot like love. She couldn't call it that. Things between them were too shaky for that. She would label it as caring. Jonah cared for her. That much she could see. But what would he think when she told him the truth?

"Just rest." He backed toward the door, his gaze on her. She couldn't look into his eyes. She couldn't bear to. She kept her own gaze averted as he left. One minute he was there and the next he was striding back across the yard. He turned back once, looking at the window, concern still such a prominent part of his expression.

Sarah gave a small wave, then turned toward her bedroom.

"Where's Sarah?" Buddy asked the question that had been buzzing around in Jonah's thoughts. Her bedroom door was shut and he figured she had locked herself in there with the excuse she wouldn't be getting anyone else sick if she stayed away.

They were taking a break from the barn to have a sandwich before they started back. He hadn't seen hide nor hair of his wife since this morning.

"She's not feeling *gut*," Jonah replied absently. But he

had a feeling that there was more to it than what she was saying. He thought back on the day before. Any problems they'd had, he thought they had talked them through. She'd seemed fine when they went to bed. Then this morning everything had changed. Maybe he should have gotten her up when his father came over, but he hadn't wanted to disturb her. Hannah had told him that pregnant women needed lots of rest. There was plenty enough food in the house to grab something quick and then head out to work. He didn't need to get her up to get his breakfast. Maybe he should have.

But waking her wouldn't stop her from getting sick.

If she really was sick.

"I'm going to see about her." Buddy's chair scraped against the floor as he stood.

"Sit down," *Dat* said, his tone stern.

Buddy stopped, then slowly eased back into his seat. "But—"

"If Sarah is sick, she needs her rest," *Dat* explained. "And you don't need to be exposed to her illness."

"*Jah, Dat.*"

Jonah took another bite of his turkey sandwich and glanced toward the hallway. He'd give her till suppertime and then he was going in, sick or not.

It was dark-thirty when his father and brothers scrambled onto their tractors and headed back home. Jonah waved to them, then made his way back into the house.

He was tired and hungry, but more than that, he was worried about his wife. He hadn't seen her at all since this morning. She hadn't come out of her room even once as far as he knew, but she might have when they were working. One more day and the barn would be complete. One more day and he'd go to his parents' house and get his horse. But until then, he needed to check on Sarah.

He absently wondered if they had any soup put up anywhere and if she might like some for supper. Stomach virus or not, she needed to eat. For her and the baby.

"Sarah?" He lightly rapped on the door.

He thought he heard the rustle of her covers but he couldn't be sure. He eased the door open and peeked inside the room. He was cautious not to scare her or rush in in case she wasn't decent. He never thought he would say that about his own wife, but here he was.

"Go away," she mumbled. She sounded tired and as if she had been crying. Was her stomach hurting her so bad that she was in tears? Maybe he should call a driver to take them into Pryor to the emergency clinic.

The room was dark as pitch, with no light filtering in from anywhere. It took a minute for his eyes to adjust. She was lying on the bed, on top of the covers, as if she had flopped there and been unable or unwilling to cover herself. She was still dressed in the *frack* she had been wearing earlier and the apron as well. Her feet were bare and her prayer *kapp* smashed on one side.

The sight of that lopsided linen drew him up short. A woman's prayer *kapp* was near sacred. The fact that she had lain down in hers and not bothered to remove it all day spoke volumes. Something was horribly wrong. And he feared it had nothing to do with a stomach virus.

"Are you okay?" he asked. It was a dumb thing to say. But he was at a loss. He moved closer to her and turned on the lamp next to her bed. Even the soft light seemed harsh in the dark interior of the room.

"I'm sick, Jonah." Her voice sounded tired, but not weak.

"Do we need to go to the doctor?"

She was quiet for so long he thought perhaps she had fallen asleep, then her shoulders shook. She was crying.

"Sarah?"

"It's over, Jonah. The baby is gone."

He blinked, trying to gather what she was saying and find the meaning in the words. "The baby?"

She pushed herself up on the bed and wiped the tears from her cheeks. "There is no baby." She seemed to pull herself together, but he could feel the distance between them. He wanted to hold her but he couldn't make his arms reach for her. She seemed as prickly as a porcupine. "Do not touch" signs were posted all around. "Just go." She pointed toward the door, but didn't meet his gaze.

He wasn't sure what to do. He wanted to stay, but if leaving made her happy . . .

Mute with shock, he stood and made his way to the door. Once there, he turned back to look at her once again.

She had left the light on but had returned to lying down. Her prayer *kapp* was askew, but at least she wasn't crying.

He quietly closed the door behind him and made his way to the living room.

The baby was gone.

He wanted to ask her exactly what that meant, but with her tears he had to assume that she'd had a miscarriage. He collapsed onto the sofa and pressed a hand to his forehead. There was no more baby.

The baby that was the very reason they were together.

He wasn't sure how he felt about it. But he knew that the pregnancy wasn't as real to him. He hadn't gone to any doctor appointments. He hadn't looked at the home test and watched the indicator turn. He hadn't done anything but hear her words and marry her. Albeit reluctantly.

Now he had no idea what to do or what to say. He had no words to make it better. No words to take away her pain. He wished Hannah was there. Or maybe even his mother. A woman to help him understand what she was going through.

Her mother. He should call her mother. He was surprised that she hadn't called her already. Or maybe in her grief she hadn't been thinking.

He pushed to his feet and headed for their garage-based phone.

Sarah's mother came almost immediately. He felt useless as he let her in and walked her back to Sarah's bedroom.

"I'll take it from here," she whispered, then slipped inside.

Jonah stared at the closed door, then made his way to his room. He had done all he could do.

Chapter Fifteen

Hilde stayed through the night. In the morning she made the men bacon and eggs, then went back home. Sarah never came out of her room.

Jonah had asked his mother-in-law what he needed to do, and she had told him to "just be patient." He wasn't sure what that meant, but the look on her face said he should have understood. So he'd nodded like it all made sense and walked her to her tractor.

Sarah didn't come out of her room for three days, not even for church on Sunday. Jonah knocked on the door several times, but she never answered. When he tried the knob, he found it locked. She had shut him out.

Jonah finally decided that she was leaving her room, but only when she knew she wouldn't bump into him. The occasional dish left in the sink and the milk disappearing from the fridge were the only clues he had. What he didn't know was *why* she was avoiding him. At least she was eating.

Be patient, her mother had said. He supposed that meant not to push Sarah. He had no idea what she had suffered. He had no idea why she hadn't come in to wake him during that night.

He had thought they were progressing, beginning to learn each other's likes and dislikes and doing everything in their power to become the couple they were destined to be. Yet this was tearing them apart, and he was helpless to stop it.

Jonah took the tractor into town the following day. He made the excuse that he needed to get paint for the new barn, when in fact the paint was already waiting for him to get to it. He asked Sarah if she needed anything, through the door, of course. But he got no answer. He could only say a little prayer that her mother was bringing over anything that she needed.

The first stop was the hardware store. He might not need paint, but he could use a few brushes and some white for the trim. He parked out front and went inside. It smelled like a hardware store should, like sawdust, rubber, and old coffee. He nodded hello to Hershel Bryant, the owner, then made his way over to where he kept the paint supplies.

He walked down the aisle slowly, looking for the right kind of brush, when a voice floated over to him from the aisle next to his.

"It's sad really." He wasn't certain, but it sure sounded like Ivy Weaver. Ivy was nice enough, he supposed, but she had gained a reputation on her extended *rumspringa* as being what the English called "a little fast." He wasn't sure by whose standards, and he wasn't about to ask.

"You don't really believe that story, do you?" He didn't

recognize the second voice, but knowing Ivy, it could have been anyone, English or Amish.

"What? That she trapped him into marrying her?"

He stopped in his tracks. Could they be talking about him?

"It's entirely possible," Ivy returned.

"So you don't think she was ever pregnant?"

"No. See, it's the perfect plan. She told him that she was pregnant, and he married her. What was he supposed to do? But now that it's time for her to start showing, she conveniently loses the baby."

"And she still has herself a husband."

"Right." Ivy laughed. "I wish I'd thought of it myself."

"Whatever. Like you're ready to get married and settle down."

"I might be." Ivy's tone took on a wounded note, and he could almost see her pout. "One day, anyway."

Her companion laughed and they moved away. He could still hear their voices, but not the words they were saying. Not that he needed to hear any more. He'd heard plenty.

He grabbed the brushes he needed, not really caring about painting anymore. He needed to get out of there and get a breath of fresh air. He felt like he was choking. As if a giant hand was squeezing the air from him.

Somehow he managed to pay and get back out to his tractor without being seen by Ivy and her friend. He didn't want them to know that he'd heard. He wasn't sure how to take Ivy's theory. He wasn't sure he could look her in the face and not say a word about it.

He swung up onto his tractor and started for home, his breath still stagnant in his chest.

* * *

Jonah sat down at the table, looking across at Sarah's empty chair. It had been days since she had left her room, nearly a week since she had lost the baby, and Jonah was running thin on patience. The ladies in the church were bringing over meals and Sarah's mother came over every other day while he was at the farm. But he was torn between wanting to help Sarah and wanting to shake her out of whatever funk she had fallen in.

There had been that brief time when it looked as if they just might overcome anything thrown their way, and then this had to happen.

But did it?

He pushed that voice aside. It was hateful and evil and had no place in his thoughts, but it had surfaced regularly since that day in the hardware store.

He knew—*knew*—that Sarah hadn't lied to him, but the doubts still plagued him. He hadn't seen the pregnancy test. He hadn't gone to any of the doctor's appointments. He didn't even know the doctor's name. For all he knew, she'd taken a Mennonite driver into Pryor for an afternoon of shopping away from the prying eyes of the district. They hadn't bought any baby things. She hadn't started decorating anything or sewing little baby gowns or crocheting booties and whatever else women did when a baby was on the way.

Was that because she was too busy settling into the house?

Or was it because there wasn't a baby, there never was, and she knew it? Why should she crochet for a child who didn't exist?

"You don't know that." He pounded one fist against the table, rattling his silverware in the process.

"You don't know what?"

He turned to find Sarah standing behind him. She

looked the same as always, morose and tired, but she was out of her room and that was a good sign, *jah*?

"Nothing." He stood as she walked around the table to her chair and sat.

"I have some casserole heated, if you would like some." Really, what else was there to say? She hadn't been out of her room when he was in the house in days.

"*Danki*."

She continued to stare at nothing, so he moved to the kitchen to get her a plate. He hadn't set her a place. He hadn't known she would pick tonight to venture out to the table at suppertime.

She took the plate from him without a word and scooped up a helping of the chicken-and-noodle casserole one of the ladies had brought over.

"You didn't make a vegetable?"

"Huh?" He hadn't expected her to say anything and he hadn't been listening. Having her back across the table from him would have been welcome if not for the conversation he'd overheard earlier.

"Why didn't you make a vegetable? Green beans, corn, something."

Jonah looked at his plate piled high with the casserole. "It's got English peas in it. Why do I need another vegetable?"

She frowned and stirred her fork around in her supper. "You're supposed to make a vegetable."

White-hot anger flashed through him. His fork clattered onto his plate as he stared at his wife. "Well, pardon me for not knowing that another vegetable was required."

Her gaze snapped to his. "Why are you being so touchy?"

"You tell me. You stay in your room for days on end, and then when you do come out it's to criticize my cooking skills."

"I wasn't criticizing. I simply said that you should have made another vegetable to go with supper."

"That, my dear wife, is criticism."

She scoffed. "I don't see how."

"How about you wouldn't have food in front of you right now if it weren't for me, and maybe you should just be thankful." This argument was getting out of hand. He could hear their words, hear how ridiculous they were, and yet he was powerless to stop it.

"You didn't make this casserole. I know for a fact this is Lettie Miller's recipe. So I should thank Lettie."

"I heated it up."

"Big deal." She pushed back from the table and stood.

He had never felt like thwarting someone as much as he did in that moment. His anger, his frustration, his hurt and sadness had all festered inside him leaving him toxic from the inside out. At least where it came to her.

"And when you heat up the next one, be sure to warm some vegetables to go with it."

With a growl, Jonah shoved his plate toward the opposite wall. It broke with a clatter, sending food sliding down the paint and onto the floor.

Saturday came and brought with it more of the same. Sarah came out of her room for meals, but they ended up in an argument over the dumbest things each time. He knew they were both on edge. He couldn't get the conversation between Ivy and her friend out of his head.

He didn't believe it, or at least that was what he told himself, but the doubts still plagued him. Sarah could have tricked him, could have lied to him, and he had just blindly believed her. He had taken her at her word, demanded no proof. She could have told him anything and he would have believed her. What a fool he was!

But deep down he knew that she had told him the truth. He had to believe that or he would go insane. Each time he took out Ivy's words, turned them over in his mind, thought them through, examined the evidence, he knew that Sarah hadn't tricked him. So why did it bother him so? Because people were talking about it like it truly happened that way.

And Sarah . . . where had the girl he had married gone? She had been so shamed at having to marry him. She had been full of dread and trepidation to move into his parents' house. But she had kept her chin up through it all, even his mother's catty remarks about her household skills and her placement with the fancy Amish. Where was that girl?

So Sarah had lost the baby. It was terrible and sad, but it wasn't the end of the world. They were married now. It wasn't like they couldn't try again. One day. But not until she pulled herself out of the blues.

Meanwhile he was elbow-deep in red. Paint, that was. He wiped an arm across his brow. He was sweating despite the cool temperatures. Painting was always more work than what it looked. But since the barn was up, it needed a bit of paint to protect it from the elements. With so much sadness floating around his house these days, he decided that red was the perfect color. It was bright and cheerful. Well, sort of. It was definitely a much happier color than white.

He went back into the barn to get the second can of paint when he heard the sound of an engine approaching. A car engine.

He shaded his eyes to see who was coming down his drive. The car was unfamiliar, one of those little four-door sedans that seemed to be all over the place. Could have been anybody, but most likely someone had gotten turned around and needed directions.

The car stopped just in front of the house. The driver cut off the engine, then a woman got out.

"April?" he breathed. It couldn't be.

The blonde smiled. "I found you."

Yes, you did. But how?

"My, my, my, don't you look cute dressed all Amish-y."

He looked down at himself, realizing that April had never seen him in anything but the English clothes he'd left at a donation site when he decided to come back home, when he decided there were no answers in the English world.

"Uh, thanks." He shook his head. "What are you doing here, April?"

"I came to find you."

And she couldn't have picked a worse time. He was happy to see a friendly face, a woman who didn't complain about every little detail like separating the big forks from the little ones and how the dish towel should be hung to dry. But he didn't need to see her now. It was too late for them and anything they could have had together. He was married to Sarah now, and Amish marriage was forever.

She sauntered closer and he caught a whiff of her expensive perfume. At least he thought it was costly. Everything about her screamed money and privilege. He wasn't sure what she'd ever seen in him. Not that they had been that serious. They'd just spent some time together during his sojourn to the English world.

"How did you find me?"

"Luke told me." She leaned in close and pressed her lips to his cheek. Then she drew back and smiled. "I've missed you, Jonah."

His heart skipped a beat in his chest. He took a step back. "Did he also tell you that I'm married?"

She gave a little shrug. "I just came as a friend."

How did she know that was the one thing he needed right then?

"*Jah*, okay."

Her grin widened. "*Jah*," she mimicked. "You're adorable, you know that?"

Well, he wouldn't go that far, but it was nice having a friendly face smiling at him.

"Aren't you going to invite me in?"

He stopped. Should he? It wasn't like there was anything between him and April. Not anymore, anyway. Why couldn't he invite a friend in for a cup of coffee and a slice of the pumpkin bread his mother had brought over the day before? "Sure. Come on in."

He led the way to the porch and held open the door for her to enter. He knew his house paled by comparison to the ones belonging to his English friends, but he had kept it neat and clean. He'd even cleaned up the casserole from a couple of days before when he and Sarah had gotten into such a terrible argument. He'd been careful not to let her rile him to that point in the days since, but she still managed to get to him every time she ventured out of her room to criticize whatever he happened to be doing at the time.

"Nice," April said as she removed her coat. She looked around the small living room and he tried to see it through her eyes. It was coming along. Once he got the barn finished he was going to start trimming the inside and getting all the rooms painted. The nursery was supposed to be the first project on the list, but now . . .

"Let me take your coat." His voice sounded rusty with emotions he didn't want to name.

He hung her coat in the front closet and gestured toward the kitchen table. "Would you like a cup of coffee?"

"That would be great." She flashed him that winning smile once again. She really was a pretty girl. Long, blond hair like spun gold, soft brown eyes that didn't accuse and blame.

She settled down at the table while he went into the kitchen to make a pot of coffee.

"Where's your wife?"

"Resting." It wasn't much of an answer, but he didn't feel the need to go into all the details, because one explanation would lead to another and another until the whole sordid story was out on the table.

He sliced them each a piece of pumpkin bread and carried them to the table as the water boiled.

April chatted about the people he had met in the English world and what they had been doing since he had come back to Wells Landing.

He poured two cups of coffee and carried them to the table. Then he slid into the chair opposite her.

"Very domesticated," April drawled, taking the first sip of coffee.

Jonah wasn't sure how to respond, so he kept quiet and took a drink from his own cup.

"Are you happy, Jonah?"

The question seemed to come out of the blue and he nearly choked. Was he happy? No. Had he been? Almost. Now each day was a struggle. But what choice did he have? The Amish married forever. Good or bad, right or wrong, he was married to Sarah.

"Jonah? Who's here?"

Great. Now Sarah was up. There would be a hundred questions about April and, he was sure, a few accusations. That just seemed to be Sarah's demeanor these days.

"A friend."

"Is that your wife? I'd love to meet her." April's words sounded sincere enough, and he had no choice but to believe her and no other options but to introduce them as Sarah came down the hallway.

Sarah drew up short when she saw April sitting at the table. "Oh. Hello."

April smiled. "Hi, I'm April Franklin."

"Sarah." A frown marred her brow as she said her name. Jonah knew she was trying to figure out the relationship he shared with the pretty blonde. It wasn't something he cared to discuss, least of all with her.

"Aren't you going to invite me to sit down?" Sarah pinned him with a hateful stare.

Inwardly, Jonah sighed. He wanted to tell her that she was a big girl and this was her house, she didn't need to be invited to do anything, but that would only lead to an argument. That was all they seemed capable of these days, tearing each other down, then retreating into their own rooms until the next encounter.

April looked from him to Sarah and back again. "Well, I for one would love for you to sit down so I can get to know you better."

He wasn't sure, but he thought he heard Sarah mumble, "I bet you would." Then she turned to him. "Is there any more coffee?"

"In the kitchen." He took another sip of his coffee to ease the sudden dryness in his throat.

"Don't worry about me. I can get it myself. You don't trouble yourself to get up at all." Sarah flicked a dismissive hand in his direction, then started for the kitchen.

He dropped his gaze to the plate in front of him. It was far better to stare at his untouched piece of pumpkin bread than to meet April's pitying gaze.

"Jonah." April's tone was soft and filled with worry.

He shook his head. "We've hit a rough patch." It was the best way he could explain without having to recite details. It was really none of April's business regardless of her sincere concerns.

"I should go." She stood and slipped her handbag strap a little higher on her shoulder.

He couldn't protest. He was touched that she had come by to see him, but it wasn't a good time. Might not ever be.

"I'll see you out." He followed her as far as the porch. He wanted to apologize for everything, disappearing like he did, Sarah's behavior, his own hand in it, but the words stuck in his throat.

"Take care of yourself, Jonah." She gave him that sweet smile. "If you ever need a friend, you know where to find me."

"Thanks," he croaked.

She gave a small wave, then skipped down the porch steps to her car.

He returned the wave and watched her back out of his drive. Heart heavy with something he couldn't name, he turned and went back into the house.

"She's gone?" Sarah asked. She was standing in the doorway that led to the kitchen. She looked as innocent as one person could.

"*Jah*."

She studied him for a moment, then gave a small nod. "You have lipstick on your face."

Chapter Sixteen

Her life was out of control. Completely. When had everything slipped from her grasp? She couldn't even say that God was in control. Her life was careening along as she was left to hold on lest she be tossed aside.

She was stiff-legged as she made her way back to her room. Jonah had a visitor. An English visitor. A beautiful visitor.

And she had kissed him.

Sarah wondered how April had met him and how far had their relationship progressed before he came back. Quite a bit, if she took the time to track him down.

But she wasn't upset about it. She wasn't. It didn't bother her that April Franklin was as gorgeous as a fashion model on the magazines at the grocery store or that she wasn't struggling. That she was happy while Sarah was fighting to keep her head above water.

And Sarah was certain that April wasn't a complete failure. Not in the way she herself was. She wasn't even able to do the one thing God had intended for women to do, have a baby.

She pushed the thought away. All it did was bring her tears, and she was all cried out.

She knew what people around town were saying about her. She knew that there was speculation that she might not have even been pregnant to begin with. She had trapped Jonah. She had set her sights on him and then maliciously and viciously gone after him like a hunter with prey. That couldn't be further from the truth. But to defend herself would only make her look guiltier. Why should she come out and face everyone's scorn?

She had taken her punishment when it was doled out. She had served her *Bann*, confessed before the church, and righted her wrong. Why couldn't it end with that? Why did she have to keep paying over and over again for the same sin?

She shut the door behind herself and flopped down in the chair she had pulled into the corner of the room. She could sit there and look out the window and try her best not to think.

One day blended into the following as the next church service rolled around. She didn't want to go, but she had to. She could get away with missing a church service after losing the baby. She could cite health reasons. But to miss again would have more tongues wagging than already were.

Jonah knew it too, so he shouldn't have looked so surprised when she came out of her bedroom fully dressed for church.

"You're going?"

"Of course." She sniffed, grabbed her coat, and headed for the buggy.

The problem with buggies was the fact that they were so small. At least Jonah's was. And riding beside him all the way to Maddie Kauffman's was near torture. Memory after memory of that night by the pond flooded back. She would never escape it. That one night had sent her life on a course she had never expected. What did God want from her? She had messed up and paid the price. Why was she still having to pay?

The buggy pitched and she brushed up against her husband. He scooted a little closer to his own door, she knew, so they wouldn't touch. It was torture to be so close to him and know that things would never be the same between them. They had almost found a happiness together. At least they were well on their way. Then tragedy struck and they were back to the beginning: her loving him and him wanting to be as far away from her as possible.

They pulled into the yard and Sarah got down without waiting for Jonah. She didn't look back, not able to even pretend that the awful truth wasn't the actual situation.

All eyes were on her as she crossed the yard. Pitying eyes, accusing eyes. If she could just find her mother or Annie, a friendly face in the crowd. But her family was nowhere to be seen and her friends were Jonah's friends and she was certain everyone was taking his side.

She pulled her coat a little closer around her even though the temperature was quite warm for this time of year. Christmas was just a couple of weeks away, then a brand-new year with the same old problems.

"Sarah!"

She looked up to find Annie waving at her from Maddie's front porch. She had never been happier to see anyone in her life. "Hi!" She hurried toward the shelter of her sister's company.

"Where's Jonah?" Annie asked.

Sarah waved a hand behind her somewhere in the direction of where they had parked. "Taking care of the horses."

Annie frowned as she slipped her arms through Sarah's, leading her to the far end of the long porch, away from listening ears. "How are you feeling?"

She wasn't. She couldn't let herself feel anything. If she did, she might fall completely apart and never be whole again. But she didn't want to say that, not even to Annie. "I'm okay."

"Sarah Sue, it is a sin to lie," Annie said in a voice so like their mother's.

Just add it to my many others. "I don't want to talk about it."

"It's good to talk, don't you know?"

Sarah shook her head. "In case you missed it, we're not English and there's nothing to talk about." The baby was gone. Jonah didn't love her, and she was trapped in a hopeless marriage with him. What more was there to say?

And the worst part of it all? She could almost hear the whispers behind her back. The bishop and the rest of the elders treated her no differently than they ever had. But she could feel the eyes of the parents on her. The scholars who were old enough to understand. She had thought that once she and Jonah got married, everything would return to the way it was before, only they would be married and having a baby. How wrong she had been. The Amish talked about forgiveness. She couldn't say it was a lack of that had caused it. But they didn't forget. No one would forget until the next big thing happened.

She made it a point not to look for her husband as she entered the Kauffman house. Lorie's fall from grace in discovering that her father wasn't really Amish and then leaving the district to marry an *Englisher* wasn't as big a stir as she was facing. Why couldn't everyone see that she was just a person with flaws and scars like everyone else? Why couldn't they look past what was happening to her to how they would feel if it happened to them? Why? Why? Why?

She kept her eyes down and her sister at her side as everyone filed into the house for the church service.

Sarah could barely concentrate on the sermon. She felt as if all eyes were on her, which couldn't be true. But it felt that way all the same. How did a person survive after loss? How did she go on? She had lost her baby, her husband, the image of the life she thought she would have. And the worst part of all? She had to live with Jonah, go on pretending that everything was all right when nothing would ever be okay again.

She sighed to herself.

Annie reached out and clasped Sarah's fingers in her own.

Sarah glanced at her sister.

Annie smiled.

At least one person was on her side.

Jonah could barely stand, his legs felt so weak and stiff. It was as if he had been put on display. At the last church service, he could smile and accept everyone's condolences. He could pretend that everything between him and Sarah was fine, even if it wasn't the truth. No one around him knew.

Then the song ended and everyone sat. Church Sunday. He wanted to shake his head at it all.

Because here, with Sarah, all their problems bubbled to the surface. Yet no one would talk about them. He imagined he could hear their whispers, could feel their stares. They had to be talking about it. It was the last thing to happen in Wells Landing and it wouldn't ease until something else happened to take its place.

The bishop was talking about their responsibilities as followers of Jesus and what God wanted from them, but Jonah could barely hear the words.

He felt someone's gaze and looked over to the women's side of the room, hoping that it might be his wife. Instead he encountered Hilde Yoder's sympathetic gaze.

He gave her a small smile. She returned it and faced back toward the front.

Distracted, Jonah allowed his gaze to roam around the room. Specifically, to the women seated across from him. Sarah was sitting a few rows ahead of him. He could see the back of her head, the slim column of her neck, and the curve of her jaw.

She rubbed the back of her neck as if she could feel his gaze on her.

How many times had he sat in church knowing that she was looking at him and ignoring the fact that she was staring? What he wouldn't give for her to turn around and look at him now.

But she stayed face forward as the bishop droned on. Normally Jonah enjoyed church. He used it as a time to get back in touch with himself and God. But lately it had become more of a chore. Something he had to do because it was expected of him. Something to endure, then run from as soon as it was over.

He wanted to get back to his old, church-loving self. He knew that if he asked his mother the way back, she would tell him that he needed to get back right with God. Maybe it was time.

Sarah did her duty after church. She helped serve the men and made sure the children had something to eat, then took her turn at the benches-turned-tables.

Annie sat right beside her, giving her strength with her sunny presence, but Sarah kept her gaze down, not daring to look up from her plate. If the women around her weren't accusing, then their eyes would hold pity. She couldn't decide which was worse. Like it mattered. They looked at her one of the two ways, and she couldn't stomach either one.

Once everyone had eaten, all the groups started migrating together to plan out the rest of the Sunday. The sun was shining, and though the wind held a bit of a chill, it was too pretty a day to let it pass without an activity or two.

Sarah stayed close to Annie even though they had separate youth groups. She needed to stay near a friendly face until Jonah finished whatever he was doing and they could go home.

Annie and her friends were putting the final details to their afternoon plans when Jonah jogged over. "Let's go, Sarah. There's a volleyball game scheduled at the rec center."

Volleyball game? She wanted to go home, not to the noisy rec center. She turned back to her sister, giving her hand a quick squeeze. "I'll see you later."

"Bye, Sarah." Annie's voice trailed behind her as she approached Jonah.

"I don't want to go to the rec center, Jonah."

He followed behind her. "Can you at least wait until we get into the buggy before you start an argument with me?"

She pressed her lips together and marched toward their buggy.

Someone called to Jonah. He paused long enough to wave, then continued after Sarah. She couldn't see him but she could tell where he was. Why did she have to be so aware of him? Why did she have to know where he was even if he wasn't in her line of sight?

She waited for him to climb into the buggy, then she scampered in behind him.

"I don't want to go to the rec center," she said before he even set the horse into motion.

Jonah sighed, but the sound was more put on than genuine. "Well, I want to go."

"So?" She was angry. Why did she have to go just because he wanted to? She was tired, worn out. This was her first outing since . . . well, it was her first outing in a long time and she was ready to go home and rest, not watch a bunch of people all happier than her chasing a ball around the gym. She just wasn't up to it.

"I can't very well go without you, Sarah."

"Says who?"

"Says everybody."

"That's dumb. I shouldn't have to go if I don't want to and you shouldn't have to stay home because I don't want to go." She crossed her arms in front of her as if to add some sort of value to her statement.

"It isn't dumb."

"Maybe it's time to start a new trend."

"And what? Embarrass myself because my wife hates me?"

She didn't hate him. She hated the situation. She hated the fact that he wouldn't be with her if they hadn't gotten pregnant. And she hated the fact that the baby was gone. She hated it all. And right now she even hated volleyball. "I doubt you'll be that embarrassed."

She looked out the window, unable to even glance at his profile. He was angry, that much she knew. But he wasn't the one everyone hated. He wasn't the one everyone pitied. And he didn't have to endure their sad stares and scorn for making the golden boy get married.

Jonah had reached near martyrdom when Lorie left.

Most folks understood that she had a family and a life that she knew nothing about. They understood, even if she hadn't known any different than the Amish world, her need to find out about this family she never knew. And they felt bad for Jonah, who had loved Lorie for so long but who couldn't compete with the lure of an unknown family in the English world. He couldn't follow her because he had already been baptized. He couldn't risk the *Bann* from his family and his church. So while Lorie had chosen the unknown, Jonah had remained with his face, and the whole community loved him for it.

He didn't say another word to her as they drove home. And that was just fine with her. Let him be angry a while. It might do him some good. He needed emotions. He had picked up after the miscarriage and carried on like nothing. Well, she couldn't do that. And if he couldn't be sad, then he could just be mad.

He pulled the buggy into the drive. She clambered down and marched to the house thinking he would be behind her once he put the horse away. But the next thing she heard was the snap of the reins as he set the buggy into motion once again. She stayed on the porch and watched him leave, wondering why he had taken her at her word.

Chapter Seventeen

He couldn't believe it. He honestly had no idea how the afternoon had ended up like this. But he had taken all he could from Sarah. He was trying his best to move forward, but she wanted to keep dwelling in the past. It went against everything they had been taught their entire lives. All things were God's will. Some were harder to accept than others, but they all came from the Maker's hand.

Well, no more. It was time to get out and start to live again. If she wanted to hole up in the house and wither away, fine. That didn't mean he had to.

He pulled the buggy into the empty lot next to the rec center and tethered his horse. Anger fueled his steps around the building and inside.

The place grew eerily silent. Everyone turned and stared. He had dared to come out without his wife. It wasn't done. At least not to couples' events. He could have gone to a men's singing or a fellowship breakfast. But he was the only married man there without his wife.

He nodded to the first person he made eye contact with and continued on into the gym like nothing was amiss.

Several couples had already started a game. The rec center set up two nets crossways on the gym floor. Currently both were being used while several other couples visited in the bleachers.

Jonah spied Luke Lambright, Titus Lambert, and Ezra Hein in the stands. “Hey.”

They all said their hellos, then a strange silence descended around them.

Finally, Luke broke the quiet. “Uh, where’s Sarah?”

Jonah shrugged one shoulder and acted as if it was no big deal. “She didn’t feel like coming.”

Maybe, just maybe, if he was lucky enough, everyone would think it had something to do with losing the baby and would forgive him his small breach of standard.

Titus cleared his throat and looked back to where Abbie sat in the stands. They would get married soon. Jonah seemed to remember the date was sometime at the end of the month. Luke was still dating Sissy, and as far as Jonah could tell, both of them were too busy having fun to worry about much else. Of course, no one expected Luke to behave a certain way anymore. Not since he had left the Amish to drive English race cars.

“It’s not a big deal,” Jonah said.

The men shuffled in place.

“It’s not.”

They all nodded, but no one met his gaze. They all knew what it meant that he came without Sarah—that his marriage was in serious trouble. The Amish might not divorce, but that didn’t mean they had to live with each other. He remembered one or two couples who had split after their children were grown. But it had been a long time since anything like that had happened in Wells Landing.

Just because he came without Sarah didn’t mean they were having such troubles, but everyone assumed that they were. Okay, so maybe they were. But that didn’t mean . . .

He was only kidding himself. His marriage was in grave trouble, and he was helpless to stop that downward spiral.

The next few days passed much the same. It seemed that now that she had made a stand and stayed at home when she didn't want to go to a dumb volleyball game, she and Jonah were living separate lives.

He had headed off somewhere today, so she had called a driver and got a ride to her parents' house. She needed to be surrounded by a few happy faces.

She paid the driver, then sent him on his way.

"*Mamm?*" She walked into the warm interior, immediately feeling as if she had been wrapped in a hug. The delicious scent of sugar cookies drifted around the room and she knew where to find her mother and most probably Annie.

"I knew I'd find you in here." She smiled at the two of them sitting around the table decorating the cookies with colored icing, eating the broken ones and washing it all down with warm coffee.

"Sarah." Annie's chair scraped against the floor as she pushed back and stood to give her a hug.

"What brings you out today?" her *mamm* asked.

"Do I have to have a special reason to come out and visit?"

Her mother smiled as Sarah crossed the room to give her a hug. She missed the hugs most of all. A woman shouldn't miss her family like this when she got married, but the love was supposed to balance out. She might be losing a little of the love from her mother and sisters, but the love of her husband was there to take up for the loss. It was the way of the world. But not her marriage.

Her marriage was doomed even before it had a chance to start.

"Sit down and you can decorate cookies with us."

It had been a tradition in the Yoder household as long as she could remember. Every year they baked the cookies together.

"I don't want to talk about it."

"Can we talk about Christmas?" Annie asked, licking the icing from her fingers.

"We can, but you need to wash your hands first." Her mother shot Annie a loving frown. Sarah wanted to laugh and cry simultaneously. She had missed them both so much. She wanted them, she loved them, she needed them.

"You are coming for Christmas?" Annie asked. "At least for pie."

Sarah flashed through her and Jonah's agreement. But that was before. Now . . .

If he could go running off any time he wanted, why did she have to keep up her end of the deal? Let him go to his parents' house and she would come here. She'd rather spend the Lord's birthday surrounded by love than under the hateful stare of Gertie Miller.

It was probably the worst decision he had ever made. Or maybe the second worst after that night by the pond.

"I was surprised to get your call." April was sitting outside the gas station in her little blue car, her cheeks flushed with heat or cold, or maybe embarrassment. He didn't know.

"You said if I ever needed a friend." And he did need a

friend. He needed someone neutral who didn't have all the Amish culture tainting her every thought.

She nodded, her blond ponytail slipping across one shoulder. "And I meant that."

His heart gave an odd thump, but it didn't feel like when he was around Sarah. This felt more like . . . guilt.

He tucked his hands in his pockets and leaned down to better see April. She was really pretty. And nice too. And not yelling at him for nothing and picking at him for the smallest imaginary infraction.

"Can we go somewhere and talk?"

She looked around. Not many customers were going into the Gas and Go, but that could change at any minute. It had gotten colder since December hit, and the clouds held the threat of snow. Anytime that happened, all the bread and milk disappeared off the store shelves. Once the grocer was out, they would start coming to the Gas and Go and clean them out as well. What everyone was doing with bread and milk was beyond him. It was just the way the world worked. "Are you sure that's a good idea?"

"No." He shrugged. None of this was a good idea, and yet he couldn't put a stop to it.

"How about some place a little public but still kind of private?"

He knew just the place. "Follow me."

He was so very aware of her behind him all the way out of town. And he was certain everyone knew that she was following him, that he had called her, that he thought she was pretty, and that his marriage was falling apart. Well, everyone knew his marriage was in trouble, but they also understood that short of leaving the faith, there was nothing he could do about the disastrous union he and Sarah had forged.

"Nice place," she said, as she got out of the car.

Jonah looked at the house as if seeing it for the first time. His father had kept it up over the years. Eli Miller took pride in his house. "Thanks," Jonah said, then started for the porch.

"Who lives here?"

"My mother, father, two of my brothers, and my baby sister."

Her steps faltered a bit, or maybe she tripped over the heels on her boots. She caught herself and straightened. "That's a lot of people."

And that was exactly why he had chosen the place. He wanted to spend some time with April and he knew that he couldn't do anything there with all his family around.

He reached for the doorknob and stopped. "About my brother Buddy . . ."

She gave him an inquisitive look that he took as encouragement.

"He's a little different," Jonah said, but before he could explain, the door was wrenched from his hand.

"I thought I heard you!" Buddy grinned from the other side of the threshold, then his expression fell as he caught sight of April. "Who's she?"

"This is my friend April. April, this is my brother Buddy."

"Nice to meet you, Buddy. Is that your real name?"

He made a face as Jonah and April stepped into the house. "No, but that's what everyone calls me."

"I like it."

"Do you want some pie and coffee?" Jonah asked.

Before April could answer, his mother bustled into the room. "Buddy, who's out here? I thought I heard—"

She caught sight of the two of them standing with Buddy. "Oh, hello."

"Hi." April's voice was confident and sure, as if it was no big thing standing in their entryway greeting his Amish family. He had heard people stutter all over themselves when they talked to an Amish person, but not April.

"*Mamm,* this is my friend April. April," he said in introduction, "this is my mother."

"It's nice to meet you," April said.

The Amish weren't big on introductions, and his mother merely nodded.

"We thought we would come by and have a piece of pie."

"Buddy," *Mamm* started, "will you take April to the kitchen for us, please?"

His brother frowned but didn't protest. "Come on, April. I think they want to talk without us here."

April's smile never wavered, but her gaze darted from Jonah to his mother, then back again. He'd have to explain later. She gave him one last look before disappearing into the kitchen with Buddy.

"What is going on here, Jonah?"

He frowned. "Nothing."

Mamm nodded. "She's not a nothing."

"She's just a friend."

"An English friend."

He shrugged. "So? What difference does it make that she's English?"

"None, I suppose, but it does matter that you are married."

He resisted the urge to sigh . . . loudly. "We're friends, remember?"

"Jonah, I know the time you spent in the English world

changed you. But you know better than this. A man and a woman can't be friends that way."

"That isn't true."

"I'm sure Sarah might have something different to say about it."

He shook his head. "When did you start taking Sarah's side?"

"There are no sides here, son."

"You have never liked Sarah. Why are you so concerned about how she feels all of a sudden?"

His mother opened her mouth and closed it again, then once more, resembling a fish pulled onto the bank of the river. "This is wrong, Jonah," she said once she finally found her voice.

"I'm not doing anything. I haven't done anything. We're just friends." He pushed past her and into the kitchen.

Thankfully she didn't follow. Maybe it was a mistake to come here. He knew he couldn't invite April to his house, and he wanted to sit and talk with her for a while. They could have gone into Kauffman's, but he would have to endure much more than his mother's scorn if he took another woman in there. No, this was the best by far. And still it wasn't perfect.

"Is something wrong?" April asked. Her soft brown eyes gazed at him sympathetically.

"No, of course not. Would you like some coffee?"

"Yes, please."

He moved to the stove to start it brewing. He had become quite efficient in kitchen chores since Sarah had slipped into her anger or depression or whatever it was.

"I got the pie." Buddy came to the table bearing three saucers with heaping slices of coconut pie.

Jonah cleared his throat. "Buddy, would you mind eating your pie in the living room?"

His brother frowned. "But you're in here."

Exactly. "I wanted to be able to visit with April a little, okay?" He slipped into the chair across from her.

"You don't want to visit with me?"

"I do. But April has to go home soon. What if you eat your pie in the living room today and tomorrow I'll come by and we can visit then."

He cast a dubious glance toward April. "Just the two of us?"

"Just the two of us."

Buddy nodded. "Okay then." He waved with his fork and started out of the room. Then he turned back and made a face. "I like Sarah better."

"Buddy!"

But he was already gone.

April covered his hand with hers. "It's okay. He's just looking out for you."

"It's not okay at the expense of others' feelings."

April gave an understanding nod. "When you get right down to it, he didn't say anything bad about me. He just reinforced his preference for Sarah."

"How'd you get so smart?" he asked.

"That's what I do. Counseling."

Was that why she was so easy to talk to?

"I work with a lot of kids just like Buddy. He was just letting you know that he thinks you're messing up. And he did it in the only way he knows how."

"By being rude?" Jonah asked, his tone lighter than his words.

"By bringing up Sarah."

The water started to boil and Jonah made his way back

to the stove. Making coffee was better than staring into those knowing brown eyes. At least they didn't accuse. But now that he knew she was a counselor . . . did that change things?

"Luke told me about the baby." Her quiet words fell like bricks between them. The words should have hurt, but he had hardened his heart. They weren't having a baby after all, but as far as their marriage went, it didn't change a thing.

"*Jah?*" He did his best to make his voice sound offhand, as if he hadn't a care in the world. But his hands shook as he carried their mugs back to the table. He wondered if she noticed.

"How are things with Sarah?" she asked once he had settled back into his seat.

"Are you asking as a therapist or a friend?"

She laughed. "A friend, of course."

"Angry." It was the one word that he could use to describe her. "But she's not angry with everyone. Just me."

"I would say that's understandable given the circumstances."

"How come? I didn't do anything."

"Nor could you. But you would be the one person who should have been able to help."

Jonah took a sip of his coffee and let that sink in. He wasn't sure he understood it all. Maybe it was just a lot of English mumbo jumbo.

"We were starting to get along, finally." He sighed. "Then she lost the baby and everything changed."

She cupped her hands around her mug and raised it to her lips, her eyes thoughtful. "Is it true what they say about Amish marriages?"

"You'll have to be more specific. They say a lot of things about Amish marriages."

"That you can't get divorced."

He nodded. "That's true." He had heard a few grumblings around that some bishops in other less conservative districts had allowed a divorce or two, but he could neither prove nor disprove this. He thought back to Cephas Ebersol. He was as fair a bishop as they came, but Jonah couldn't imagine him allowing them to get a divorce based on "I don't want to be married any longer." For some reason Jonah had yet to understand why God had brought the two of them together. And they would just have to ride it out to see all the reasons.

"Wow."

"You think that's a bad rule?"

She shook her head. "I'm not saying one way or another, but it seems to me that a lot of people could benefit from following that."

"And the others?"

She frowned. "Not so much. But maybe it would keep people from getting married without really giving it some thought."

It hadn't done anything for him and Sarah. "Maybe," he went ahead and said anyway. It seemed the right thing to say.

"Are you going to eat your pie?" Jonah asked. They had been talking so much neither one had even taken the first bite.

"It's an awfully big piece."

Jonah laughed. "That's the only problem with asking Buddy to serve sweets. His helping is twice anyone else's."

"Got a sweet tooth, does he?"

"One to match his sweet heart."

April forked up a bite of pie. "Oh, my gosh."

"What?"

"It's definitely true what they say about Amish food. This is delicious."

He nodded and took another bite. No one could beat his mother's coconut pie. "You'll have to come back and have dinner sometime. You can meet the whole family."

April flashed him that sweet, sweet smile. "I would like that."

Gertie waited until the woman left before she grabbed Jonah's arm. "What are you doing, son?"

He looked down at her fingers wrapped around his arm. "I'm going home."

"So you do remember where you live."

"What's that supposed to mean?"

"I thought perhaps you forgot since you saw fit to invite that young woman back here again."

"It's nothing, *Mamm*. Just dinner."

"It's not *gut*, Jonah. Not *gut* at all."

"There's nothing going on," he said. Not that there had been at one time. She could see the guilt in his eyes. He hadn't kissed the girl good-bye before she got in her car and left. Gertie knew. She had been watching from the window, but just because he wasn't physically cheating didn't mean he wasn't cheating in his heart.

"You need to keep your heart pure," she warned. "Follow God's bidding."

He pulled his arm from her grasp, his expression suddenly guarded. "What if God wants me to be friends with her?"

"You owe Sarah more than that," she said. She might not like the circumstances by which Jonah and Sarah came together, but the Bible was clear: let no man put asunder what God hath put together. The two of them were married, forever. And he'd do best to remember it.

"I've given Sarah my life, a house, and everything she could want to go in it. I can give April my friendship." He turned on his heel and headed for the door.

Gertie watched him go, Matthew 6:24 ringing through her head. "No man can serve two masters."

Chapter Eighteen

Sarah heard the tractor and moved away from the window. She hurriedly sat down on the couch, smoothing her hands over her prayer *kapp* and wayward hair, then pressed them against her apron. She didn't want Jonah to know that she had been looking at the window watching for him to come home.

But whether he saw her or not, she knew where he had been. Her cousin Libby had called over an hour ago to tell her that Mandy Burkholder had driven past the Gas and Go and seen Jonah talking to an English woman in a small blue car.

That was all she needed to know. He had said he was going to the hardware store, and instead he'd gone into town to meet April. And she had no idea how to handle it. What did English women do when their husbands went out with other women? Was she supposed to get angry? Well, she was angry, but was she supposed to let him know how badly he had hurt her? Or was she supposed to act like nothing happened? If that was the case, maybe she should lock herself in her room.

Too late.

The front door opened, and Jonah stepped into the

house. He took off his coat and hat before giving a start. Evidently he hadn't seen her sitting on the sofa. Or maybe he just hadn't expected her to be there.

"Sarah."

"Hi, Jonah. Get everything you needed at the hardware store?"

He nodded, but kept his gaze locked on the far window in the living room. "I'm going to start the bookcase after Christmas." He seemed so honest and sincere, and yet she knew he was standing there lying about where he had been. He might have stopped by the hardware store to say he'd done it, but it wasn't the only place he'd been.

She nodded, not knowing what else to say. Maybe she should make her own English friend who could tell her how to handle the situation she was in now.

Christmas was just a week away, and she had no idea where her life was heading. How could she celebrate the Lord's birth with all this hanging over her head?

"About Christmas."

He had started toward the kitchen, but her words stopped him. He turned back. "What about Christmas?"

"I don't want to spend Christmas with your parents."

He blinked a couple of times as if he was having to translate her words. "But that was the agreement."

"I changed my mind." There was no way she was going now. She felt childish, like she was punishing him for meeting April. Well, maybe she was. But she couldn't get back at him any other way.

Why do you have to get back at him?

She pushed the thought away. "You don't want to spend the holiday with my family. So why don't we do each other a big favor and spend it with the people we love?"

"What about Second Christmas?"

She shrugged. "Why should it be any different?" The

words kept falling from her lips, but she barely recognized her own voice. When had she gotten so cynical and uncaring?

For a moment she thought he might protest. "You know what? Fine," he said, then he moved on into the kitchen.

Sarah watched him go, then sat back against the sofa cushions. That didn't go exactly like she had expected, though she got everything she asked for.

What is wrong with him?

But she really didn't need to ask that question. He didn't love her the way she did him. And pushing him away was only pushing him away.

To make matters even worse, she had turned ugly and bitter.

How could she even think he might fall in love with her? Not even God could perform a miracle like that.

Jonah stood at the kitchen sink looking out over the yard and the newly built barn. The gray and cloudy sky reflected his mood as surely as if it had been planned that way.

Sarah didn't want to spend Christmas with him. She didn't want to spend an evening with him. She didn't want to do anything with him. She didn't want to be married to him.

He didn't know why the thought stung, but it did. He was satisfied enough being married to her. Life wasn't all about love and roses and sunshine.

The clouds outside were surely a testament to that. The entire sky was blanketed with them, thick, heavy clouds that never moved. How did the sky get clear? How could he find his way back to where he and Sarah were before she lost the baby?

Or maybe the real question was would he ever be able

to get back to that place? Only time would tell, and it seemed it was the only thing they had on their side.

"I thought Sarah was coming over." Buddy frowned at Jonah, then glanced out the door as if maybe he had missed her.

I did too, Buddy. "She, uh . . . well, I'll tell her you missed her."

Buddy shut the door behind Jonah as he started to unload the presents. "Where is she?"

Jonah straightened. "Is Hannah here yet?"

Buddy shook his head. "Aaron and Mary are in the kitchen. Where's Sarah?"

Jonah warmed his hands by the fire. Buddy wouldn't be the only one with questions. "She decided to spend the day with her *mamm* and *dat*."

Buddy seemed to think about it a moment, then he gave a small, understanding nod. "But she'll come over tomorrow."

Jonah shook his head. "I think she's going to see them for Second Christmas too."

"But—"

"Buddy." Jonah cut his brother off before he could get really going. "Sarah is going through a rough time right now."

His brother nodded sagely. "Because of the baby."

It was a simplistic explanation, but definitely one Buddy could understand. His mother had told Buddy that Sarah had lost the baby she carried. That much he could understand. Jonah couldn't expect his brother to comprehend much more. How could he when Jonah himself didn't understand it?

"So we have to be patient with her? Do nice things for her?"

"*Jah.*" But what had he done for his wife? He'd tried to understand, that was what. He'd tried to empathize, then he'd started to move on. What else could be done? Living in the past wasn't good for any of them. But Sarah, it seemed, wasn't ready to move forward. And the fact that he was seemed to bother her beyond measure.

"I'm going to draw her a picture." Buddy started from the room, then stopped. "You'll take it to her, *jah*?"

Jonah smiled at his brother. Buddy had such a big heart. He wanted to help Sarah, but he had limited capabilities. Still, that didn't stop him. He did what he could, and it always came from the heart.

"*Danki.*"

Jonah watched as his brother hurried away, wondering where everything had gone so wrong.

Christmas. It was supposed to be the happiest time of the year. So why did she feel so sad? Sarah looked around at all of her family gathered at the dining table. Jonah had gone to his own parents' house for the holiday while she had come home. It was what she had wanted, so why wasn't it making her happy?

"Help me clear the table," Annie said.

Both their brothers' wives had children to attend to and babies to feed. Sarah tried not to be resentful, but the thoughts kept creeping in. *Why can't that be me? Why did Ellie and Linda get to keep their babies while mine was snatched from my grasp?*

"Sure." Kitchen chores were better by far than mooning over what never could be.

"I'll wash and you can dry," Annie offered.

Sarah nodded and got out a dish towel.

"You sure are quiet today," Annie mused.

Sarah shrugged.

"See?" Annie nodded in her general direction. "You aren't normally this quiet."

"Maybe I find I need to be because you like to talk so much." She tried to put on a smile, but it felt forced upon her lips. So much for that.

"Do you want to talk about it?"

She shook her head. "There's nothing to talk about." Jonah didn't love her. It was as simple as that. And even if he did, nothing would change between them. Their marriage had been for all the wrong reasons. Yet they were trapped in it. She had trapped him. At least that was what everyone was saying. When they weren't talking about him and April Franklin.

She had only come to town once that Sarah knew of. That was a couple of days ago. Sarah knew because Jonah came home with a new pair of leather gloves, much too nice for farm work. Only an *Englisher* wouldn't know that gloves like that were a luxury and had no place on a farmer. And the only *Englisher* she knew who would give him such an extravagant present was April Franklin.

Sarah did her best not to be jealous or resentful, but it seemed those were the only emotions she could have these days. If she let any others in, she was afraid that loneliness and heartbreak would follow thereafter.

"I think there's a lot to talk about."

Just then their mother came into the room. Though she had cooked most of the meal herself, she started gathering up the jars of jam, pickles, and chow chow that had been brought out for the meal and loading them back into the icebox.

"I've been thinking," *Mamm* said.

That's when Sarah realized she had been boxed in, with her sister on one side and her mother on the other.

"What?" Sarah tossed down her dish towel, trying to get ready for whatever it was she was about to face.

"You."

"And?"

"I think it's time for you to come home for a while." Her mother said the words so calmly that Sarah wondered for a moment if she had heard her wrong.

Come home? How could she come home? She was married. And that just wasn't done. Her place was with her husband. Even Helen Ebersol had said that when Sarah was asked to give up her teaching job.

Sarah opened her mouth to protest but no sound came out. It was perhaps the furthest thing from her mind when her sister said they should talk. A married woman didn't just up and leave her husband.

But all she could manage by way of protest was a small squeak.

"Now hear me out," *Mamm* said. "You've hit a tough time in your life and you need all the support you can get. I'm just not convinced that Jonah can fill that role for you right now."

It was more than the truth. Maybe if she and Jonah loved each other. Maybe if they had been married a year or so before getting pregnant. Maybe if they had dated or even spent a little courting time together, things might be different. But none of those things were their truth. They didn't have those solid foundations to help them heal. And she was floundering. She knew. She could feel it every day, yet she was helpless to do anything about it.

But this . . .

"You can come home for a while. Give yourself a chance to get back right with yourself and God, then see where that takes you."

Her heart gave a small leap of joy. She could move home. She would be surrounded by her family, the people who loved her. That was what she needed to heal. That had to be it. Surely Jonah would understand. And if he didn't? Well, she wasn't going to worry about that. Right now she had to do what was best for her, and what was best was moving home.

She smiled at her mother, and this time the action was as real as it could be. "I think that's a great idea."

She couldn't just leave without talking to Jonah. Sarah felt cowardly enough for needing a break, and she would feel doubly so if she took off without even telling him where she was going and how long she was staying.

So she packed her bag and waited for him to return. Annie hadn't wanted her to come alone, but she had insisted. This was something between her and Jonah, and it didn't need witnesses. So she had borrowed her parents' tractor and chugged on over.

Jonah came home around four thirty. "Hi, Sarah." He seemed surprised to see her. She couldn't blame him. She had left after him this morning, and when she was at home she spent the bulk of her time in her bedroom. She could only take so much of staring at him across the table and knowing that he would never love her.

Then his gaze fell to the suitcase at her feet. "What's that?"

Sarah stood and smoothed her hands down the front of her dress and apron. "I've decided to go stay with my parents for a while."

He propped his hands on his hips, his expression unreadable. "What's a while?"

"I don't know. A while."

"Until after the first of the year? Valentine's Day? Easter?"

"A few weeks maybe."

"Whatever you want, Sarah. But hasn't that always been the way?"

What was he talking about? It had never, ever been about the things she wanted. She had dealt with his scraps of attention, the whispers when no one thought she was listening, and she had spent her entire marriage knowing he would rather be married to Lorie.

She folded her arms and steeled her stare. "This is best for everyone."

"You need some help getting out to the tractor?"

She shook her head.

He stared toward his bedroom without so much as a look back in her direction. "Enjoy your *mamm*'s."

"And then she left," he said into the receiver.

"Just like that?" April asked.

"Just like that."

After Sarah had chugged off down the road, Jonah had rattled around the house for a while, then he went out to the barn to call April. He hated to bother her with his problems on Christmas Day, but he needed a friend in the worst way. It seemed his marriage was not going to improve. Not without some help, and even then, he wasn't sure Sarah cared if it got better. She had found her solution, running away. But Jonah had nowhere to run.

"I know this is going to sound a little crazy, but do you think maybe she wants you to come after her?"

"And what? Make her come home?"

"Maybe she simply needs to know that you want her there."

Could that be the problem?

"Did she say why she left?"

"No."

"And you didn't ask her?"

"No." The thought had never crossed his mind. She wanted to go to her mother's, and he let her. "I'm tired of everything being an argument."

"I'm sure she feels the same way."

"She starts it."

Only silence met his words.

"Okay, maybe I don't do anything to help, but I'm at an end. I can't do anything to make her happy, why should I even try?"

"They haven't by chance okayed divorce in your district, have they?"

Jonah almost laughed. Almost. "No."

"Then you have two choices: figure out what your wife needs, or leave it all behind."

Chapter Nineteen

"I'm so glad you're here." Annie's voice floated to her in the dark.

Once she had gotten back to her parents' house, it almost seemed as if she had never left. She and Annie took turns taking a bath. Then they sat on the bed and brushed their hair talking about everything and nothing, just like they used to do.

Now they lay in their beds just as they had so many times before. It was just like it used to be, and so different.

"I'm glad I'm here." And she was. But she couldn't help wondering what Jonah was doing now. Was he getting a snack before he went to bed? He loved a little bite of something just before he went to sleep. He said he slept better if his stomach wasn't empty. The day he had told her that, she laughed and said there was no way his stomach was empty considering how much he had eaten at supper. He had laughed and chased her around the house until she promised that she was only joking and he could eat as much as he wanted whenever he wanted.

And for a moment she thought he might kiss her, then the moment passed. Would things be different if he had?

Of course not. That was just fanciful thinking on her part.

"What are you thinking about?"

"Nothing."

"Uh-huh." Annie didn't sound convinced.

But what good was it telling her sister that she wished things between her and Jonah had been different?

"Let's make more Christmas cookies tomorrow," Annie suggested.

"Didn't you get enough of those already?"

"Never. I could eat Christmas cookies all year long."

"You do. They're called sugar cookies."

The bedsprings squeaked as Annie turned over. "They taste better when they're cut into shapes." It was typical Annie logic.

"Round is a shape," Sarah pointed out, just to see what her sister said. It was a great distraction, and she'd much rather talk about sugar cookies than dwell on all the problems with her marriage.

"Not a very *gut* one." She shifted in the bed once more. "You know what would be fun?" She didn't wait for Sarah to answer. "To get a cookie cutter shaped like an egg. Then at Easter time, we could decorate it instead of eggs!"

"You don't like decorating eggs?"

"I didn't say that. It's just that cookies taste better."

Sarah laughed and she realized it was the first time in a long while. "That they do, sister. That they do."

Sarah slid the next sheet of cookies into the oven and looked around for something to wipe her hands on. "Where's the towel?"

Annie shrugged and kept sprinkling the snowflake-shaped cookie with glittery sugar.

This second round of "Christmas cookies" was more

winter themed, with two sizes of snowflakes, white and pale blue icing, and glittery-looking white sugar for decoration.

"Is that someone at the door?" Sarah swore she heard a knock, but no one knocked around these parts. That could only mean one of two things: it was either someone they didn't know or someone who didn't think they'd be welcome.

"Sounds like it." Annie didn't bother to look up from her cookie.

"Can you get it?" Sarah looked around for something to wipe her hands on.

"I'm busy."

Sarah sighed and wiped her hands on her apron as she walked to the front door.

"Jonah!" To say that she was surprised to see her husband on the other side might be the understatement of the year. "What are you doing here?"

"Can I talk to you for a bit?"

"I just put some cookies on to bake."

Something flashed through his eyes so quickly she thought she had imagined it. Could that be remorse? "I can sit in the kitchen with you."

A part of her wanted to give that time to him, hear what he had to say. But there was another part of her that needed to give that time to Annie. After all, she had promised her sister last night. "Annie's in there." It was a compromise and maybe a coward's way, but let him decide.

"I can come back later this afternoon."

He must really want to talk. "Let me get these cookies out, then we can talk, okay?"

He nodded, his relief clearly evident. "*Jah*." He stepped into the house and shut the door behind himself.

Sarah turned back for the kitchen as Jonah took off his hat and coat, hanging them by the door.

"Annie?"

"Hmmm . . ." Her sister didn't bother to look up.

"Jonah's here."

"What?" Her head jerked to attention, swiveling from Sarah to Jonah and back again. "Hi, Jonah," she said, her gaze finally resting on him. "What brings you out?"

Sarah stared wide-eyed at her sister. "He wants to talk," she said, her teeth clenched to warn her sister against saying anything else. But that was the thing about Annie. She wasn't very good at picking up on those sorts of things.

"Do you think that's a *gut* idea?" she asked, but Sarah couldn't tell who the question was directed toward.

"I told him we were making cookies, but after I get this batch out of the oven, I'm going to the other room to talk, okay?"

Annie studied her for a moment, then gave Jonah a once-over. Until that moment Sarah hadn't realized how handsome he looked. What was it they said? Absence makes the heart grow fonder? One night away and she had almost forgotten how good-looking he was. But it was also the first time that she had noticed how tired he looked, like he hadn't gotten much sleep. But she had only been gone one night. Or maybe that sad tilt to his eyes and the small downward turn at the corners of his mouth had been there longer than she realized.

"*Jah*, okay," Annie finally said.

The kitchen timer dinged, and Sarah instinctively moved to get the cookies. Jonah hovered nearby.

She hated that her hands shook as she moved the cookies to the stove top to cool. She should take them off the cookie sheet to cool on the rack, but the way she was trembling, she was bound to tear them all in half. Better leave them where they were for now.

She nodded toward the entryway that led into the family room.

Her heart thumped in her chest as she settled down on the couch. The last time they were here, they were telling her parents about the baby. Now . . .

"What's on your mind, Jonah?"

"April said I should come by and talk to you."

The name was like a slap in the face. "You've been talking to April?"

He nodded, obviously missing the hurt in her voice. "She's easy to talk to and—"

"Then why aren't you talking to her now?" Sarah resisted the urge to jump to her feet and hustle him to the door. Until this minute she had thought he had come to make up with her, tell her that he wanted her to come back home. Then he busted out with April.

Sarah wasn't sure what hurt the most, the fact that he'd been spending time with another woman or that the other woman was the only reason why he had shown up here today.

Jonah's face turned red. "I'm not married to April."

Sarah crossed her arms, more to stop their trembling than to shut him out. "According to all the gossips, you might as well be."

He was on his feet in a heartbeat. "Is that what you think of me?"

"I don't know what to think, Jonah. All I know is what you show me. I thought you came here today to maybe work through a few things, but I can see now I was wrong."

"It seems I was too." He limped, stiff-legged, toward the door.

Sarah watched, helpless as he crammed his hat back onto his head and grabbed his coat. He was out the door without even putting it on. He couldn't get distance between them soon enough.

She should have known.

Sarah flopped down on the sofa and gave into her tears.

The weatherman had been talking about snow for days, but so far none had fallen. Today was entirely too warm for it now, but Jonah didn't care. He was just happy he and April could sit out on the porch and talk without the wind cutting straight through them.

"You told her what?"

"That you and I were talking, and she just went crazy. She started telling me that I should just go talk to you."

"And what did you say?"

He shook his head, chagrined by what had transpired between him and Sarah. "It turned bad from there."

"And you walked out."

"How'd you know?" he asked.

April shook her head. "Amish men are more like English ones than most people realize."

He picked at the peeling paint on the bench where he sat.

"Do you love her?" April asked.

The question took him off guard. "Love doesn't matter. We're married, and that's all there is to it."

"Unless you decide to leave the faith."

"*Jah*."

"Is that something you would consider?"

Would he? He didn't know. What he did know was that his wife was angry all the time and marriage hadn't turned out anything like he'd planned.

Who was to blame?

He just didn't know.

"That doesn't mean anything." Annie opened the oven to peek at the bread, then turned back to Sarah.

She didn't want her sister taking up for Jonah. She wanted to stay mad at him. "It means a lot, actually."

Annie straightened and turned off the oven. She left the bread inside to cook a few minutes in the remaining heat. "How so?"

"Annie, he's running around with an English girl." Had her sister somehow become deaf in the few minutes they had been talking? True, Annie seemed to be in her own little world most days, but it was one of the things that Sarah enjoyed about her sister. However, today it was beginning to grate her nerves a little.

"And?" Annie nodded, encouraging Sarah to continue, but there was nothing else to say.

"Isn't that enough?"

Annie shot her a look that was half pity, half astonishment. "It's nothing. That's what it is," she said, turning away and removing the bread from the oven. She set it on the stove top, then faced Sarah, her hands still folded around the pot holders as she propped them on her hips. "You are looking for something to be upset with him about. And it seems like you've found something even though it is ridiculous."

Sarah wrinkled her nose despite the wonderful smell of freshly baked bread that surrounded them. Annie might live in her own world at times, but she was about the best cook Sarah knew. "It is not."

"Did he tell you he loves her? Or that he regrets marrying you?"

Tears stung the back of Sarah's eyes. "He didn't have to."

Annie shook her head sadly. "I know that the two of you got married under . . . unusual circumstances, but that doesn't mean he doesn't care for you."

"Doesn't it?"

"If he didn't, then why did he marry you to begin with?"

"Because he had no choice." Sarah wanted to hang her head in shame, but this was Annie, the one person she knew she could depend on to not pass judgment.

"Everyone has a choice, Sarah."

Those words stayed with Sarah all that evening and into the night. Annie climbed into bed and wanted to talk, but Sarah feigned sleep. She had too much on her mind to participate in idle chitchat.

Did Jonah really have a choice?

No. Not in their world. She had heard tales of English girls having babies with no husband around to speak of, but the Amish didn't allow such behavior. The night that she and Jonah had spent together had brought enough shame to them both. And though her reputation seemed more fragile by far than his, he had to maintain appearances as much as she. But could he have walked away?

She supposed that he could have. But he would have most probably gone to live with the English and let her alone to raise their child.

But there was no child.

She smoothed a hand over the flat plane of her stomach. She usually carried a couple of extra pounds, but she had lost weight after the . . . miscarriage. How she hated that word. Each day it grew a little easier to say in her mind, but uttering it out loud was almost more than she could bear.

The bedsprings creaked as Annie turned over in her sleep. It felt good to be home, surrounded by all the people she loved and who loved her in return, but there was something wrong, something missing.

She sighed and punched at her pillow, trying her best to get relaxed enough to sleep.

"I know you're awake." Annie's voice was clear and free from the cobwebs of sleep. Perhaps she had been pretending too.

"We need to be resting," Sarah replied, though her thoughts were anything but peaceful.

"What are you thinking about?"

"Nothing."

"It is a sin to lie, Sarah Miller."

Sarah Miller. That was her name now. And would be until the day she died. She had tied her life to Jonah's, but he didn't want that connection. What was a girl to do?

"It's not important," Sarah finally replied. At least it wasn't to Jonah. And she couldn't let any of it be important to her, or her heart would be shattered into a million pieces.

"Do you love him?"

Sarah didn't bother to ask who she was talking about. "*Jah*." Once upon a time she had believed that she had loved him with all her heart. Heavens, had she been wrong. Back then she had only *thought* she loved him. That was before he had bought her a house and tried to soothe her after the loss of their child. That was before the rides on his tractor, the trip to the county fair and all the wonderful days she had spent with him. Before she had loved him with a young girl's heart, but now? She loved him as a woman loves a man—wholly, deeply, completely.

"If you love him, then why are you here with me and not home with him?"

Why not? Because she was the only one in love and always had been. And in love alone was no place to be.

* * *

"Jonah, this has to stop."

He shook his head at his mother's words. "I'm not doing anything wrong." It was just after Christmas, and once again he'd met April at his parents' house. They had sat in the living room discussing their different Christmas traditions and drinking hot cocoa. His family had filed in and out at odd times. His mother knew for a fact that they had just been talking, sitting in opposite chairs as they enjoyed each other's company.

Didn't she understand that he just needed a friend? A friend who didn't judge or cite chapter and verse to him about the sanctity of marriage? His marriage was in trouble. That was no big secret. What he was going to do about it was another matter altogether.

"Everyone's talking," *Mamm* said. "It's not right."

"Who other than God can say what is right or wrong?"

"The bishop, the deacon, the *church*."

He scoffed. "I'm not doing anything wrong."

"Don't bring her here again," his mother warned. "If you do, she won't be welcome in this house."

Shards of pain shot through his skull as he ground his teeth together. So that was how it was going to be. "Fine," he growled. "Then I guess I'm not welcome here either."

He slammed the door and hustled over to his tractor. He was surviving, couldn't she see that? Why did everyone have to be so judgmental? The English had it right: "Live and let live."

But you're not English.

He could be. He had half a mind to pack his stuff and head over to Luke Lambright's. He knew his longtime friend would find room for him to stay. That would serve them all right. If they couldn't accept him as he was, then they wouldn't have him at all.

* * *

"I came to say that I'm sorry." The words didn't come easily for Gertie. She took a deep breath and studied Jonah's face. He looked tired and edgy, as if his heart had no peace.

How could it?

She had waited as long as she could to see if he would come around, but after only two days, she knew she would have to be the one to make amends. That was fine with her as long as she could get Jonah back in the fold.

She had mistakenly thought that giving him an ultimatum would help to bring him around to clear thinking. She had been wrong. Now she was working to repair the damage those impulsive words had cost.

He seemed to think about her apology for a moment, then gave a small nod.

Gertie resisted the urge to sigh in relief. She wasn't in the clear yet. "Can I come in?" She had forgone the tradition of walking into a loved one's house, deciding to knock instead. The next move was entirely up to Jonah and would set the course for her little plan.

He paused, then stepped to the side, allowing her to enter.

Gertie stepped over the threshold, grateful for the small measure he had given her. "I brought some banana bread."

"*Danki.*" He followed her as she hurried into the kitchen. She wasn't sure how long he would allow her to stay. Especially after she said what she came to say. When had things gotten so complicated? When had she lost her son? Not when he married Sarah Yoder, but long before that. Maybe even when Henry Kauffman died. She shook her head at herself. That wasn't even his name, but he was Lorie's father, and his death had sent her into a spiral of grief and bad choices that had deeply touched Jonah and made him a victim as well.

"Would you like me to make some coffee?" she asked.

"I can do it." But he shouldn't have to, Gertie thought as he moved toward the stove. That was his wife's job, but Sarah wasn't here, and that was the exact reason for Gertie's visit.

She sat at the small kitchen table and unwrapped the bread while Jonah went about making coffee. In no time they had their snack of buttered banana bread and a steaming cup of coffee in front of them.

"What's on your mind?" Jonah asked.

Gertie took another sip of coffee. "That is *gut*," she commented, stalling for time. She had to make sure that everything was right. She wouldn't want to blow this opportunity before she even truly had it in her grasp.

"*Jah*, it is," Jonah returned. "But I very much doubt that you came here to discuss my coffee-making skills."

"Can a mother not visit her son to just pass the time and enjoy his company?" She took another sip and eyed him over the rim of her cup.

His eyes, so very much like her own, were narrowed in speculation. "Tell me why you're really here."

Gertie lowered her cup. "*Jah*, okay then, I'm here to talk about counseling."

He sat back in surprise. "Counseling?"

"*Jah*." She nodded, hoping the idea wasn't completely out of the question.

"What sort of counseling?"

Gertie leaned forward and took one of his hands in hers. "Jonah, marriage is a sacred endeavor. Everyone in Wells Landing knows that you and Sarah are having difficulties. But it's time now to correct those problems and look to the future."

A flash of hurt streaked through his eyes. In less than a heartbeat it was gone, leaving her to wonder if it had ever truly been there at all. "Sarah and I don't have a future."

His words broke her heart. She may not have ever wanted the pair to be together, but God had other plans. His will was the most important, and she had to believe that He knew best. "Please tell me that you don't really believe that."

He eased his hand out of hers and sat back, away from her. "*Jah.* I do."

Gertie shook her head. "You can't go against God's will, son."

"This has nothing to do with God's will. It was just the mistake of two people who were needing something they couldn't find anywhere else. God had no hand in it."

"You've been hanging out with the English too much. God has a hand in everything."

He didn't want to acknowledge her words. If he did and he was being honest with himself, he would have to admit that she spoke the truth. But he wasn't ready to examine all the details. Not when Sarah wanted nothing to do with him.

"You're missing something," he told his mother.

"What is that?"

"Sarah doesn't want to be married to me any more than I want to be married to her. Why should I make us both miserable by insisting that we go to counseling?"

"Because she's your wife. Forever."

Forever. That was a long time when two people didn't know how to love one another. "Does it really matter?"

"It does if you want to save your marriage."

There was nothing to save, but he knew she wouldn't believe him.

"You can't just leave your wife, Jonah."

"I didn't leave her. She left me."

"She's not here," *Mamm* pointed out.

He had no response.

"There is no divorce among the Amish. The only way you can walk away from this marriage is to go over to the English."

He snapped his attention to her, teeth clenched in rage. Or was it frustration? "I know, *Mamm*. Believe me, I know."

Jonah watched his mother back out of his driveway, her words still ringing in his ears.

God has a hand in everything.

Did God have a plan for him and Sarah? Did that plan include them living separate lives?

He shook his head. His thoughts were as fanciful as an English fairy tale. Sarah wanted nothing to do with him. She only had scorn for him.

He wished she would listen to him the way April did. April was kind and considerate and didn't look at him like he'd crawled out from under a rock when he walked into the room.

But Sarah hasn't always looked at you like that.

He pushed that voice to the side. Sarah might have cared for him once, but she had more than shown him that the time for her love was over. He thought that they had a shot. Everyone knew that they were forced to get married. He had foolishly believed that somehow they could make it work. They would have a baby to bind them together, to keep them focused on the same goals. But all that was over now. The one thing he was certain of was gone in an instant, as if it had never even been there at all.

He had heard the talk around town. He knew what some of the less kind members of their community were saying. No one would dare speak it to his face, but they believed that he had been tricked into marriage with a child who never existed. There was a time, a brief moment when the thought had crossed his mind as well, but after seeing Sarah's heartbreak, her tears and all-consuming depression, he knew that it was real. At least it had been to her. And that was what made it so sad.

He hadn't had the time to think about the baby, a breathing, living creature who would be born, walk and talk. A child they could teach their ways and raise in the church. None of those ideas had been real to him, but they had been to Sarah. He could see it in her eyes, yet he was powerless to help her in her grief.

Maybe if it had been real, maybe if he could have helped her, maybe then things would be different and she wouldn't be back living with her parents with half the district between them.

Maybe . . .

"I'm worried about you, Sarah."

She started and turned around as her mother approached. "There's nothing to worry about," she lied. Or maybe it wasn't so much of a lie. There was really nothing to worry about. It was over between her and Jonah, if there was anything between them to begin with. Only in her dreams.

"You're living here and your husband is living miles away. I'd say that's something to worry about." Her blue eyes filled with concern.

Sarah shook her head in disbelief. "I'm here because you encouraged me to come home."

"*Jah,* I know. But . . ."

"But you didn't think I'd stay this long."

"*Jah.* Something like that."

Sarah hated worrying her mother, but it couldn't be helped. "There's nothing I can do about that."

"I beg to differ," her mother said.

Sarah shook her head and made her way to the kitchen table. Annie was out gathering eggs and their *dat* was at work. Sarah had the feeling this conversation wasn't going to be a quick one. She might as well be comfortable while her mother had her say. She slid into one of the chairs and waited for *Mamm* to continue.

Her *mamm* took the chair opposite her and rested her forearms on the tabletop. "No one said marriage was going to be easy. We all know that. But there are many things couples can do to work through their problems."

Sarah waited.

"I talked to the bishop about you and Jonah going through marriage counseling."

Sarah was on her feet in an instant. "You what?"

"Sit down, daughter."

She returned to her seat, wondering who her mild-mannered mother had been talking to. Who had put these ideas in her head? "Why would you do such a thing?"

"I hate seeing you mope around here, pining for your husband and the family that you thought you were going to have."

"It's too late for that." The words might have come from her mouth, but they stabbed through her like a sword.

"It's only too late when God calls you home. Surely you know that."

"I don't know," she mumbled, not knowing how to respond. There was a time when she had believed in love, believed that God would see them all through, but now . . . now, her faith was thin and her ideas of love shattered.

She had loved Jonah with all her heart. Well, she had thought so, then she married him and learned what love really was. Then it slipped through her grasp like smoke. And she knew. She would never get that back.

"Well, I do." Her mother sat back with a knowing smile.

Sarah could see the confidence in the curve of her lips. She thought she had convinced Sarah to try counseling, but Sarah knew what was in her own heart. And she knew how her husband felt about her. "I'm not the only one in this marriage." It was the best way she knew to tell her mother that hope was slim.

Hope is nonexistent.

"I'm sure if I talk to the bishop about this, he'll make sure that Jonah shows up for the sessions."

"No!" Sarah slapped a hand over her mouth to keep any more words from falling out. "I mean, I don't think that's a *gut* idea."

Her mother frowned. "Why not? It is what we do."

Sarah knew that. She didn't need her mother telling her as much. But how could she explain her own shortcomings? "It's complicated," she muttered.

"Not so complicated that God can't sort it out." Her mother gave her a kindly smile.

Sarah returned it, but in her heart she knew: God wanted no part of the mess she had found herself in.

"Are you asleep?"

For a moment Sarah thought about pretending that she was, but her conscience kicked in. "No." She had been ignoring her sister too much.

"Are you going to do it?"

"Do what?"

"Go to counseling?"

"How do you know about that?"

Sarah heard the rustle of covers and knew that Annie had shrugged. "I overheard you and *Mamm* talking today."

"I thought you were out gathering eggs."

"I was, and then I wasn't."

It was a typical Annie answer.

"Well?" she asked again.

"Well what?"

"Are you and Jonah going to marriage counseling?"

"No."

There was another rustle as Annie turned onto her side. "Why not?"

Sarah wanted to jump from the bed and shout that it was no one's business but hers. But that wasn't exactly the way a faithful Amish woman conducted herself. She had finally admitted it to herself—her faith had slipped, practically fallen away entirely. These days she was going through the motions. But not just at church. Every step she took was more effort than the last.

Lord, when does the pain end?

But she didn't expect an answer.

"Jonah doesn't love me," she finally said. How could she say the words out loud, that she was terrified that he wouldn't want her if she couldn't have a baby? What would she do? The one thing she had wanted most in her life wasn't to be hers.

There were plenty of women who suffered the same fate. So many that they had started their own group. She didn't want to be one of them. She knew that the other women talked about them, prayed for them, pitied them.

But she wouldn't be one of them if her marriage was at an end. And she would never know what a complete failure she was as a woman and a wife.

No, it was much better this way.

"Sarah?"

She snapped back to the matter at hand, her sister across the room, well-meaning but breaking her already shattered heart into even more tiny little pieces.

"I've seen it with my own eyes."

Sarah shook her head even though she knew her sister could barely see her in the darkness of their room. "You must need to go have your vision checked, sister."

"I may not have a suitor of my own, but I have seen love on many of the faces in our church. I have seen how Andrew looks at Caroline, how Elam looks at Emily, and how Titus looks at Abbie."

"How's that?" Sarah asked.

"The same way Jonah looks at you."

Chapter Twenty

It was a far-fetched plan if there ever was one.

But it was the only one Gertie had. It was what God had given her, and she was grateful.

She pulled her tractor into the driveway at the Yoders' house.

The plan had come to her late last night as she had stared at the ceiling, sleep eluding her. She was worried about Jonah. Very worried. But if she couldn't talk sense into him, maybe she could appeal to Sarah.

So it was a long shot at best. But what was a mother to do?

It was true that she had never truly approved of Jonah and Sarah's union, but the time for protest was over. The deed was done, and their futures were tied together for life. And it was no life if the two of them weren't even living in the same house.

She parked her tractor to one side of the house. She had thought about calling before she came over, but she was afraid that Sarah wouldn't agree to talk to her and would conveniently disappear. She figured an ambush was in order.

No one came out onto the porch to greet her. The laundry line was heavy with clothes, flapping and snapping in the Oklahoma wind. Hanging clothes didn't mean anyone was home. But she could hope . . .

Gertie made her way up the porch steps and rapped lightly on the door. She wasn't on friendly enough terms that she felt comfortable just walking into their house, and once again she wished she had called first.

The door jerked open and Hilde Yoder frowned at her in confusion. "Gertie Miller. What are you doing here?" The words were spoken in surprise and not anger, a fact Gertie was happy about. This whole marriage thing between Jonah and Sarah had not turned out like anyone had planned.

"I came to speak with Sarah."

Hilde's frown deepened. "She's not here."

Gertie glanced into the house but couldn't see much as Hilde blocked her view. "Is she really not here, or are you just saying that so I'll go away?"

Maybe not the best thing to say. Hilde propped her hands on her hips and shot Gertie a stern look. "Are you calling me a liar, Gertie?"

She took a deep breath and did her best to gather her thoughts. "No, Hilde. I would never say such a thing about you. But I really need to talk to Sarah."

"About what?"

"She needs to go home. Back to Jonah. I came to convince her to do just that."

Suddenly the starch went out of Hilde's spine. Gertie hadn't realized that Hilde had been holding herself so stiffly until she practically wilted before her eyes. "She's not here, but come on in."

Gertie considered telling her no, that she would come back later, when Sarah was home, but decided that to turn down Hilde's offer would be rude.

She stepped into the house and followed Hilde toward what she supposed would be the kitchen. It was.

"I'm glad you came by," Hilde said over one shoulder as she motioned toward the kitchen table. "Have a seat. Would you like a glass of water? Cup of coffee?"

Gertie nodded dumbly. "Anything's fine," she mumbled. "Why are you glad I'm here? I mean . . . that's nice of you to say but . . ." She was making a mess of this. She and Hilde had never been friends, and their children getting into trouble and marrying surely hadn't changed that.

Hilde didn't answer right away. She poured them each a glass of water and brought them to the table. Gertie noticed that Hilde had started water to boil. Truly it was a little cold outside to drink something like cold water. And even though the Millers and the Yoders didn't live very far apart, Gertie's tractor didn't provide her with much protection from the frigid Oklahoma wind.

Gertie took a sip of water and waited for Hilde to continue.

Sarah's mother slid into the chair opposite her and twirled her glass around as Gertie waited.

"I'm worried about Sarah," Hilde finally said. She heaved a great sigh after the words were spoken, as if a huge weight had been lifted from her shoulders.

"I'm worried about Jonah." Gertie did her best to keep the annoyance from her voice. If Sarah would just move back home . . .

"Those kids . . ." Hilde shook her head. "They need to be living under the same roof."

"I agree."

Hilde's gaze jerked to hers. "You do?"

Gertie nodded. "*Jah*." She didn't need to add that the Amish married for life. Oh, she had heard tall tales of Plain folk in other states and settlements who had divorced for one reason or another, but she had considered them just that. Tales.

"I'm so relieved to hear that."

"I don't know why. It surely doesn't change anything." Gertie hadn't meant to sound so sharp, but if being worried about a child would help them, then Jonah and Sarah would be living happily in the little converted English house he'd bought at the edge of town.

"What if we can?" Hilde's eyes twinkled as if she had a secret. But instead of divulging it, she pushed up from the table and moved to the stove to finish the coffee. While they had been talking, the water had started to boil.

Gertie wanted to shout that she didn't want any coffee, she wanted to hear Hilde's plan or idea or whatever it was, but she managed to keep her manners like a good Amish woman should.

It seemed like forever before Hilde poured them both a cup of coffee, but the clock above the sink told a different story. Only seven minutes had passed.

"Would you like some cream? Sugar?"

"I would like for you to come back and tell me what's on your mind."

If Hilde was offended, she didn't show it. Instead she brought the two cups of coffee to the table and slid back into her chair. "I think we should get them back together."

Gertie's excitement deflated like a leaky balloon. "I thought you had a *gut* idea."

Hilde sat back in her chair, her eyes reflecting her internal hurt. "It is a *gut* idea."

"But we need a plan. Ideas aren't going to help us."

"Of course they will."

Gertie frowned. "Is there more to this idea of yours?" They needed more, enough more to make it a plan. Some action they could take.

"Last time I was at the doctor's in Pryor, I saw a show on the television."

Gertie's eyes widened. "You were watching television?"

Hilde shook her head even as her cheeks flushed deep pink. "It was right there in front of me. What was I supposed to do?"

Gertie supposed she could have averted her eyes, but if she were being honest with herself, she would have been watching too. She hadn't had many opportunities to watch English TV, but she had taken every one. It was fascinating watching people move around in a plastic box. Of course, Eli would have a fit if he knew that she walked through the electronics department very slowly, staring at the miraculous boxes, even though she knew it to be a sin. "Go on," she said. Hilde's transgressions weren't the important thing here. This was all about Jonah and Sarah and saving their marriage. Someone had to do something.

"Well," Hilde continued, "the new year is about here."

"*Jah.*" Gertie hated to even make a sound for fear that Hilde would be off on another tangent.

"I've heard Sarah talking about Caroline and Andrew Fitch having a party to celebrate. A couples' party."

Gertie shook her head. Such a thing to celebrate, turning

over a day on the calendar. That was an event for the English, not the God-loving Amish. But these young people today kept getting more and more like the world. Sometimes it scared Gertie. If it kept on like this, in a few years one might have trouble telling the English youth from the Amish. That was something she hoped she never saw. "If it's a couples' party, how are Jonah and Sarah going to get an invitation?"

Hilde smiled. "You leave that to me."

If Gertie remembered correctly, Hilde and Esther Fitch were good friends. Perhaps she was going to use that relationship to make sure that Caroline and Andrew invited the couple.

"Do you really think this is going to work?" Gertie asked.

"It has to."

Gertie thought for a moment that Hilde was going to follow up with *we don't have any other choices*, but she didn't. "Did you really see this on English television?" Gertie asked.

Hilde nodded. "The Dr. Bill show or something like that. He had all these couples who were having problems."

"What did they do?"

"It wasn't them. It was their families. They called it an invention or something like that. They got the couple together and made them sit down and talk it out."

"Did it work?"

Hilde shrugged. "I don't know. They called my name and it was my turn to go back for my appointment."

Gertie considered that for a moment. "What if this doesn't work?"

"It has to," Hilde said. "It's the only idea I have, and I don't go back to the doctor for another six months."

* * *

"I thought it was a couples' party." Sarah looked from Caroline to Emily, then over to Julie.

"Not a couple-couple party," Julie said.

"Right." Emily nodded, sending her prayer *kapp* strings bobbing around her shoulders.

"But there are a lot of couples coming," Caroline added.

"Just not only couples." Julie shrugged one shoulder. "Our buddy bunch group."

That didn't make Sarah feel any better. Most all of their buddy bunch had gotten married in the last few years. Most everyone there would be married.

You're married.

She ignored that little voice. Yes, she was married, but what difference did it make really? She was still living with her parents. Jonah was still living at their house. Well, she thought that was where he was living. She hadn't heard anything different. And she surely hadn't talked to her husband.

"I don't know." How uncomfortable would she be hanging out with all her friends watching them celebrate the new year? It wasn't like Amish couples were openly loving, but she would know. All their friends were in happy marriages. And hers was beyond repair. How had things gotten so twisted around?

One night. One moment of weakness. One hope that things could be different for them. And that one moment had changed everything. And not to the better.

"Sarah, you have to come." Julie clasped Sarah's hand and squeezed her fingers.

Sarah frowned. Something was up. She wasn't sure

what, but what difference did it make if she went to the party or not?

"You haven't been to anything in so long," Emily said. "We miss you."

Sarah immediately regretted her suspicions. She hadn't been to any functions in a long time, preferring to hide out at her parents' house and pretend that the last year hadn't really happened. It was cowardly, and she knew she wouldn't be able to keep it up for much longer, but she wasn't about to stop now. Not until she had to. "It's just . . ."

"Hard," Julie supplied. "we understand."

Sarah wanted to shake her head at it all. Her friends had all had wonderful relationships. Well, maybe it had been a little rocky at first for Caroline and Andrew, but everything had worked out in the end. And Emily and Elam, it had looked a little touch-and-go for them, but Julie and Danny had a courtship straight out of one of those English romance novels Sarah's *mamm* read when she thought no one was around.

Sarah had always thought she would have a relationship like that. But now . . . That was never happening. She was a married woman. Separated from her husband and doomed to live her life with a man who didn't love her. He would never love her.

Tears filled her eyes. She had thought she was past all this, but apparently she had been wrong. She ducked her head to hide her despair, but she was too late.

"Don't cry."

Suddenly she was wrapped in three pairs of loving arms.

"Shhh . . ." Emily soothed. "It's going to be all right."

The words were meant to console her, but Sarah knew. It would never be okay again.

And that was something she would have to learn to live with.

"And it's at Andrew's house?" Jonah narrowed his eyes. His friend Eli had just invited him to a party at the Fitches' house.

"*Jah*. Everyone's going to be there."

"Everyone?"

Eli Glick shook his head and turned his wheelchair to the side as if seeking help from some of the other men gathered around. Eli had been paralyzed from the waist down in the accident that had killed Alvin King and sent Titus Lambert to prison for five years. Jonah had been friends with them all, and the loss had been devastating for their circle of buddies as well as the entire community. But since Titus's return, much healing had been accomplished. It wouldn't be long before it was something that was mentioned in passing and not the horrific event that it truly was.

"Who's everyone?"

Eli whirled back round. "Me and June," he said, starting off with his surprise relationship with June Lambert, Titus's sister. "Titus and Abbie, Clara Rose and Obie, Julie and Danny. And Caroline and Andrew, of course. Just the buddy bunch, you know."

And the buddy bunch included Sarah.

"I don't know," he started.

"What's not to know?" Eli asked. "It's a New Year's Eve party, and the buddy bunch is going to be there."

Which included Sarah.

He had been avoiding her, not knowing what to say to

get things back on a better footing. She had moved out. Why should he make all the effort for a reconciliation?

"Maybe you should go by and talk to her." Eli's quiet words broke through his thoughts.

"Why would I want to do that?"

"Let me see . . . because she's your wife."

Some wife. Some marriage. It had been doomed from the start, and nothing would get it back now. "Uh-huh" was all Jonah could manage. What good would it do to rehash all of the mistakes they had made? None at all.

"So will you come?" Eli asked. "Will you at least think about it?"

Jonah nodded. "I'll think about it." But his mind was made up. There would be no new year's celebration for him.

Chapter Twenty-One

"It didn't work," Gertie said on the morning of January first.

"I know it didn't work." Hilde bit back her sigh. What an unlikely partnership she had formed with Jonah's mother.

Hilde wouldn't say that she and Gertie Miller had ever been close. Nor were they enemies or adversaries. It was just that Gertie was a little too much of a busybody for Hilde's liking. But desperate times called for desperate measures, at least that was what the English said. Hilde still wasn't completely sure what that meant, but she thought it had something to do with using every resource a person had when desperation set in.

And that was where she was. Smack-dab in the middle of Desperation Town.

Their plan had been simple, and Hilde had hoped and prayed that there would be success in simplicity. Gertie had contacted Jonah's friends while Hilde had called all of Sarah's. They would get them to invite Sarah and Jonah to the same party in hopes that close proximity would bring them to talk. And then, by talking, they would work through some of their problems.

Okay, so she knew that last part was definitely on the

side of wishful thinking, but they surely couldn't work out anything if they weren't talking, and they couldn't very well talk if they weren't in the same room.

She had watched them after church, and they did everything in their power to avoid each other. That in itself gave Hilde hope. If they didn't care and really wanted to remain apart, they wouldn't have to work so hard to stay apart.

But despite their best efforts, neither Jonah nor Sarah had shown up for the party.

Hilde heard Gertie's sigh on the other end of the phone line and felt like releasing one herself. The Christian in her knew the situation was in God's hands, but the mother in her couldn't sit around and do nothing while her daughter's marriage fell apart.

Jonah and Sarah had made more than their share of mistakes, but that didn't mean they didn't deserve a happy marriage.

"So what do we do now?"

"I don't know." She could almost see Gertie shake her head.

"But there's something. *Jah?* There has to be something that we can do."

Gertie sighed once again. "Pray, Hilde Yoder. Praying seems to be the only answer we have right now."

Valentine's Day. It was the day of romance, couples, and love. And she was going to be all alone.

"Are you sure you don't want to come with me?" Annie asked. She was going to a "hen party" that included all of the unmarried or unspoken-for girls in her youth group. It was a fun idea for the unattached girls to have a sleepover and fun time while their couple-oriented counterparts were out celebrating in true romantic style.

"I'm not really a 'hen,' now am I?" She was an old married woman.

An old married woman whose husband was off doing heaven knew what. She had heard the stories. Jonah had been gone for days. No doubt he was off with the English girl April who he seemed to like so much. Sarah wondered if perhaps he loved April, but the thought hurt so much she had to store it away. Maybe later she could take it out and look at it, but not yet.

But she knew. One day, word would get around town that Jonah was gone, that he had moved in with Luke Lambright, and once that happened, Sarah's fate would be sealed. She would end up living in a little house on someone else's property and taking in mending like ol' Katie Glick.

"You don't have to make up your mind right now," Annie said. She used the glue to make the shape of a heart on the red construction paper. "Can you hand me the glitter?"

Sarah passed her the small tube filled with shiny silver flakes. "What are you doing again?"

"We're exchanging friendship Valentines with one another."

"Cute." A part of Sarah felt it was a tiny bit pathetic, but it was the part of her that wished she had a better relationship with her husband, or at the very least, friends like her sister had.

"Cute enough to make you change your mind about coming with me?"

"*Danki*, but I think I'll sit this one out."

Annie shook her head. "Suit yourself."

* * *

"What are you doing, man?"

Jonah turned from the sink where he had been rinsing out a coffee mug. One thing he loved about staying with Luke Lambright was the fancy English coffeemaker that made one cup at a time. It seemed a bit wasteful, but Jonah enjoyed it all the same. "Cleaning a coffee cup."

Luke limped into the kitchen, his cane in his left hand, and braced one hip against the counter as he calmly eyed Jonah. "What are you doing *here*?"

For a moment Jonah thought about playing dumb and repeating his claim to only be washing a coffee mug, but decided it was time to come clean. "I have some decisions to make."

Luke nodded. "Go on."

Jonah fully turned, coffee momentarily forgotten as he talked to his friend. "Sarah."

"Listen, it's not really any business of mine, but it seems like you could use a friend."

Jonah nodded. "But—"

"But you think I've been too long with the English." Luke smiled, the action taking the sting from his words. "Remember this: the biggest difference between English marriages and Amish marriages is divorce."

"There is no divorce."

"That's what I'm saying."

Jonah shook his head, confused. "It's no good," he finally said.

"What's no good?"

"My marriage to Sarah. It's no good. It should have never happened."

"That might be," Luke said. "But knowing this isn't helping anything."

"What's that supposed to mean?"

"Your marriage is only as good as you make it."

Jonah thought about it a second and decided that he didn't want to think about it anymore.

"You can go around all you want and talk about how the two of you never should have gotten married and how the two of you have nothing in common now, but the truth of the matter is you *are* married. You can give up your broadfall pants and homemade shirts and start living the life of an *Englisher*, but she will always be your wife."

Jonah didn't want to think about that either. "It's more complicated than that."

"No. It's not." Luke shook his head. "Everyone in town knows about the two of you. They know about the baby. I know we try to keep these things a secret, but you and I both know how word gets around."

"So?" Jonah hated the defensive tone in the one word. It spoke things he'd rather be left unsaid.

"Two people don't make a baby when there's nothing between them."

"But—"

"Maybe I should have said two Amish people."

Jonah shook his head. "There is nothing between me and Sarah."

"There once was, there could be, there would be again. But you can't have that standing here in my kitchen."

"Are you asking me to leave?" *Jah*, he had been here for a couple of days. Okay, more than a couple, but the house had gotten too hard to live in. It seemed big and empty. Every room smelled like Sarah. Every piece of furniture, every picture on the walls brought her to mind. And with thoughts of her came the thoughts of how he had failed. There was only so much of that a man could take.

So he had packed what he could into a duffel bag and caught a ride into Tulsa with Ezra Hein.

Right now he much preferred Ezra's company over Luke's. Ezra hadn't tried to talk him into returning to Wells Landing. He hadn't told Jonah how wrong he was, nor had he pointed out all of the faults in not doing everything he could to win his wife over.

You tried that, remember? And it hadn't gone as planned. He had gone to Sarah's house with the thought of courting her in the way they had never had the time for, but once they were together they started bickering once again. It was exhausting to always be at odds with another person, especially one that he was supposed to be close to.

And if he was tired of all the constant strife, she had to be as well. So he was doing this for the both of them.

"I'm thinking about staying here."

"Here?" Luke's eyes widened. They were the exact color of the pictures of the ocean Jonah had seen. If he went English, he could go visit the sea in person.

You could do that Amish and go to Pinecraft like Zeb Brenneman.

"In Tulsa," he corrected. Luke had finally set the date with his girlfriend of two years, Sissy Hardin. Jonah wouldn't do anything to mess up their plans.

"Why would you want to do that?"

He shrugged. It was his out. He could become English, divorce Sarah, and move on. If she wanted to get married again, all she had to do was follow him.

It's not that easy and you know it.

He pushed that voice aside. Like it or not, Sarah was going to be hurt no matter what. At least this way she had a chance to start again.

"You're not in love with April, are you?"

Was he?

Jonah shook his head. "No, but I'm tired, Luke." It was the best explanation he had.

Luke clapped him on the shoulder. "Brother, we have all been there."

But he didn't have an answer as to how to get over it.

"I don't know," Jonah said into the phone.

"I think *Mamm* is worried about you."

And she probably was. The truth of the matter was he was a little worried about himself. Once he thought he knew what he wanted in life. Things had been simple then, back when he and Lorie were a couple. Back before she had found out her father had led a secret life. Looking at those times now, he could see that things weren't quiet and simple as he wanted to believe, but at the time . . .

"I'm not trying to worry anybody," Jonah told his brother. This was the third call Aaron had made in as many days. Jonah was about ready to say yes, he would return to Wells Landing for a bit if only to get everyone off his back about it. Then again, he supposed that was playing right into their hands. And he wasn't ready to return. Not yet. Not when he still had so many questions.

"Jonah?"

He inwardly groaned. "Hey, Buddy." Ivan was perhaps the last person he wanted to talk to. He loved his brother with all his heart and wouldn't do anything to disappoint him.

"Please come home. There's a party and *Mamm* says I can go if you'll go with me."

The excitement in Buddy's voice was almost solid. "That's great, but can't you go with Aaron?"

He could almost see his brother make a face even though they were miles apart. "Aaron wants to go out with Mary."

Of course he did. After all, Aaron and Mary had only been married a couple of weeks longer than he and Sarah had been.

So why aren't you spending Valentine's Day with your wife?

"Maybe Jonathan can take you."

"*Mamm* said it has to be you. Please, Jonah, pleasepleaseplease!"

"*Jah*," Jonah said with a sigh. "Okay, then. I'll come home and take you to the party."

"Hip hip hooray!" Buddy cheered.

But only his brother's enthusiasm brought a smile to his face. The last thing he wanted was to be in Wells Landing on the biggest day for couples, when his couple had fallen apart long ago.

"Sarah, did you hear what I just said?"

Sarah jerked back to attention and faced her cousin Libby. "*Jah*, of course," she lied. But it was a small fib that she only told to keep from hurting her cousin's feelings. Sarah's mind had been wandering lately, mostly to places it shouldn't go, to the what-if of her and Jonah.

He had been living with Luke Lambright, or so the gossip vine declared, and had been for some time. She was certain everyone was speculating on how much longer before he jumped the fence completely and turned English. And that would leave her in line to be the next oddball old maid in Wells Landing.

Not that she was truly an old maid, but the result would be the same. Jonah would be off living his life and she would be stuck in limbo, unable to do anything but live.

Move over, Katie Glick, here I come.

"If you were listening, then what did I say?"

Sarah blinked, unable to even make anything up.

"That's what I thought."

Sarah forced an apologetic smile. "I'm sorry, Libby."

Libby frowned. "I'm worried about you, cousin."

Get in line. That seemed to be a common sentiment these days. "I'm okay."

"Good, then you will come with us to the party." Libby clapped her hands.

"Wait . . . what party?" Who was "us"? And when were they going?

"You really weren't listening, huh?" Libby gave her an indulgent smile. "The party is on Valentine's Day. It seems that the bishop is a little afraid for all the single people in the district going out together . . . alone—"

Sarah could no more stop her blush than she could prevent the sun from coming up the next day.

"So he convinced the church board to rent out the rec center so that everyone could come and have a great time together."

"He what?" She had never heard of such a thing. Then again, the English influence on the district had grown stronger lately. And with Luke Lambright and Sadie and Lorie Kauffman all leaving the church, she supposed that Cephas was a bit worried about all the English influence.

"Is your hearing going too?" Libby laughed.

"I mean, why would he do such a thing?"

Libby shrugged. "I have no idea, but it sounds like a fun time. And everyone's going to be there."

"Everyone?" Everyone but Jonah. She could only imagine that he would be out celebrating with April. Wasn't that what the English liked to do? Make a big romantic deal out of February the fourteenth?

But Jonah wasn't English. Not yet.

"Everyone." Libby nodded. "Say you'll come."

Sarah wanted nothing more than to stay at home and pretend like Valentine's Day wasn't even on the calendar, but she had been hiding out for long enough. Her friends were starting to get impatient for her to go out with them to singings and the like. She didn't feel right going to events for couples, and she certainly couldn't attend events for singles. That was one thing Katie Glick had over her. At least she was well and truly single and could one day get married.

"Please, Sarah." Libby tugged on her arm as if that could persuade her to come.

"All right," she said. "If everyone is going to be there, I guess I should be too." But she knew the one person she wanted to spend time with the most would be far, far away. She just wasn't sure how that fact played a part in her decision-making process.

"Everything is in place." Hilde whispered the words on the off chance that Sarah or Annie were around somewhere listening. If either one of them found out, the whole plan would be ruined.

"Perfect," Gertie said, satisfaction evident in her voice.

"Are you sure this is going to work?" Hilde asked. "Didn't we try this once before?" And she so desperately wanted this to work. If Jonah left and went to the English, then Sarah's life would be completely ruined. As far as Hilde was concerned, her daughter had suffered enough.

"That was child's play compared to this."

Hilde wasn't sure what made Jonah's mother so confident that everything was going to work out, but Hilde had placed her faith in God. She refused to believe that it was in God's will for her not to have any grandchildren, for

Jonah to leave Sarah, and for her eldest daughter to be the ridicule of Wells Landing. "If you're certain . . ."

"I am. The bishop has agreed to say that he was the one who rented the rec center, Buddy's talked Jonah into coming back for the party, the only thing we're waiting on is Sarah."

"She'll be there," Hilde assured her. "Libby made sure of it. Now if everyone keeps their secret, the two of them should be well and truly back on their way to being a happy couple once again."

It sounded like a good plan, but Hilde wasn't sure when Sarah and Jonah had ever been a happy couple.

"I think you should wear a red dress," Annie said, hopping off the bed and heading toward their shared closet.

Sarah had long since stopped protesting about this party and all things associated with it.

"Or a pink one. You know, like a rose color."

She could take it no more. "There aren't many red dresses in Wells Landing." Most everyone wore darker, more conservative colors or sweet pastels. Not flashy red. Though Sarah had seen Ivy Weaver wear one from time to time. And everyone in town knew her rotten reputation.

"*Ach*, the bishop won't mind for one night."

Sarah shook her head. "I don't have a red dress, and I'm not making one for this occasion," she continued before Annie could voice a second protest.

Her sister turned, a garment clutched to her chest and her eyes sparkling. "I have one."

Sarah's eyes widened. "You have a red dress?"

Annie nodded, but what she held looked to be a beautiful rose color, perhaps the prettiest pink Sarah had ever seen. "I think you should wear this."

She shook out the dress and apron and Sarah immediately recognized it as the dress Annie had worn to Easter last year. "I can't wear that." The two of them might be sisters, but they were about as different as two people could be. Annie was thin—willowy, she had heard people say—with beautiful, straight, flax-colored hair. Sarah's hair was dark, curly, and unruly, and she had always seemed to carry a few extra pounds around her middle. Only their blue eyes connected them as sisters.

"Of course you can." She thrust it toward Sarah. "Try it on."

Sarah shook her head. "You are so much smaller than I am. It would never fit me."

"It might. You've lost so much weight since . . . well, you've lost some weight. And wouldn't it be fun to wear something new to the party?"

Sarah shot her a look.

"Okay, so it's not new, but it's different. And I hardly ever wear it. Come on. Give it a try."

Sarah started to protest once again, but the excited look in Annie's eyes stopped her. She wasn't sure why it was so important to Annie for her to wear the dress—after all, her sister wasn't even going to the same event—but she could tell it was.

"Please." How could she tell her baby sister no?

With a small sigh she reached for the dress. That was when she understood. She didn't want to wear it because she didn't want to give herself hope about the day.

Like there was any hope to be had. Jonah had gone off with the English, the baby that had once been a dream was gone, and her life would never be the same.

Sarah pulled off her dress and pulled the rose-colored fabric over her head. It settled easily around her hips and fell softly to just below her knees.

"It's perfect," Annie gushed.

"It's too short," Sarah protested. But only halfheartedly. There was something about the beautiful rose color that warmed her from the inside out. Maybe that was a good sign to find joy in the little things once again. It had been a long time since she had that.

"We can let it out and then it'll be perfect."

Sarah moved from the center of the room to the door, closing it so she could peer into the mirror there.

She must have lost a lot of weight since she and Jonah had parted ways. It might have even started before that. Regardless, she had shed enough pounds that Annie's dress fit her to a T.

"Say you'll wear it, Sarah."

She turned back to face her sister and her pleading blue eyes so like her own. "Why does it mean so much to you for me to wear this?"

In two steps, Annie wrapped her arms around Sarah and hugged her close. "You've been so unhappy lately. I just want you to have something *gut* in your life."

Even if it was only a dress at a non-couples party remained unsaid, and for that Sarah was grateful. She didn't need her sister to point out how sad her life had become.

Sarah returned her sister's hug. "*Danki*, Annie. I'd love to wear your dress to the party."

Chapter Twenty-Two

"This is going to be so much fun." Buddy skipped ahead of Jonah toward the doors of the rec center, then caught himself. He cleared his throat, straightened his coat, and pulled his shoulders back.

Jonah wasn't sure whether to laugh at his brother's lightheartedness or cry that he felt he needed to change for this party.

"Do you think there'll be girls here?"

He chuckled. "It wouldn't be much of a party without girls."

Buddy nodded. "I mean I would like to meet a girl. Maybe one like Sarah."

Despite the cold, Jonah stopped in his tracks. He had never imagined that his simple brother could want more from life than what he had in that very moment. But it seemed that he was wrong.

"You, uh . . . want to meet a girl?"

Buddy nodded as Jonah started his feet back into motion. The weather had turned extremely cold, and the weatherman was calling for snow later in the wee hours of the morning. Jonah planned to be at home warm in his bed long before the first snowflake fell. "*Jah*." Buddy started skipping once again, then caught himself and slowed his steps. "Do you think I can meet one? You know, a nice Amish girl?"

How did he explain to his brother that his disabilities might prove to be a hindrance in finding a date? The entire community had seemed to adopt him as their own, but such a relationship would put a damper on any budding romance.

"I mean, I know I'm not as smart as you and the other guys, but I can farm and take care of a wife." He puffed out his chest as if to prove his point, and Jonah felt more like crying more than ever before.

How ironic that he had a wife he didn't want and Buddy wanted a wife yet would probably never marry. Most Amish women had been raised to not care about such matters as looks and such, but could any of them see past Buddy's mental limitations to the gifts he truly had to offer?

"Hey, slow down there, brother."

Buddy slowed his steps, then seemed to realize what Jonah was saying. He nodded sagely. "You're saying that I'm moving too quick."

"That's right," he said as he opened the door to the rec center. "Let's worry about finding you someone to play Rook with before you get married off, okay?"

Buddy smiled. "Okay, Jonah. Whatever you say."

Sarah wrapped her coat even tighter around her and wished she had thought to wear her sweater underneath it. With the chill in the air tonight, she could use any extra layer she could get.

Her father had been talking about the coming snow. Even though the wind held the promise, the storm wasn't supposed to hit until sometime before sunrise the following day.

Too bad. Any earlier and she might have been able to beg off going to this party and stay at home. But as it was, she had dropped Annie off at her gathering, then headed over to the rec center.

She hated walking into the place alone, but that was where she found herself. The good news was since she had driven, she could leave anytime she wanted. And Annie had promised to find a ride home with one of her friends. So Sarah had a new plan. Go in and show her face, then leave and hightail it back home. *Jah*, she wanted to prove a point, that she was back to living again. But that didn't mean she had to go all out on the first day. Once she tested the waters she could do this living again at her own pace.

"Go in, make sure everyone knows I'm here, then leave." She should be in and out in less than an hour.

She felt put on display as she walked in. It seemed that everyone had turned out for the party and all eyes swung to her. Okay, so maybe it was something of a novelty to see her out. She and Jonah hadn't been together since Christmas, and she hadn't been to anything other than church since then. She was certain the looks were of surprise, but she decided to hold her head high and face whatever curiosity was about to come her way.

"Sarah!" Libby broke away from a group of friends and headed her way. Sarah knew everyone in the little bunch of people, but none of them were what she would call friends. Still, she was grateful for her cousin's greeting. For all her vows about keeping her head up, it was almost more weight than she could bear.

"Hi." Sarah squeezed her cousin's hands, needing any strength she could get from them.

But in Libby's eyes she saw remorse and . . . pity?

"What's wrong?"

"Jonah's here."

"What?" Her voice was like the squeak of a mouse, high-pitched and feeble.

"I know. I'm sorry. I would have never suggested that you come here if I had known."

"Who's he here with?" She could barely form the words. Did she really want to know? What if he had brought April with him? What would she do then? How could she hold her head up in town? It was one thing to know that he had moved on and had gone English to be with her and quite another for him to bring her to an Amish party.

"Buddy."

"What?"

"He brought Buddy."

"His brother?" Her heart leapt with relief, but she wouldn't give in to the emotion until she knew for certain.

"You know any other Buddys?"

"*Gut* point."

So Jonah was here with his brother. She couldn't let that get her hopes up. Just because he brought his brother to the party didn't mean he wasn't still hanging around with the English beauty. They could have plans another night. After all, Valentine's Day had fallen on a Thursday night. Some couples weren't celebrating until the weekend, which might explain the large turnout.

"It's going to be okay, though," Libby said, threading her arm through Sarah's. "Just stay close to me. It's not like you have to talk to him or anything."

The party was set up like a carnival, with tables and

booths complete with games, face painting, and a place to make Valentines. For who Sarah didn't know, seeing as how this was supposed to be a non-couples party. The games included a dart throw, fishing, and a bean bag toss. She noticed several people, men and women alike, wearing cheap plastic bead necklaces and bright molded rings as well as red paper party hats. It seemed perhaps that these were the prizes for the many games.

She smoothed her palms down the front of her dress, er, Annie's dress, and gathered her courage around her. She noticed a few people openly looking at her, no doubt wondering why she had picked tonight of all nights to finally make her way back into the Amish social calendar. Thankfully she wouldn't have to actually answer that question. She had no idea what to say.

"Let's go make a Valentine." Libby led the way over to a table. Actually there were two tables pushed end to end with chairs all around. The tables were covered with construction paper, markers, and all sorts of embellishments.

"Who exactly are we making Valentines for?" Sarah asked as she allowed Libby to drag her over to the tables.

"For each other, of course." Libby laughed and pulled out one of the chairs, settling in with ease.

Sarah decided right then and there that she was going to have a good time. It was time, after all. Apparently Jonah had moved on, maybe even with the English. It was time for her to do the same. She gave her cousin a bright smile and reached for the red paper.

"Did you see her? Did you?" Buddy's cheeks were flushed with excitement. He wore a shiny red party hat that sort of resembled an Amish hat, though Jonah thought the English called them top hats. Whatever that meant. Around his neck hung several strands of beads, white, red, and pink. One even had a plastic heart every couple of inches or so.

"Have I seen who?" He decided playing dumb was his best course of action. Then again, maybe Buddy wasn't talking about Sarah but someone else. He could hope.

"Sarah! Sarah's here! Have you seen her?"

He had been trying his best not to look at her since she had arrived almost twenty minutes before. But even in the small amount of time he allowed himself to watch her, he took in so much. She was slimmer now. When had she become so thin, her face nearly gaunt?

Despite the weight loss, everything about her seemed the same, from her chocolate-brown hair to her soft blue eyes. She was wearing a pink dress, one he had never seen before, and he wondered if she had made it special for the occasion. He decided he liked the color on her. It made her skin glow and her eyes even bluer.

Not that he cared or anything.

"I saw her."

"You should go talk to her." Buddy pulled on Jonah's elbow as if that would serve as good motivation to get him next to Sarah.

But he didn't have anything to say to her.

Well, that wasn't exactly true, but anything he had to say could wait.

"Why would I want to do that?" he asked.

"Because she's your wife."

And she was, but . . .

"It's kind of complicated, Buddy."

His brother frowned. "It doesn't seem so complicated to me. The two of you are married and you should be talking."

One would think. "Things aren't so simple as that,

Buddy." Sometimes he wished more than anything that the world could be the way it was in Buddy's mind.

"I don't understand."

Jonah patted his brother's arm. "It's okay, Buddy. Most times I don't either."

"Maybe you should do something about it."

"Maybe." But what? Go over and talk to her? Tell her that he missed having her around?

At least that was the truth. The house seemed twice the size it really was once he started knocking around in it by himself. It was too big for him to have all on his own. And he still hadn't made up his mind about moving to Tulsa.

But more than he enjoyed the freedom of the English world, he needed the option. He needed to know that he had some place he could go. A place where no one cared about his sins and the troubles in his marriage. A place where marriage wasn't the most important aspect of his life. He wasn't sure why he needed it. He only knew that he did.

"You should go talk to her." Buddy nudged him in the ribs.

"Maybe," he said again. He watched her sitting there next to her cousin. Sarah looked as if she hadn't a care in the world. But he knew better. He knew the pain she had suffered. He knew the depression she experienced. He alone knew how much the baby had meant to her.

He had thought for a time that she cared for him. But he shouldn't have listened to all the idle talk. She had wanted the baby, not him. Had she ever really loved him at all?

As if sensing his stare, she turned, her gaze locking with his.

He was right about one thing. That dress made her eyes

as blue as the sky just after a spring rain. He raised one hand and gave her a small wave.

She turned back to the project she was working on without even acknowledging that she had seen him. It shouldn't have bothered him, but it did. She had seen him, of that much he was certain. So why didn't she give a little wave in return? They had been through too much together for her to just ignore him now. Yet that seemed to be her goal.

And he knew. It was well and truly over between them, if it had ever really been there at all.

Her heart lurched in her chest. It was one thing to be told Jonah was at the party and quite another to lock gazes with him from across the room.

He looked good. Better than good. It seemed the English world agreed with him. And then he had given her that little wave as if he hadn't a care in the world. What did he expect, for her to wave in return?

He had made his feelings clear. She wasn't a part of his life, if she had ever been.

She knew now. All she had wanted to do by moving out was give herself a little space to heal. She had needed time away from Jonah. Time that she didn't have to spend working on their relationship but that she could use on herself. But that time had passed, and she had needed the reassurance that he wanted her to come back. Instead he had gone off to explore the English world.

All their good times together, even as small as they were, could not compare to the lure of the forbidden. He wanted other things more than he wanted her. She understood that now.

Understanding didn't make it hurt any less, but at least she had a foundation on which to rebuild.

But her life would only take her so far.

"Watch out, Katie Glick. Here I come," she muttered under her breath as she tried to concentrate on the Valentine she was making.

"What?" Libby asked.

Sarah pushed up from the table. "I need to use the restroom."

"Wait a second and I'll come with you."

She shook her head. "That's not necessary. You stay and finish your Valentine."

She turned away even as her cousin asked, "What about your card?"

She flicked a dismissive hand and kept walking. "I'll finish it later." And she hustled out of the gymnasium and into the hallway.

As expected, there was a line at the restrooms. She crossed her arms and studied the items on the bulletin board and otherwise pretended that no one was staring at her as if she was a rare exhibit at the zoo. But she supposed her situation was as unique as one. How many women in Wells Landing had been through everything she had? Not even one. The closest was Caroline Fitch, but she was nowhere to be seen.

Sarah wasn't even sure why she waited in the line. She really didn't have to go. But she couldn't sit at the table any longer and pretend everything was all right. How soon before she could leave without everyone thinking she had left because Jonah was there? Why did she even care?

After her unnecessary turn, she splashed cold water on her face and dried her hands. For once her hair was staying in place and didn't require any smoothing. She dried her hands and walked out to find Jonah hovering by the door.

The girls who had been standing behind her in the line

were watching him as if the two of them were part of some live show brought in for their entertainment.

"Can I talk to you?"

The words sent joy zinging through her. This . . . this was what she had wanted for so long. Yet she reined in her joy. What if he just wanted to tell her that she had toilet paper stuck to her shoe?

She looked down at her short, lace-up black boots, but she had nothing attached to either one of them.

Still, she couldn't get overly excited until she heard what he had to say. It might very well be nothing.

Or the most important thing ever.

"*Jah.* Sure." He waited for her to come closer, then he glanced at all the faces anxiously waiting to hear what he was about to say.

"Let's find someplace private." He motioned for her to come with him down the hallway, away from the gym and the Valentine's Day festivities.

Sarah followed Jonah as he checked a couple of the rooms as they passed. The rooms were used for a variety of classes, including English as a second language and art.

The third door he tried gave way and he entered, turning on the light as she came in behind him.

She willed her heart to remain true and not thump completely out of her chest. She wanted this. How she had longed for another chance. She had hoped and prayed, and it seemed as if her patience was about to see her through.

"I didn't expect to see you here tonight," he said.

She couldn't read one nuance of his expression. Even his maple syrup eyes were guarded and closed. "I didn't think you'd be here either." Did that mean that he wouldn't have come if he had known, or was he merely saying that he was glad to see her?

"Are you doing okay?" he asked.

How did she answer that? She wished some part of his expression would give her some clue as to his thoughts, but it remained as closed as all the doors they had passed. "I suppose."

He nodded. "That's *gut*."

"How are you?" Why were they acting like small acquaintances who hadn't seen each other in years?

"*Gut, gut*."

She searched her brain for something else to say. Should she ask about his family? What he was doing these days? April?

"I'm going to sell the house."

Pain shot through her. He was selling the house? Her house.

No. Not her house any longer.

"You can't sell the house." The words escaped her before she had time to think them through.

"I can. I have to. There's no need in me staying there if you . . ." He gave a small shrug. "I'm moving back in with my parents."

Not *I love you. I miss you. I want you to come back home*. If he had said any of those, she would have returned in an instant.

But Jonah didn't love her. He never had. They had pretended for a while that they could make it, but that time was over.

"Talk around town is you're thinking about joining the English."

He shrugged. "I've thought about it."

How could he even consider such a thing?

"I just didn't want you to be surprised if you drove by and saw the sign."

Why would she drive by the house? There was nothing for her there, not even him.

"I can't believe you, Jonah." Tears spilled over her lashes and slid down her cheeks. He looked as if he was about to take her into his arms and comfort her, then he pulled back.

"You aren't living there anymore. Why do I have to live there too?"

Why, indeed?

"What do you want from me, Sarah? The entire time we've been married I could never figure that out."

He was selling the house. Somehow she had it in her mind that as long as he lived in their house, there was a chance for the two of them. A FOR SALE sign in the yard would mean the end of her hopes for the two of them.

"All I wanted was for you to love me."

Jonah watched Sarah stumble from the room. He wanted to go after her, but what could he offer her? She wanted his love, and that was something he couldn't give. He had given it all to Lorie and watched her walk away. He wouldn't do that again. Sure, he cared for Sarah. He would even be a good husband to her, but he couldn't give her the love that she wanted. And he didn't think he would ever be able to.

So he remained where he was.

He wouldn't follow her. He wouldn't give her false hope. He cared enough about her to at least give her that much.

Chapter Twenty-Three

Sarah dashed the tears from her eyes and dried her cheeks on the hem of her apron. With any luck, Libby wouldn't notice and she could get out of there without having to answer a lot of painful questions.

She managed to paste a pained smile on her face as she approached the craft table where her cousin still sat.

"There you are. I was beginning to think you had run off with the circus."

Sarah shook her head and pressed one hand to her stomach. "I'm not feeling *gut*. I think I should go home."

Concern wrinkled Libby's forehead. "What's the matter? Do you need me to ride with you?"

Sarah shook her head. "No, you stay and have fun. Don't leave on my account."

Libby didn't seem convinced. "If you're sure."

Sarah widened her fake smile. "I'm positive."

Somehow she managed to get her coat and get out of the rec center without having to talk to anyone else. She thought she heard Buddy Miller calling her name, but she pretended she didn't hear him and hustled across the parking lot to her waiting tractor.

In the short time she had been in the rec center, the

snow had started. The flakes were falling fast, stinging her cheeks as they connected with her skin. They mixed with her tears as she wiped the snow from the tiny windshield and climbed into her tractor.

She just wanted to get home.

It took a few tries for the engine to turn over. The cold was definitely working against her, but finally the motor caught. She pulled onto the street and started for home.

It was slow going. She didn't drive much in these types of conditions. It snowed at least a little every year in Oklahoma, but the weather was infrequent enough that most times she could avoid getting out in it. Tonight was an exception, to be sure.

The road was completely white as she chugged along. Any tracks that had been there before her were filled in as the snow fell faster and faster.

But her tractor seemed to be slowing down. It *was* slowing down. She pressed a little harder on the accelerator, but it only went slower. She looked at the gauges. She was out of gas.

Her father's warning to fill up the tank rang through her mind. She hadn't stopped for gas. She had been a little too concerned about getting Annie to her party on time and then obsessing over the fact that she was finally going out. And on Valentine's Day.

She eased her tractor to the side of the road. She had stayed on the back roads, as was their custom. It was easier by far to travel the little roads than the highways in their slow-moving tractors and horse and buggies.

She left the lights on to help it be seen by a passerby, but who would be traveling out here at this time of night? Not many folks, that was for certain.

She couldn't remember the last house she passed by or

if it had been Amish or English. Regardless, she couldn't stay here. But should she go forward or backward?

Forward, she decided. Just like her life, she needed to get on, face front, and head out. She grabbed the flashlight from behind the seat and slid from the cab.

She wrapped her coat a little tighter around her and pulled her scarf over her head. Oh, how she had wished she had listened to the weather report before she had headed out tonight. But one could never tell with Oklahoma weather. It could drop ten degrees in less than an hour, or six inches of snow in the same amount of time.

The snowfall had softened, but there were at least five inches of snow on the ground. Little trickles of cold seeped down in her boots with each step she took. She should have brought her rubber boots, but when she had gotten ready tonight she hadn't thought she would be trudging through a winter wonderland. The snow wasn't supposed to arrive until early morning. It was barely past nine.

She trudged on, her light only piercing the darkness and snow a couple of feet in front of her. She knew she couldn't be the only one caught unawares, though she figured most people would just stay put, spend the night wherever they were and worry about getting home in the morning.

Her feet were freezing and wet, her stockings growing increasingly soggy with each step. She pulled her scarf a little closer around her ears as the strong Oklahoma wind tried to pull it from her head. She couldn't tell if the snow had picked up once again or the wind was just blowing it around. Whatever it was, it seemed to cling to every inch of her, soaking through her coat, the bottom of her dress, the gloves on her hands.

She kept her eyes on the ground trying to determine if she was actually still following the road. Using the heel of one of her boots, she scraped a patch clean. Part of it was asphalt, part was frozen dirt and grass. At least she hadn't wandered out in the middle of the roadway.

She thought she caught a glimpse of a mailbox up ahead, but it seemed the more she walked, the farther away it was. Or maybe she was seeing things, making out shapes that weren't really there through the flurries of snow. Her feet sloshed in her wet shoes as she blew on her gloved fingers, hoping her breath would warm her frozen digits.

Was that . . . ?

She cocked her head to one side and listened over the wind. Was that the sound of an engine? Maybe someone was coming.

She only had a few moments to decide if she was off the road enough. She stepped off the road a bit more, careful not to slip down the incline into the ditch. She waved the flashlight in the air, hoping whoever it was would be a good Samaritan and help her.

The engine grew nearer and she could tell it was a tractor. Most likely an Amish couple heading home from their Valentine's Day celebration. Her joy over them being Amish was tainted by the fact that they were most likely in love and not wanting to give a stranger a ride.

"Sarah?"

She recognized that voice. "Buddy Miller?"

He swung down from the cab of the tractor and hustled over to her. "Jonah! Jonah!" he called over his shoulder. "It's Sarah and she's cold."

"Why are you out here?" He turned his attention back to her.

She shivered as he wrapped one arm around her. "My tractor ran out of gas a ways back."

Buddy led her toward Jonah's tractor. "Hey, brother, you were right. That was Sarah's tractor back there."

She had never been so happy to see anyone in her life. Even him.

Jonah's eyes crinkled with what looked like concern. "What are you doing out here? You're soaked through."

She didn't have the energy to comment. She just climbed in beside him, thankful to be out of the weather.

She closed her eyes, then barely stirred as warmth snuggled around her.

"Shhh . . ." Jonah's voice soothed her. Jonah's scent surrounded her. He must have covered her with his coat.

"*Danki*," she whispered, then closed her eyes and drifted off.

"She's asleep, Jonah." Buddy held Sarah's hand as Jonah navigated his tractor through the piling snow.

He hoped she was only asleep. How long had she been out in the snow? She was soaked to the skin and as cold as ice, her face as pale as milk.

"Her gloves are wet," Buddy said.

"Take them off and try to warm her hands with yours, can you do that?" He would give anything to be able to stop the tractor and see to her himself, but the most important thing was to get her someplace warm.

Buddy had learned to drive a tractor long ago, but Jonah didn't want to give him the stress of driving in this terrible weather.

He had heard the snow might possibly turn into blizzard conditions before the night was over. He and Buddy had decided to go home while others were deciding to stay at the rec center and see how the weather was once the sun came up tomorrow. Boy, was he glad he had taken that chance. Who knew where Sarah might be if he and Buddy had stayed at the rec center.

The mere thought made his stomach churn and his heart drop. She could have been out here for hours, maybe even until morning. He didn't even want to think about it. She would have been frozen solid.

He swallowed hard and kept his eyes on the road.

"Are we almost there?" Buddy asked. He sounded concerned, as concerned as Jonah himself felt.

"Almost." Actually he had no idea. He couldn't see any landmarks as the snow continued to fall with a vengeance. But he didn't want to worry his brother any more than necessary.

He wanted to reach down and touch her face, feel the rise and fall of her chest as she breathed. He needed to make sure she was alive. She was as still as death and twice as pale. Thankfully it was cold enough that he could see little puffs each time she exhaled. Her breathing was a little shallow but steady, and that was good. Wasn't it?

"I'm worried about her." Buddy turned his blue eyes to Jonah as if his big brother had all the answers. But Jonah didn't have an answer for this one.

It was slow going on the slick, snow-covered roads. After what seemed like an eternity, but could have only been half an hour, Jonah spotted their mailbox.

He almost cried with relief, but they weren't out of trouble yet. He still had to get them down the driveway. He needed to get her inside and warm. He needed to make sure that she was going to be okay. Then and only then could he breathe a sigh of relief.

It seemed to take years to get down the driveway. "Buddy, run ahead and open the door."

"Are you going to bring her inside?"

"Of course," Jonah said, turning off the tractor. "Now go on."

Buddy, bless him, ran ahead as fast as he could.

Jonah swung down from the tractor and gently scooped Sarah into his arms. She weighed next to nothing, and for that he was grateful. The snow was piling up at an alarming rate and he fairly waded through it to get to the porch.

"Jonah?" His mother stood in the doorway, her sturdy form outlined by the lights inside the house. "What on earth is going on?"

He stomped as much snow as he dared off his shoes and legs, then continued into the house.

"Buddy, build up the fire, okay?"

"*Jah*." Buddy gave a big nod, then started piling logs on the dwindling fire.

Jonah carried Sarah in and laid her on the couch. He needed to get her out of her wet coat and dress or she would never warm up.

"*Mamm*, get me one of Hannah's old dresses and some blankets. Buddy, can you get me a couple of towels?"

"*Jah*." Buddy hustled from the room as if the devil was on his heels.

"What are you going to do?"

"She's soaked to the skin. I need to get her out of her wet clothes and into something dry and warm."

"You can't change her clothes." His mother gasped in surprise.

"*Mamm*, she's my wife. Who else should change her clothes?"

It seemed as if she had forgotten that small detail. She hesitated for a minute more, then left the room.

He had no sooner gotten Sarah's coat off than Buddy

rushed back in. "Here." He thrust two towels at Jonah, then stood back as if waiting further instructions.

"Buddy, *Mamm*'s gone to get Sarah some dry clothes, but I can't change her out of her wet ones with you standing there. You understand?"

Buddy shook himself out of his deep stare. "You want me to go upstairs?"

Jonah wanted to smile, but his heart wouldn't let him. "That would be great."

"Are you staying here tonight?"

Jonah didn't think any of them were going anywhere anytime soon. "*Jah.*"

"*Gut.*" Buddy beamed his most brilliant smile. "I'm glad." Then his expression fell. "I mean, I'm not glad Sarah is hurt, but I'm glad you're staying here. I mean . . ."

"It's okay, Buddy. I understand."

His brother wilted with relief.

"But I need you to do one thing for me, okay?"

"*Jah*. Anything,"

"I need you to run to the barn and call Sarah's parents. Tell them that Sarah's tractor ran out of gas, but she is fine and staying here for the night. Can you remember all of that?"

Buddy nodded. "But is she? Going to be okay, that is."

Jonah looked down at his wife's milky pale face. "I'm going to make sure of it."

Buddy hadn't pulled off his coat and he hustled back out the door. Jonah vowed to give him fifteen minutes, then he was going after him. This snow was unlike anything he had ever seen.

Gently he removed the scarf from around Sarah's head and the pins that held her prayer *kapp* in place. The linen-type material was soaked through and had lost much of its starch. She would probably have to buy a new one. One by one, he took the pins from her hair, releasing the curly brown tresses and drying them with one of the towels Buddy had brought.

"I found this." His mother thrust a pale aqua-colored dress toward him. He could see it had a stain right on the front, as if his sister Hannah had been eating something and spilled it down herself. But it was dry, and that was all that mattered. As he held it up, he could tell that even with her weight loss, the dress would never fit Sarah.

"It's too small," he said, his disappointment clear. Not that it mattered. He would dress her in his clothes if need be.

"I was worried about that, so I brought this as well."

It was one of his mother's nightgowns, a soft white garment with a row of tiny pink flowers stitched across the yoke. He had seen it before hanging on the clothesline to dry, but he had never really thought about the garment or the whimsical little flowers that were so unlike his no-nonsense *mamm*.

"This is perfect. *Danki*."

His mother gave a quick nod. It seemed like she wanted to say more, but she shook her head and swallowed hard. "I'm going to bed now. Let me know if you need anything."

Jonah nodded.

"Anything at all," his mother repeated.

But all he needed was his wife to wake up and start arguing with him about something. Anything, as long as she was okay. But there was no one on earth who could give that to him.

Jonah was just about to start changing her clothes when Buddy burst through the front door. He removed his coat and hat and hung them by the front door, then toed off his black walking shoes. "Is she awake?" he asked.

"Not yet." He hoped those words proved true. If she wasn't awake yet it meant she would wake up. Eventually.

"I need to change her clothes," Jonah said with a nod.

"You do. And I need to go upstairs while you do that."

"It's time for bed, Buddy. Maybe you should try to get some sleep."

He could see his brother was torn between wanting to do as Jonah had asked and needing to see this thing with Sarah through.

"Will you come get me when she wakes up?"

"I think she'll sleep through the night." At least that was what he hoped. That she would sleep through the night, heal from the blows she had suffered, then wake in the morning her argumentative and stubborn self.

But she didn't look like his strong-willed wife. She looked soft and fragile, like a china doll he had seen once at the mall. She looked as if one solid blow would break her all apart.

Where had his Sarah gone?

He barely registered Buddy's retreating footsteps as he gingerly uncovered his wife. Her skin still held a bluish tint, and it scared him. How long had she been exposed to the elements? In his daze, he couldn't remember passing her tractor, but visibility had gotten worse and worse as he had driven home. He could have gone right past it with only inches to spare and never seen it sitting there.

As gently as he could, he removed her dress. She was soaked through to the skin. He rubbed her with a towel to warm her, all the while saying quick little prayers that everything would be all right. It had to be all right. He didn't know what he would do otherwise.

She stirred, her blue eyes open, but not quite focused. "Jonah?"

"Shhh," he said. "I'm here. Just rest now. We can talk in the morning."

He used that time to pull the nightdress over her head. It was miles too big for her, so he tucked it around her, hoping the extra fabric would do its job to keep her warm.

"Okay." She snuggled down into the blanket and closed her eyes.

He leaned in purely on instinct and pressed a kiss to her forehead.

She smiled and released a small sigh.

Everything was going to be all right. He just knew it.

But with the morning came a fever.

His *mamm* pressed the back of one hand to Sarah's forehead. "She's burning up."

He could see that without laying a hand on her. Where last night her cheeks had been the color of cool buttermilk, today they were pink like the flowers his mother grew at the edge of the garden.

As pink as the dress she had worn the night before.

The dress was still hanging by the fire where he had placed it to dry. He had stayed up most of the night, holding her hand and just being close to her. He felt responsible. She had left the party because he had told her that he wanted to sell the house. He could see that the words had adversely affected her. And heaven help him he had wanted to get a reaction from her. He wanted her to say something, *anything*, to him, so he had said the most hurtful thing he could think of. Sarah loved that house, or at least that was what she said. And he knew she would be sad if he sold it.

The plan hadn't come to him until that very moment. In an instant he'd known that it was a logical plan. He would sell the house and move in with his parents, or Luke Lambright. But more than anything, he had wanted to shock Sarah.

Boy, had that worked. She had run off in the snow, risking life and limb to get away from him. This was all his fault.

"Do something to help her." He looked to his *mamm*. She was the one person he could always depend on, but he knew that this was out of her hands.

She pressed her lips together and gave her head a little shake. "I'll get her some Tylenol and a wet rag."

Jonah looked out the window to all the snow piled all around. The sun was shining and the temperature was above freezing, but it would be a couple of days before the roads were clear enough for them to get out. He didn't know what he would do. He had to help her. He had to.

His mother came back in with a glass of water, two small pills, and a wet washrag.

Jonah knelt by the couch and lightly shook Sarah's shoulder. "Sarah." His voice cracked and he cleared his throat to try again. "Sarah." Louder this time.

Her eyelashes fluttered, then she peered at him. Her eyes looked at him, but it wasn't as if she truly saw him at all.

"Sarah, sit up and take this medicine." He slipped one hand behind her and helped her to sit up enough to take the pills, then settled her back onto the couch. He folded the washrag and laid it across her forehead. He wasn't sure what a wet rag would actually do to help, but it seemed to be his mother's solution in times like these, and he couldn't question her judgment this far in.

Sarah shuddered. "So cold," she murmured. "Cold."

Jonah pulled the blankets farther up on her shoulders and tucked them in to cut out the chill. But he knew that the cold came from inside. He could only pray that the Tylenol and the cool rag could work a miracle. Somehow in his gut, he knew that would be the only thing that could help.

"Her parents called on the phone and left a message." Buddy slammed the door behind him as he hustled back into the house just after noon.

Jonah stirred, surprised he had been asleep. He had pulled a kitchen chair into the living room so he could sit close to Sarah, just in case she woke up, her fever broke, and she needed him.

He placed a finger over his lips to quiet his brother, but Sarah didn't stir, and that worried him. He felt helpless and useless and worthless.

"What did they say?"

"They left a message. They said they were glad to hear that she was okay and to have her call home later." His gaze dropped as he studied Sarah's flushed face. "She's not going to call, is she?"

"Of course she is." It was a lie, but he wanted to believe it. He didn't know what was wrong with her, if she had the flu or pneumonia. The Tylenol hadn't touched her fever. He wasn't sure what would. She needed a doctor. But there was half a foot of snow on the ground with drifts twice that high. Until the sun melted some of it away, no one was going anywhere anytime soon.

Buddy continued to stare at Sarah. "Is she going to be okay, Jonah? And don't lie to me."

"Why would I lie to you?"

Buddy propped his hands on his hips and swung his

gaze to Jonah. "You don't think I know all of you lie to me when it suits you?"

Was that how he saw it? "We love you." It was the best excuse he had without admitting what his brother said was true.

"You're not supposed to lie to the people you love."

Jonah opened his mouth to respond, but no words would come out. Buddy's words struck him like a poorly thrown baseball.

Had he been doing that? Lying to the people he loved? Only if he loved Sarah.

He looked into the flushed face of his wife and he knew. He loved her. He wasn't sure when it happened. So much had transpired between them. So many bad memories, but they were mixed with good ones, the two of them buying a house, sharing a meal, working side by side getting the house ready to live in. All the while knowing they had a baby on the way.

Then tragedy had struck and the good times had turned sour.

But wasn't that what marriage was all about? Life, even. Good times turned bad, but God got them through. Bad times turned to good, and families flourished. As long as they remained strong and together . . .

But Sarah had left. And he had let her. He had hurt her.

And now . . .

"Jonah?" Buddy knelt beside him.

Tears slid down Jonah's face. "What am I going to do if she's not okay?"

Buddy crunched Jonah in a Buddy-sized hug and rocked him from side to side. It might not have been the gentlest embrace, but it was exactly what Jonah needed. He'd spent his life taking care of Buddy and redirecting him when the time warranted it. It was only right that his brother comfort him in this time of need.

"Shhh," Buddy crooned. "Don't talk like that. She's going to be okay. Let's pray for her."

Buddy released Jonah to kneel beside him. He wrapped Jonah's hand in his own and bowed his head. Jonah had no idea what he prayed for, only that he squeezed Buddy's hands tight as if the touch alone was a direct line to God.

Maybe it was.

Jonah could only hope and continue to pray. He couldn't lose his wife now, not after he'd finally found her.

Sarah felt as if she was floating on a sea of red. Everything should have been hot. She could almost see the smoke, but she was cold. So very cold. How did she get here, on this crimson ocean? And what was sitting on her chest?

She couldn't breathe, not well, anyway, and each breath of air she managed to drag into her lungs burned like fire.

She was floating, of that she was certain, but she felt anchored. Someone had her hand. She looked down, but her vision was blurry, or was that the smoke? She couldn't tell.

"Jonah?" She tried to shout for him, but she couldn't manage more than a squeak. Why did she call out for him? He despised her. At the very least he hated being married to her. She should call for her mother or Annie, someone who loved and cared about her, but she had used up all of her strength.

The snow. Now she remembered. That was how she got here. It started snowing and she was walking, then . . . nothing. But snow wasn't red and it certainly wasn't hot. But she was cold, she reminded herself. So very cold.

She needed to speak to someone about starting a fire. A real fire, not this red light that surrounded her. Yes, a fire. That was what she needed. And she would ask for it, right after a little nap. After all, she was so very tired.

Sarah closed her eyes on the endless waters of red and drifted off to sleep once again.

Chapter Twenty-Four

Two days after the snowstorm, the roads were clear enough to travel.

Mamm had kept Sarah's fever at a manageable level using the medicines they had on hand, but Jonah had endured all he could. He was taking her to the doctor. She had the flu or pneumonia or something, and it was more than he knew how to take care of. Only the weather had kept him from taking her, but now that the roads were passable, he was having her seen to.

"Did you sleep here all night again?"

Jonah lifted his chin from his chest and stretched from side to side. "*Jah*."

His *mamm* came down the steps, her face freshly washed and her prayer *kapp* pinned firmly in place. "You need to sleep in your bed, son. A chair is no place to rest your body."

She had a point, but he didn't want to leave Sarah, not even for a minute. If her fever broke, he wanted to be right there. If she woke and needed something, he wanted to get it for her immediately. He couldn't leave her, not when he had only just found her.

She had been right there all the time, but he had been too blind to notice. Well, no more. Never again.

"I'm taking her to the doctor today."

Mamm looked out at the melting snow. "You should call Bruce."

He shook his head. He didn't want to wait. He could take her into Wells Landing, and if she was too sick for the clinic to handle, they could take her up to Pryor. But the main thing was to get her to help as quickly as possible.

"Jonah?"

He spun around to see Sarah finally awake. Her cheeks had lost their too-pink hue, though her voice held a rusty, unused quality. "Sarah," he breathed. He was by her side in an instant as she struggled to sit up.

"Where am I?"

"You're at my parents' house. Don't you remember?"

She shook her head, then reached up as if to search for her prayer *kapp* or maybe the reason why her hair was hanging down around her shoulders.

"Your tractor ran out of gas and it started to snow. Buddy and I brought you here."

Her expression was beyond confused, but he could almost see the pieces of the puzzle falling into place. She had to be remembering something, he just didn't know what. He could only hope that she didn't remember their fight in the classroom at the rec center or the things he had said about selling the house. But judging by the hurt light creeping into her eyes, she remembered at least some of it.

"I want to go home."

"The roads are a mess, but in a day or two I can take you back to our house. Where you belong."

She shook her head, then closed her eyes as if the

motion caused her great pain. Or maybe she was just dizzy.

"You haven't had much to eat or drink for a couple of days."

"A couple of days?" she whispered.

"I'll get her something." *Mamm* bustled from the room.

"Lie back down." He clasped her shoulders and did his best to get her to relax back on the sofa. But she didn't want to, her body straining against his even as she reclined against the cushions.

"I don't want to. I want to go home."

He was saved an answer as his *mamm* hurried back into the room with a glass of orange juice and large piece of white bread.

"Eat this. You'll feel better."

She shook her head, but accepted the juice. "My throat hurts."

At least she would get some nourishment. He had a feeling she had been letting herself go in the last couple of weeks. That would explain all the weight loss and how hard the flu had hit her.

She drank only half of the juice, then settled back down. "I'm going to rest for a while, and then I want to go home. To my parents' house." She sounded like a spoiled child.

"We'll see," he said, unwilling to agree or disagree. He wasn't taking her anywhere but to the doctor, then to the house they shared to start their lives—their *marriage*—over again.

Sarah slept off and on for the remainder of the day. Since her fever had broken, Jonah opted not to risk the roads and take her into the doctor, but he stayed by her side in case she needed anything.

She refused food, but he managed to get two cups of warm coffee down her to go with the juice. He would feel so much better if she ate, but she was on the mend, and that was really all he could ask for.

"Are you going to just watch her sleep all day?" Buddy asked. He came down the stairs, pulling on layers of clothing. "Jonathan and I are going to build a snowman with Prudy."

Just then his baby sister skipped down the stairs wearing no more than her dress and a pair of flat girlie shoes.

"Prudence Ann Miller. You get back up those stairs right now and get on a pair of long johns and pants before you come back down."

Jonah thought she might protest, but she seemed to sense her mother's bulldog attitude and reluctantly trudged back up the stairs.

"And don't forget the hat I crocheted for you."

"Yes, *Mamm*." But Prudy's voice sounded anything but enthusiastic, and had Jonah not been so worried about Sarah he probably would've laughed.

His mother shook her head and disappeared back into the kitchen.

"Go out with us," Buddy said.

Jonah shook his head. "I need to be here for Sarah."

Buddy studied him, his blue eyes intense. Jonah knew that a lot of people felt Buddy's intelligence was less than average, but what he lacked in book learning he more than made up for in wisdom. "If you love her, why do you live apart?"

"It's complicated."

"Everybody always says that. But I think that's just an excuse for you don't know." And with that Buddy marched to the front door, pulled on his coat, his hat, and his boots, and made his way out into the snow.

"Wait for me!" Prudy ran down the stairs, her rubber boots clunking against the floor as she hurried along. She grabbed her coat and followed behind Buddy. Jonah noticed she didn't have her hat.

A few seconds later Jonathan came down the stairs bundled up like Jonah's other siblings and carrying Prudy's hat. "Are you sure you don't want to go with us?" he asked.

"I'm sure."

"Suit yourself." With a jaunty wave, Jonathan followed Prudy and Buddy out the door.

Someone had tied cinder blocks to her arms and legs. And to her eyelids too. Sarah felt heavy and sleepy, the floating sensation giving way to a sinking feeling she couldn't seem to shake.

She was at Jonah's house, and he was there with her. She still wasn't certain how she ended up at the Millers' house, but here she was. No denying it.

She felt a warm touch and knew someone had pushed the hair back from her face. She sighed and snuggled a little deeper into the blankets covering her. She was tired, so very tired, and heavy. She couldn't have moved if she had wanted to.

She was sick. That much she knew, but she would worry about that later. When she wasn't so very sleepy.

"I wish she would eat something." Jonah's voice floated to her from very far away.

"She'll eat when she's ready. Right now her body is trying to heal itself. You're going to have to be patient."

Who were they talking about? Whoever it was must be pretty bad off, judging by the level of concern in their voices. But she didn't have time to worry about anyone else right now. Her limbs felt lighter than they had before, but she was still as weak as a kitten. And all she wanted to do was sleep. Maybe later she would ask them who they were talking about and what was wrong with her, but first she needed a small nap.

She sighed and allowed herself to drift back off to sleep.

Jonah talked to her parents, assured them that Sarah was on the mend, and never left her side. They moved her into the sewing room downstairs. There was an extra bed in there for when they had company, though Jonah couldn't remember the last time they had used it for such. For three more days he kept his vigil. Her fever came and went, but never reached as high as it had been that first morning.

"Jonah?" He jerked awake, confused that he had been sleeping. What time was it? Early, by the looks of the dark sky out the window. Or late. Really, really late.

"I'm here, Sarah."

"Okay." Her voice grew sleepy once again. "I was just checking."

And for some strange reason her words gave him hope. He found her hand in the dark and squeezed her fingers. She squeezed back and he smiled. Everything was going to be fine. He just knew it.

* * *

She'd had the strangest dream. She had been floating along in the sky, drifting as if she were some sort of bird. And Jonah was there with her, holding her hand and smiling at her as if he really and truly loved her. And for a moment that dream had been her only reality. Then everything had changed; her limbs grew heavy and she had crashed to earth.

She had heard somewhere that if a person had a dream that they were falling, if they hit the ground they would have a heart attack. She could now say that wasn't true. She landed on the ground in a bright field of corn, every bone in her body feeling as though it had shattered. She managed to pull herself to her feet even through the pain, but that pain was nothing as she watched Jonah fly away with April. She might not have looked like her in the dream, but Sarah knew who the girl was.

Jonah was on his way to the English world with his true love, and she was left behind, alone, in her Amish home.

"I love you," he had called as he flew away. But she knew that to be a lie. How could he love her if he was leaving?

Sarah jerked awake, once again feeling as though she was falling.

"Sarah?"

Jonah hadn't flown away. He was sitting right there by her bed. That part of the dream might not be true, but the rest of it was right on the mark. He didn't love her, and he was leaving her for April. She had heard all the talk. He was selling their house so he wouldn't be weighed down by the responsibility.

"What time is it?" she asked. There was no clock in the room, at least none that she could see.

Jonah chuckled. "Just after lunch," he said. "But you might want to ask what day it is."

Okay. "What day is it?"

"Wednesday."

Wednesday. But the Valentine's party had been on Thursday. That would mean . . . "I've been asleep for six days?"

"You've been sick."

Why couldn't she remember that? But she could believe it. Her hair hung in lank strands around her face, and her mouth tasted like ash. "*Jah,*" she said. If she had lost six days, that had to be the truth, whether she could remember it all or not.

The last thing she could remember was talking to Jonah at the party, him telling her that he was selling the house, and then leaving the party and getting caught in a snowstorm.

She looked at the window across the room. There was no more snow to be seen. It seemed Jonah was telling her the truth.

"Would you like something to eat?"

Would she? "*Jah, danki.*" She decided she was hungry, or at least she could eat something. Her belly felt empty and raw even if it wasn't growling for food.

Jonah got up and hurried from the room, leaving Sarah blessedly alone. His presence was disturbing her, though she hadn't realized it until he left. He seemed concerned about her, and for that she was grateful. He had made sure that she had been taken care of these last few days, but she couldn't help but question the sincerity of that concern. He must be putting on for his family, pretending that everything was okay for now when she knew that it wouldn't be long until he left for the English world. It was going to break his mother's heart. Though Sarah and Gertie had never been close, she didn't want that for the other woman. She would have to be heartless not to care.

Jonah came back into the room carrying a tray with a steaming bowl of something that smelled delicious and a thick slice of bread on the side. "*Mamm* made you some soup. It's chicken noodle."

"It smells good."

She pushed herself into a better sitting position, and Jonah placed the tray over her lap.

She wasn't wearing a prayer *kapp*, but she bowed her head regardless and said a small prayer for getting through this illness and the food she was about to eat.

She finished her silent prayer and picked up her spoon. She blew on the steaming spoonful of soup as Jonah watched her like a hawk watches its prey. Or an overprotective mother watches her rambunctious child.

"What?" she asked.

"I've been worried about you."

Be still, heart. They were just words. Pretty words, but only words. She knew his true feelings. "I'm okay." She dunked her bread into her broth and savored the warmth as it filled her. She hadn't realized how hungry she was until she actually started eating. Now she was having to temper her movements to keep from eating like a pig.

Perhaps someone was at the door watching. But she ignored Jonah as she continued to eat, and he continued to watch her every movement as if she were some fascinating creature instead of the wife he didn't want.

She finished the last bite with a satisfying sigh.

Jonah was on his feet in an instant. "Do you want some more?"

She shook her head. "I'm really kind of tired. I think I'll take a nap." It was anybody's guess as to how she could sleep for days, then need a nap. She guessed that was all part of being ill.

"*Jah.* Sure." He picked up the tray and left the room.

Sarah rolled over, so surprisingly exhausted. She closed her eyes and fell immediately asleep.

For the next two days, Jonah attended her every need. It was tough lying in bed most of the day, her body weak, but her mind willing and ready to go. And it was even more difficult since Jonah hovered, hardly letting her out of his sight for any more than a trip to the bathroom.

Each day she walked—with his help, of course—into the living room. She would play Chinese checkers with Buddy and a silly game called Ants in Your Pants with Prudy.

At least Sarah was growing stronger with every day that passed.

"I'm ready to go home," she said on Friday morning. The snow was gone, she was better, and nothing was holding her at the Millers'. She would miss Buddy and Prudy and Jonah most of all, but she had to get back to real life and stop pretending that she and Jonah had a future. But it was so easy to do when he hovered over her, making sure he didn't want for even the simplest of things.

Guilt. It hadn't taken her long to figure out that Jonah felt guilty, as if somehow his words had caused her to be out in the snow and get sick. She wasn't sure how he factored that in, since she had been responsible for filling up the tractor. Or not, as the case was. She wasn't sure that little detail concerned him at all.

But she couldn't stay here and pretend forever, and she certainly couldn't allow him to continue to fawn over her out of misplaced guilt.

"About that . . ." Jonah started. He looked over to where Buddy sat playing with his yo-yo. He had been trying all week to learn a new trick. Baby in the Cradle, she thought it was called. "Buddy?"

He looked up from his toy, then flipped his gaze to Sarah. "I guess I need to go straighten up my room. *Jah*, that's what I need to do." He hustled up the stairs as if the seat of his pants was on fire.

Something was up, but she had no clue as to what.

"I'll take you home, but not to your house."

She frowned. "Then how can you take me home?"

"I'm going to take you to our house."

"I thought you were going to sell it." As far as she knew, he could have sold it already.

"About that . . ." It was the second time he had used that phrase, and it was starting to make her suspicious.

"About what?"

"I'm not going to sell the house, Sarah. I want to live there."

She shouldn't have been surprised. After all, it had been an English house once. It was wired for electricity and would be nothing to get back up and running for his budding relationship with April. Sarah ignored the pain as the thought seared through her. It was past time to face facts.

Wait a minute. "If you want to live there . . ." She couldn't finish the sentence. It made her hopes rise for things that could not be.

"And I want you to live there with me."

Sarah blinked at him, wondering if the flu had somehow damaged her hearing or maybe her brain had overheated when she had a fever. Something wasn't working right. This was Jonah. Jonah who she loved with all her heart who had never really wanted anything to do with her.

Until that one night.

She pushed the thought away and concentrated on what he was saying now.

"What do you say, Sarah?"

She pushed to her feet, needing to put some distance between them. "What do I say?" She stomped over to the fireplace and stared into the flickering orange flames. Words escaped her. She braced her hands on the mantel and ducked her head between her arms.

"Sarah?"

She whirled around to face him. "Why are you doing this to me?"

He had the nerve to look confused. "Doing what?"

"Pretending like you want to be my husband." She bit back the tears that threatened. She would not show that weakness. Not now.

He stood and came close to her, but Sarah moved away. She had a hard time when he was standing close. "I do want to be your husband."

She shook her head. "After all we've been through, the very least you can do is tell me the truth."

"This is the truth."

She shook her head. She wanted to believe it but she couldn't. "Take me home, please, Jonah. And don't put us through any more of this." She turned and made her way to the kitchen. One thing she had learned since she had been staying here: if she wanted Gertie Miller, look in the kitchen.

Jonah's mother stood at the counter kneading a wad of dough on the floured surface.

"I just wanted to come say *danki* for allowing me to stay here when I was sick. I appreciate all you did for me."

Gertie's gaze flickered to something over Sarah's shoulder, and she knew that Jonah had come up behind her. She looked back to Sarah, brushing the back of her arm against her forehead. "It was Jonah."

Sarah didn't know quite how to respond. "Well, *danki*."

"He loves you, don't you know."

Behind her she felt Jonah stiffen. What was Gertie trying to do?

"That's what he's telling me." But he hadn't really said those words. Only that he wanted to be her husband. And that he wanted them to live in their house together.

But she knew that it didn't mean anything more than him trying to assuage his guilt for not loving her. She'd had a lot of time to read as she was recovering from her flu. It was amazing the stories that found their way into *The Budget* and *Die Botschaft*. Sandwiched between tales of Elmer Byler's donkey who had twins to the best whoopie pie recipe ever recorded were stories of a rare divorce in an Indiana community and a couple who were living separate lives but still in the same house.

But she didn't want a sham of a marriage. Maybe she could have handled it years from now, when she and Jonah had grown apart after so many happy years together. But everyone in the district, in the entire community, knew why he had married her. She wouldn't be able to stand the pitying looks. She couldn't take it now. She would rather be an outcast and live on the fringes like Katie Glick and Merv King the coffin maker than live a lie.

"So he's taking you home now?" Gertie asked.

"That's right," Sarah said. "He's taking me back to my parents' house. *Danki* for everything."

Jonah couldn't get it through her head. What was wrong with her that she didn't believe what he was saying? He couldn't make it any clearer than he had already.

He helped her up onto the tractor and thought for a

moment about taking her to their house and making her stay there, but the whole point was to get his wife back. He wasn't sure that would do the trick. In fact, it might just make things worse.

What would April do?

She would tell him that if he loved Sarah, he would grant her request and take her where she wanted to go.

Love wasn't a right; it was earned, and he had done nothing to earn Sarah's love. At least nothing in the last few months. After she lost the baby, he had lost his direction as well. But no more.

He used the excuse of the tractor engine noise to stay any conversation between them. He needed the time to gather his thoughts. And he had a lot to gather. He lined up his mistakes and examined them one by one. It was time to change things between them. Past time.

He pulled down her driveway and parked his tractor in the side yard. One of the Yoders had fetched the tractor home once the roads had been cleared, and he parked next to it.

He swung down and reached out to help Sarah, but she scrambled down without his assistance.

"Sarah!" Annie rushed out onto the porch, her smile so wide it covered most of her face. "You're home! I'm so glad you're home!"

He had wanted another bit to talk to Sarah, tell her once again that he wanted her home, but Annie skipped down the steps and wrapped Sarah in a huge hug. Together the two of them walked arm and arm up the steps and into the house.

Jonah followed them like a lapdog.

He shook the thought away. It had taken some time to

get into this mess with Sarah, and it was going to take some time to find his way back out.

Her mother and father greeted him at the door.

They thanked him for caring for Sarah while she was sick. What had they expected him to do? Leave her on the snowy roads? They offered him a snack, but he refused. As much as he wanted to stay and spend as much time as he could with his wife, he had plans to make.

Chapter Twenty-Five

"Jonah's here." Annie let the window shade fall back into place and looked to Sarah.

"What do you mean he's here?" Sarah put aside the book she was reading and frowned. Just yesterday he had dropped her off with promises to come back and see her "soon." She thought it had been just talk, sweet words to fool her parents into believing that he actually cared more about her than he did. Now he was outside?

"He's talking to *Dat*." Annie studied her with a critical eye. Sarah squirmed under the perusal. "Do you want me to redo your bob?"

"No."

"Why not? Your husband is here, and he looks like he's come courtin'. Why would you not want to look your best for him?"

"Because I'm not courtin' my husband." The idea was ridiculous. And it sent her heart fluttering in her chest. She couldn't afford that. She couldn't afford to fall for his sweet manner and pretty words. She had already been down that road, and it led to nowhere.

Annie frowned. "I'm confused. I thought you loved him."

"I do. But that doesn't mean he loves me in return."

Sarah picked up her book and continued to read. Well, she pretended to, but she couldn't concentrate on the words knowing that any minute a knock would sound at the door.

The sound shouldn't have made her jump, but it did.

Annie's eyes widened. "He's here," she whispered.

"Tell him I'm gone," Sarah returned in the same hushed tones.

"That's not the truth," Annie protested.

"I don't care about that. Tell him I've gone somewhere."

"Where?" Annie asked.

"I don't know. It doesn't matter. Just tell him I'm not here."

But it was too late. The front door opened, and Jonah stepped into the room.

Sarah was on her feet in an instant. She whirled around to face him, barely registering that her sister did the same.

"Hi." He smiled when he said it, and she was sorely reminded of how weak in the knees just his presence could make her. Why would God let him affect her so? Or maybe it was the devil's handiwork, especially since she had vowed to remain strong where he was concerned.

"Hello, Jonah." Her words were cool, aloof even.

Annie poked her in the side with her elbow.

Sarah smiled and shot her sister a "quit it" look.

Sarah turned her attention back to her husband. "What are you doing here, Jonah?"

"I brought you some flowers." He thrust an odd-looking bouquet toward her, his grin widening.

"What?" Sarah took an involuntary step forward, looking at the unusual flowers he held. Each was wrapped in cellophane, with a small matching bow around the stem. "Are those . . . ?"

"Cookies." He tempered his grin a bit, but she could tell that he was proud of himself for the gesture.

"I wanted to bring you some flowers, but well, it's winter and all. Then I went by Esther Lapp's."

"Esther Fitch's, you mean," Annie corrected.

Jonah nodded. "I guess she will always be Esther Lapp to me. Anyway, she and Caroline Fitch have been making these for special occasions. They told me they had heart ones for Valentine's Day, but they switched to flowers since March is approaching."

Sarah hated to admit it, but it was perhaps the cutest thing she had ever seen. The flowers were actually cookies, each covered with a different color icing—turquoise, orange, yellow, and green. The cookies themselves were different shapes, a few looking like tulips and some like daisies.

"Are they sugar cookies?" Annie asked.

Jonah shook his head. "They're chocolate chip."

"Too bad," Annie said. "Sugar cookies are my favorite."

"But chocolate chip is Sarah's favorite."

How did he know that?

Sarah looked at the unique bouquet once again, this time seeing it with different eyes. Chocolate chip cookies and icing? Could this get any more perfect?

"I can't accept them."

"What?" Annie and Jonah whirled on her, each speaking over the other.

"Why not?" Annie asked.

"Stay out of this, sister."

"Sarah, they're just cookies. Why would you not be able to accept them?" Jonah took a step toward her when she wished he would turn around and take his pretty cookies that made up the sweet bouquet and head out the door.

She shook her head. Didn't he understand it was much

more than cookies? Every time she saw him, just his smile gave her hope, and hope was a dangerous thing.

"I have plans, Jonah, and they don't include you." It was perhaps the hardest thing she had ever said. Given half a chance—a *real* chance—she would change those plans and live as his wife forever. But this wasn't a real chance, this was about guilt. How long before his guilt eased up and he was running off to the English world again? How long before he decided he really didn't love her after all and he wanted to be with April?

Her heart couldn't take that kind of blow. No, the best thing was to end it now while she still could. Because later she might not be able to let him go.

"What plans?" Annie scoffed. "Your plans are pathetic."

"Don't you have something better to do?" Sarah asked.

"Nope." Annie crossed her arms and rocked back on her heels. Why was she making this so hard for her?

"I for one would love to hear about these plans," Jonah said.

Sarah stepped toward him, hoping he would retreat toward the door. Of course he stood his ground. "It's time for you to go home, Jonah."

He crossed his arms much like Annie had and stared indifferently down at Sarah. "If you don't tell me about your plans, I'll ask Annie."

"And she won't answer if she knows what's *gut* for her."

Jonah chuckled. "That sounds suspiciously violent for a *gut* Amish girl."

"As I meant it to." She took another step toward him, but still he held fast.

"Can I?" Annie bounced on her toes in excitement. "She's going to take over being the town oddball from Katie Glick."

Jonah looked at Sarah, his expression mockingly serious. "Does Katie know this?"

"Annie doesn't know what she's talking about."

"I do too." Annie nodded for emphasis.

"There's only one problem with that," Jonah mused. "Katie Glick never married."

"Once we divorce, no one will remember."

Jonah frowned. At last she had gotten to him. "We can't divorce. We're Amish, remember?"

"It won't matter when you leave to go English."

His frown deepened. "Who said I was turning English?"

"Everybody."

"Well, 'everybody' is wrong."

Despite the serious edge in his voice, she didn't believe him. She knew he might say that now, but ever since Lorie had left, Jonah had been walking with a foot in both worlds.

She would love to be the one who brought him around to his raising, who showed him all the joys of remaining Amish, but she knew that would never come to pass. Too much had happened for her to believe that it ever would.

"I think you should leave, Jonah." Bravely Sarah grabbed his arm and led him toward the door. She pulled his coat and hat from the pegs off to one side and thrust them into his arms. She didn't bother waiting for him to put them on before she opened the door and gestured him out into the clear February day.

"But—" he protested.

She shook her head. "Be safe driving home."

Suddenly Jonah's view was filled with the white-painted wood of the Yoders' front door.

What had just happened?

He looked down at the bouquet of cookies he held. They were supposed to charm Sarah, show her just how much she meant to him. But instead she had ushered him out the door and closed it in his face.

He raised a hand to knock and thought better of it. He hesitated, then set the cookies on the bench just outside the door before loping down the steps toward his tractor.

"Going home so soon?" Otto Yoder, Sarah and Annie's father, chose that moment to come out of the barn.

Jonah shrugged. "This may not be as easy as I had hoped." That was putting a nice spin on things.

"Women can be tricky."

Especially when they had been through as much as Sarah had. But Jonah had foolishly believed that he would tell her that he loved her and she would fall into his arms, kiss him, and not care who was around watching.

It wasn't her conservative Amish nature that had kept her from his embrace, though. It was Sarah herself.

"She says she's going to take over for Katie Glick."

Otto frowned. "Taking in mending?"

"Being the town oddball." Jonah grimaced, not realizing until he said them out loud how harsh his words really were. "I didn't mean that like it sounded."

Otto nodded. "I understand. There's always one." He gave a small smile.

"Well, Sarah seems to think Wells Landing needs another."

"Just give it time," Otto said.

It was sound advice, but Jonah had wasted so much time already. He didn't want to take any more time than necessary. He wanted his wife back. He wanted to get started living again. For so long his life had been on hold for others. Now he was waiting for the most important person in his life to realize that she loved him still.

But until then, he was going to take every opportunity he could to show her how much she meant to him. And hopefully with the grace of God, he would break down her defenses and prove his love once and for all.

"Uh-oh." Annie moved away from the window and came to sit on the couch next to Sarah.

"What?" She placed the hat she was crocheting on her lap and eyed her sister.

"Nothing."

Sarah opened her mouth to tell Annie that lying was a sin when a knock sounded on the door.

"Is that Jonah?" she asked in an urgent whisper.

Annie picked up this week's paper from the coffee table and shrugged.

"It is." Sarah stood and motioned toward the door. "Go tell him I'm gone."

"You go tell him."

Sarah propped her hands on her hips while Annie continued to pretend interest in the paper. The thing was upside down. "Fine."

She marched over to the door and jerked it open. "I'm not here," she said, pushing past Jonah and out into the yard. She didn't even bother to put on a coat. Thankfully the day had turned out fairly warm for the time of year. March was coming up fast, and though the weather could be very unpredictable, a person could count on a few pretty days mixed in with winter's finale.

"You're not here?" Jonah asked, obviously confused.

"I'm fixing to not be." She looked around, but it seemed that her father had taken the tractor somewhere.

Maybe she should have listened when he poked his head inside and talked to her mother earlier. But as usual she was mired down so much in her own problems she couldn't see anything else. Now her only hope of actually leaving was taking the horse and buggy.

So be it.

She marched over to the barn and got her horse, leading the gentle mare out into the sunshine.

The horse danced a little to the side. She was excited to be going out on an odd day.

"What are you doing?" Jonah called.

Like her actions weren't completely obvious. "Sorry. I have an appointment and I'm late."

"I don't believe you."

She shrugged. "You can believe whatever you want." She continued to hook her horse to the buggy, her hands shaking with some emotion she couldn't name.

"Sarah." Jonah's voice was soft and cajoling. She loved it and hated it all in the same instant.

"What?" Finally finished with the horse, she stood up straight and propped her hands on her hips. She was hoping to strike a saucy "don't mess with me" pose, but she was starting to just feel tired.

"Where are you really going?"

The thought hit her in an instant. Why hadn't she thought of this before? Of course! It was the solution they had both been searching before.

"I'm going to talk to the bishop," she said. "I'm going to ask him to give us a divorce."

Jonah's heart stopped in his chest, then he realized exactly what she was saying and had to stifle his laugh. "He's not going to grant us a divorce. We're Amish, remember? Married for life."

She shook her head and climbed into the buggy. "He might. I'm going to ask. Lots of married Amish are getting divorced now."

"That's not true."

"Maybe not, but it's the way of the future."

"No. it's not."

She pulled the reins through the front window. "An annulment, then. Why couldn't we have an annulment?"

"Because we're Amish." Honestly, he was starting to feel like one of those birds they had at the pet store in town. One that could only say a couple of sentences, so he said them over and over.

But it seemed Sarah wasn't listening. She set the buggy in motion and started for the road. Jonah had no choice but to climb on his tractor and follow her.

He thought she would start off, realize how ridiculous she was being, and turn back for home, but the closer they got to the Ebersols', the more he started to believe that she might just be serious about this.

And his heart sank a little as he watched her turn into the bishop's driveway.

He shook that feeling away and followed her. She could ask for a divorce or an annulment and other such nonsense, but that didn't mean the bishop would grant her one.

Cephas Ebersol was a good Amish man.

He was a fair man.

But he's progressive as well.

Jonah pushed that thought away. Just because the bishop was progressive didn't mean he would grant Sarah her crazy wish. But being progressive might mean he would see their marriage as the mistake Sarah had convinced herself it was. And if Cephas thought that . . .

He shook his head and pushed the gas pedal a little harder. He had to stop Sarah. He couldn't let her ask the bishop. Cephas couldn't say no or yes if she wasn't permitted to ask. He had to stop her. But how?

He pulled his tractor around her carriage. She shot him an angry look as he passed her, the road so narrow he could almost reach out and take the reins from her hands.

Instead he drove his tractor into the Ebersols' yard, using it to block the end of the drive. Sarah had to stop and walk past him to get to the bishop's house.

She stopped her horse, her blue eyes flashing anger and something else he couldn't identify as she climbed down from the buggy. Was it resignation? Disappointment? Whatever it was, it was gone as quickly as it appeared.

"Get out of my way, Jonah Miller. I'm doing this for the both of us."

He shook his head. "I don't see how. I don't want this."

"Would you stop doing that? You don't have to pretend."

"Who says I'm pretending?"

"I do."

"Well, you're wrong."

That stopped her in her tracks. "You're not pretending?"

"No."

She thought about it a second, then nodded sagely. "I get it. You're pretending not to be pretending."

Jonah shook his head. "You're giving me a headache."

"You're giving me a heartache."

"Then listen to me."

She closed her eyes and he wondered if she was saying a prayer, probably because after a moment she opened them again. She pulled on the band of her apron, then started around him.

"Where are you going?" He hadn't been expecting her attack or he might have stopped her from getting past him.

"To talk to the bishop." She said each word clearly and slowly, as if speaking to a preschooler who hadn't learned English yet.

"Sarah," he called and started after her.

She was small and quick and somehow she reached the Ebersols' front door before he could catch her.

She looked back at him once, then knocked on the door. She opened it, no doubt to slip inside and away from him, but before she could take another step, Cephas Ebersol stepped out onto the porch.

"What's going on out here?" He looked from one of them to the other, and Jonah had the feeling he had been in his house listening to the ruckus all along. Maybe he had been hoping they could work it out between themselves.

Well, that had been Jonah's hope as well. So much for that.

"Jonah is trying to stop me from coming in and talking to you."

"Is this true?" Cephas turned his knowing blue eyes to Jonah.

"*Jah*. She's lost her mind and thinks you will grant her a divorce."

"Or an annulment," Sarah quickly broke in.

"That's a mighty big request."

Sarah nodded, stepping to the side as Jonah made his way onto the porch to stand next to them. "You know as well as I do that this marriage was doomed from the start. At first I thought this was God's will that the two of us were to be together. I wanted to see that because it's what I had wanted for so long."

The bishop nodded. It was no secret in the district that Sarah had had a crush on him for a while now. But he had been too in love with being in love with Lorie to see Sarah for what she was: a beautiful young woman with so much to give. Almost losing her to the flu had shown him that he truly did love her. He just wished that it hadn't taken him so long to see that.

"And it wasn't God's will?" Cephas asked.

"Of course it was," Jonah said while Sarah replied, "No, it wasn't."

She glared at Jonah, then turned her attention back to the bishop. "Why would God want us to get married just to take that baby from us?"

Cephas shook his head. "I don't pretend to understand all the ways in which the Lord works."

"God is *gut*," Sarah said. "Why would He want us miserable for the rest of our lives?"

"Are you miserable?" Cephas asked.

Jonah swallowed hard as he waited for her to answer.

"*Jah*."

She was miserable? "Why?" The word slipped from his lips before he could even think twice about it.

"You're not?"

With those two words she turned it around on him. "Maybe . . . at first, but I was stupid."

She shook her head. "No, you were truthful. Neither one of us wanted to be in the situation we found ourselves in, but that's where we were. Back then you didn't pretend that our marriage was anything more than it was. Now you're going around declaring that you want to be my husband, and we both know that's not true."

"It's not?" Jonah asked.

The bishop turned to him. "What is it?" he asked. "Do you want to be her husband or not?"

"I do."

Cephas nodded. "*Gut*, because I will not grant you a divorce."

Sarah opened her mouth, but he interrupted. "Or an annulment."

"But—" She looked heartbroken at the bishop's words, but gave a brave nod. Then she turned to him. "I'm sorry, Jonah. I've done everything I can. If you want to go be English and marry April, I won't stop you."

Just then a car pulled up into the drive. He recognized it as belonging to April. What was she doing here?

They all watched as she parked the car and got out.

Sarah moved down the porch steps and went over to April. Jonah held his breath. "I won't begin to try and understand what God has in His plans for us all, but I won't keep Jonah from you."

April's forehead creased in a confused frown. "Thanks. I guess."

"The bishop won't grant me a divorce, but if he goes with you—" Her breath caught and for a moment he thought he heard a sob, but he must have been mistaken. It seemed Sarah was telling the truth when she told him that she had given up on him and that she didn't love him anymore. And he had been counting on that love to see them through. But he had been too late.

April turned her gaze to Jonah. "I didn't think Amish got divorces."

He shrugged. "We don't."

"But if he goes English, he can divorce me and marry you."

"Marry me?" She laughed. "Is she serious?"

"Of course I am," Sarah said.

Jonah nodded. "I'm afraid she's lost her mind."

"Would you stop saying that!"

"It seems like something is definitely amiss," Cephas added.

"I'm standing right here." Sarah looked at each of them in turn. "Why are you talking about me like I'm not around?"

"Well," Jonah started, "you don't seem to be listening to anything we have to say."

She took a deep breath, and Jonah knew they had pushed her to the end of her patience. "I've done everything I could to help you be happy. I can do no more. What you decide from here is all up to you." She shook her head and started for her buggy.

"I'm not happy," Jonah called just before she hoisted herself into the carriage.

Sarah looked to the bishop. "Should I even ask why?"

He nodded. "Might as well."

"Okay," she said. "I'll bite. Why aren't you happy?"

Jonah started down the porch steps needing to be closer to her as he said the words. "See, my wife . . ." He shook his head. "She used to love me once upon a time, but I don't think she does any longer. At least that's what she says."

She kept her hands on her carriage as if she was about to pull herself up and leave any second. "*Jah?*"

He nodded. "That's right." He came closer still. Now she was so near he could reach out and touch her sweet face. "And I don't know what to do to make her love me again."

Sarah watched him like prey watched a predator. Her eyes were wide and a little fearful, as if she held a hope she knew would take her nowhere. Now was the time for him to show her that he meant what he said. "Why does it mean so much to you?"

"Because I want things to go back the way they were

before. Well, maybe not exactly the same way. We've had a few rough patches, you see."

She nodded, but kept ahold of the buggy. "Go on."

"But I want her to come back home. Move back into our house and start a family with me."

"Have you told her that?"

"I've tried to, but she doesn't seem to want to listen."

"Do you love her?"

"Of course I do."

Her blue eyes darkened until they were as deep and bottomless as a nighttime sky. "Have you told her that?"

He stopped. Had he? He shook his head. Not in all of the times he had tried to talk to her had he told her how much she meant to him. What a fool he had been. "No," he whispered.

"Maybe you should." Her voice was equally soft, perfectly matching his own.

"I love you, Sarah Miller."

It was all she had been waiting for and more, yet she couldn't make herself move closer to him. What if this was a dream? What if she reached for him and woke up empty-handed? She had waited so long for Jonah to see what they could have together, and she couldn't take the chance that he would disappear into thin air and leave her heartbroken once again.

"You love me?" Those were the only words she could squeeze past the lump in her throat. He loved her? How long had she wanted to hear those words from his lips? How could she believe them? "Why?" Not exactly what she meant to ask.

Jonah chuckled. "Sometimes I'm not so sure myself.

You can be strong-headed and uncompromising, but I think it's your smile."

She held her breath and waited for him to continue.

"When you smile your whole face lights up. Not just your eyes. You smile with every ounce of your expression. It pulls me in and makes me want to smile right along with you.

"And when you cry, my heart weeps with you. I may not show it, but I feel every tear on the inside.

"I can't say why God put us through so much before He brought us here, but I do know this: He brought us here for a reason, and that was to love one another always."

Always. It was the best word she had ever heard.

"Sarah?"

Once he spoke her name she realized that he had been talking all this time and she hadn't said one word. She hadn't even moved from her position of half climbing onto her buggy.

Her mare stamped her feet with impatience.

"*Jah?*"

"Are you okay?"

She nodded. "*Jah.*"

He frowned and those sweet maple syrup eyes clouded over. "But you don't feel the same. Listen, just give me a chance. I'll make you love me again, I promise. Just please say you'll come back home."

"*Jah.*" The word burst from her like a lit bottle rocket. "*Jah! Jah! Jah!*"

She launched herself at him, and thankfully he braced himself as he caught her.

She loved the feel of his arms around her. Loving arms that she had been waiting for her entire life. She and Jonah had been through trials and tribulations that most never suffered. But they would be stronger for it.

He held her close, so close, and she loved every minute of it.

"It looks like my work here is done," the bishop quipped. He disappeared back into his house.

Sarah laughed and Jonah rocked her back and forth.

"Mine too," April said.

"What made you come here?" Jonah asked.

"I wanted to talk to you. I left messages on the phone but you never called me back."

"Buddy," Jonah grumbled. He released Sarah but kept her close, her fingers tucked into his palm.

"You think Buddy erased April's messages?" Sarah asked.

"I know he did. It seems you have a fan club," he said to Sarah.

She smiled a little to herself, knowing someone would have to talk to Buddy about personal boundaries. But until then . . .

"What's on your mind, April?" Sarah tempered her voice to sound caring and concerned. She may have viewed April as her competition, but she would learn to treat her as a friend. It wouldn't be hard.

"I realized that all Jonah was doing didn't include telling you he loved you. And that was the most important thing of all."

"You drove all the way out here for that?" Sarah asked. She had heard stories of non-caring *Englishers*. That term didn't describe April at all.

"Well, yeah. I want the two of you to be happy."

Jonah squeezed her fingers. "We will be."

April nodded. "I know." She flashed them both a smile, then with a small wave she got in her car and left.

Jonah pulled her close to his side. "Let's go home."

Sarah nodded. She wanted nothing more. She might not understand the hows and the whys. One day she might, but for now she knew: God had led her home.

Epilogue

The last hour of church was always the longest. Jonah never understood why, but it simply was. He glanced over to where Sarah sat. They were separated by the walkway between the benches, but only that.

As if sensing his gaze, she looked up and smiled.

The gesture was so sweet he wanted to hold her in his arms, but they still had an hour of sermon and an afternoon of fellowship before he could have her alone. But he could have the next best thing. He nodded toward their daughter she held in her arms.

Elisa Mae Miller had just turned three months old, and he was pleased to say that she was the image of her mother. A soft tuft of dark hair graced her tiny head, and her eyes were the blue of the sky after a refreshing rain.

Sarah smiled and he was reminded once again what a wonderful mother she had become. Perfect in every way, much like the daughter she had given him. She gave Elisa Mae a small kiss on the forehead and passed her to him. She smelled like baby lotion and all things good and fine in the world. He cradled her to his chest and breathed in her innocence.

After all he and Sarah had been through, Jonah knew that Elisa Mae was more than a blessing; she was the promise of the future. A future he and Sarah would spend together.

He held his daughter close and let the words of the bishop wash over him.

"Blessed are the merciful: for they shall obtain mercy. Blessed are the pure in heart: for they shall see God."

He allowed his gaze to roam around the congregation. Mercy was abundant, to be sure. The last couple of years had brought about a great many changes. Lorie had moved on, married Zach Calhoun, and joined the English. He knew she kept a foot in each world, but with the English was truly where she belonged. She was still painting, still teaching at the senior center.

Jonah gazed into the tiny, sleeping face of his baby girl and he wondered when Lorie would have such a blessing. He wished that for her and more.

Luke Lambright had moved on as well, but no one had truly expected him to stay with the Amish. He was too adventuresome to be confined with something like religion. Jonah just hoped he remembered to leave room for God.

And Sadie Kauffman Hein visited from time to time, bringing her Mennonite husband Ezra along as well. Their son, Jake, was almost a year old now and the spittin' image of his father.

But for all the faces that were absent, there were more still present. Caroline and Andrew Fitch along with their children, Emma and Holly, had surely become as important to their community as if they had been born there. And baby number three was due sometime in the fall.

Titus and Abbie Lambert were successful raising their camels for milk. Though the Lord had not blessed them with any children, Jonah had a feeling that it wouldn't be much longer now. All things in time. And for now, Wells

Landing had been more than blessed with new citizens. Clara Rose and Obie Brenneman had a new baby boy, Emily and Elam Riehl had two baby girls, and Mariana and Reuben's twins were growing by leaps and bounds. Tess and Jacob Smiley hadn't been blessed with any children yet, but they were still raising kids. The goat kind, that was. And despite the problems they'd had, the couple seemed happier every time he saw them.

Elisa Mae stirred in his arms and fussed a bit. He adjusted her onto his shoulder, loving the feel of her tiny body against his chest. He patted Elisa Mae on the back to soothe her.

He had never imagined he would be here. Not when Sarah had come to his house to tell him the devastating news of her unplanned pregnancy. He never thought that he would be living this moment. Never dreamed how happy he could be.

The bishop talked on, but Jonah's favorite verse came to mind even over Cephas's lesson.

"Delight thyself also in the Lord; and He shall give thee the desires of thine heart."

But Jonah knew, the Lord had surely delighted in them.

Visit us online at
KensingtonBooks.com
to read more from your favorite authors, see books by series, view reading group guides, and more.

Join us on social media

for sneak peeks, chances to win books and prize packs, and to share your thoughts with other readers.

facebook.com/kensingtonpublishing
twitter.com/kensingtonbooks

Tell us what you think!

To share your thoughts, submit a review, or sign up for our eNewsletters, please visit:
KensingtonBooks.com/TellUs.